VERGANGENHEIT

A TALE OF FORGOTTEN DREAMS

BY E. SCOTT SPENCER

Copyright 2011 Thomas M Dodington

ISBN: 978-0-9785587-4-1

Published by Horsington Press,
Martindale, Texas

Also by E. Scott Spencer:

SENIORS HAVE IT TOUGH

HAUNTED STEEL ADVENTURES

GYPSY WAVES

For further information, please visit
www.escottspencer.com

AUTHOR'S NOTE: This book, its characters and actions, are fictitious: locations and names, if real, are used fictitiously.

NOTE TO THE READER

This book is a sequel to the main body of SENIORS HAVE IT TOUGH, by E. Scott Spencer, and the action below begins in 1982. There is a GLOSSARY with technical and unusual words at the end of this book.

CHAPTER 1

A MYSTERY IN OLD FILM CANS

Keith's grip tightened on the handle of a razor sharp butcher knife as Jessica struggled to take it from him. Just one slip and he, or Jessica, would lose a finger or much more. With his left arm he tried to push his beautiful young wife away without hurting her soft gentle body. Jessica moved quickly, dodging the blade as she worked to pry it from his grasp. Their little kitchen was no place for a fight: what had gone wrong? "Keith, stop it, you don't know what you're doing, killing him won't bring Kristin back, you'll land in the gas chamber."

"I've got to do something, he killed Kristin, he did it on purpose to save that worn out old bag and collect a fat fee transplanting her parts."

"It's not that simple and you of all people should know it. Kristin wants you to live, to be happy, to carry out her dreams even if she can't be here to share them with you. She's watching from up above, crying to see you rise above your misery."

"Shit". Keith breathed heavily as he slowly relaxed his grip, letting Jessica take the knife back to the rack where it belonged. Jessica's words confused him once again as he walked away into the living room mumbling to himself, "Kristin is dead, you're just claiming to talk with her spirit to make me feel better."

Before she realized what had happened, Jessica's crying body fainted to the floor in a flash of dizziness. An emotional old French song, *J'Attendrai*, ("*I Will Wait*") had suddenly run through her head as tears of sadness clouded her eyes. She heard the words to the old French song which women sang as their lovers marched off to war in 1939. In her eyes she saw a montage of soldiers marching, thin uniformed bodies with short cigarettes, children waving good-bye, old trains steaming slowly away in grainy black and white footage, then as the words changed she saw the flowers, clouds and the seasons passing, and then the battlefield craters and finally the white tombstones, row upon row in the gathering dusk. The music continued, "*J' attendrai.....*" ("*I will wait, day and night, I will wait for your return, the seasons pass, the flowers fade, the fire*

3

dies, the birds leave, the shade slips into the garden, the wind brings distant sounds, the autumn leaves fall, I wait by my door, I will wait forever for your return"). She saw the women waiting, standing by the windows, always staring into the distance, while she knew that their lovers would never return. Jessica slowly regained control over her emotions and dried her tears as she lay on the floor. What did this mean? Why such a vision from the past? Was Keith about to die while she waited for his return? It made no sense, the emotional music was a memory from her past, from her time in France. Slowly she told herself, "Calm down, the song means nothing, it's just a memory, push it away, look at the beautiful roses Keith picked for you." She opened her eyes and smiled at the flowers, but knew deep inside that the song was a portent of something that would happen in the future: one day she would sing this song and cry as she waited for a lover who might never return; she knew also that the flowers in the song faded to dust, ". . . *Les fleurs pâlissent*".

Keith focused on his breathing, walking around the house slowly, forcing himself to calm down. A strong young man, twenty-five, and handsome with everything to live for. Whatever the facts actually were, Keith interpreted them to mean that doctors had killed his first love Kristin on purpose and that he, Keith, had been so intimidated by their big words, bloody green scrubs, and medical-Latin B.S. that he hadn't fought back. In his view, he could have sought other opinions, he could have taken her from the hospital, he could have hired lawyers and made a stink, but no, he had accepted the quacks' version of reality and let Kristin's beautiful life fade to dust. A cardboard box full of ashes left on his doorstep was all he had to show for their life together.

Jessica saw his need for revenge taking over his life, yet she couldn't stop it no matter how hard she tried to distract him. Although she was uncommonly pretty with long dark hair and a beautiful body, a difficult childhood had left deep scars that were far from healed. Keith and Jessica were the same age and had only been married a few months, but their joyous union was turning into a nightmare. She watched as Keith's mind filled with hate. He had already turned down several projects, and was unable to focus on the realities of daily life. And she realized that his depression was affecting her own life, dragging her down instead of helping her solve her own mental problems. What a twist of fate: she had been the crazy person in need of help, in need of rescue by a stable strong young man, and now she had to take care of him instead.

4

Keith and Jessica hadn't had a moment's happiness except for their first joyous night together. On Christmas Eve Jessica had pledged her love to Keith while he had been in a trance. Jessica had probably hypnotized him, while she pretended to be Kristin, but nothing was very clear to Keith about the experience. The more that he thought over what had happened, the more it didn't make any sense to his scientifically-trained mind. All that he really knew about that night was that when he had regained his senses, he and Jessica were naked and wrapped in each other's arms, madly in love, and planning to marry immediately. This beautiful event had been a wonderful change, coming as it did after the disaster that had occurred at the completion of his first major motion picture. But his joy had collapsed less than twenty-four hours later when he had met the doctor who had cut choice pieces from Kristin's mangled body to save the life of another woman.

Jessica walked down the hall, slowly approached Keith and cautiously wrapped her arms around him, her tears falling on his shoulder as she cried her heart out. "Keith, what happened to our happiness, to our joy in each other, to our plans for the future?"

"Tell me, please tell me if you know. I feel terrible, I can't concentrate, I just can't focus on normal things."

"When we were making your film, every day, every minute from dawn to midnight was consumed by work, there was no time for worry or personal thoughts. Now we've been cast adrift and our minds are wandering, imagining the worst."

"So many things happened. For a while I was a big deal, at least among our friends, and now it's all gone, all except you, and your soft warm body pressed against me. I don't deserve you, you're far too wonderful."

Keith gently pushed Jessica away so that he could see her tearstained face, then kissed her softly. "Jessica, if somebody from outside looked at us now they would say that we're acting like spoiled brats: we have the world in our hands and sit around crying because it isn't perfect. You're a great painter, your career is only beginning, and my first screenplay is already a feature motion picture even if few have seen it. We're just starting to conquer the world. Doors are opening all around us, but it's dark and we can't see them yet."

Jessica smiled and started to laugh, "Tell me about the doors you imagine, where do they lead?"

Before he could invent an answer, they heard a knock at the front door. Keith and Jessica both laughed spontaneously and rushed to open it: the coincidence was almost too good to be true. Harry Smithson, an old Cameraman and a close friend of Keith and Jessica, had driven over in his 1949 tomato-soup red MG. They hadn't seen Harry since the fateful Christmas party in his daughter Angela's home. Keith and Jessica, glowing in their new-found love, had been the toast of the party. Then Angela had introduced them to the doctor who had saved her life. Keith had fainted to the floor as psychic Jessica cried out in the anguish of death, reliving Kristin's pain in the midst of the festive Christmas gathering. She had realized in a blinding flash that Angela was the woman who lived, drawing her every breath through dead Kristin's transplanted lungs.

Now Harry stood at the door, the expression on his wrinkled face a mixture of anticipation and worry. Although close to ninety, he moved with the speed and control of a much younger man. His hands carried two large rusty thirty-five millimeter film cans as Jessica answered his knock. Without a word, Harry wrapped an arm around Jessica, hugging her tightly in silent greeting. Keith watched, struggling to control his emotions. He knew that Harry had nothing to do with Kristin's death, and that probably Harry was as saddened and confused by what had happened as Keith. But how to express his feelings, how to greet the father of the woman who lived. Jessica broke through the turmoil.

"Harry, come in, come in, how are you? It's been too long. We miss you and Angela very much."

"Thanks Jessica. I didn't dare ask you to come over to our place, I didn't know how it would go with Keith and Angela, there're so many feelings under the surface, and Angela is as broken-up as Keith: she had no idea of the connection, of who her transplants came from."

Keith moved forward and took Harry's hand in both of his, "Sorry Harry, I'm a wreck; I can't get over it, even though I try. I know I'm driving Jessica crazy, but I can't help it."

"Someone a long time ago told me that working hard is the best cure for depression, so I'm bringing you a complex puzzle, and maybe an important film project, to take your mind off the past."

Jessica noticed the film cans in Harry's hand, "What's in the cans? A funny movie from the old vaults to cheer Keith up?"

"Nothing that simple. I need your help. I want to borrow your young legs, your energy, and your clever brains, and we'll need a big dose of luck. I've been wanting to come over and enlist your help for days, but the business with Angela has been holding me back. Something happened this morning that made me drive straight over regardless of what your feelings might be. We've got to get moving."

They sat down in the living room of Keith's little house on Le Conte Street in Westwood, part of Los Angeles, a perfectly-manicured group of old homes between Beverly Hills and the UCLA campus. The house had belonged to Keith's parents years ago, and Kristin had lived here with Keith before she was run over by a huge car on Wilshire. The driver had escaped to Libya and diplomatic immunity in his private jet, leaving Kristin's flattened body for the doctors to fix, or cut up for parts.

"Would you like coffee Harry, or something stronger?" Jessica asked.

"Not yet, but maybe in a while as this is going to take a bit of explaining."

"Come on Harry, don't keep us in suspense, what's in the cans?"

"Last week I received a strange phone call: almost knocked me over, and that doesn't happen often. A foreign voice was on the line and without introduction he asked me two questions. First he asked if I was the Harry Smith who had shot film in Bavaria in 1937, and I answered yes, vaguely remembering the trip. Then he really startled me by asking if I still had an old camera from Germany with initials carved inside, and what the initials were. Nobody knows about that camera, nobody except two other people, and the initials are L.R. The guy hung up as soon as I answered."

"What camera, what happened?"

"In a minute, that call's not the whole story. So I pulled the old camera from its box in the cellar and reminisced about Bavaria and why the guy could have called me. No ideas. Then yesterday I opened the front door and these cans, and other stuff, were on the steps, in an old wooden box. No notes, no explanation, no nothing. So I brought them inside and looked carefully. I had no idea if they were exposed movie film, or what. They were taped shut with old tape, the kind we used during the war, and they're not Kodak, they're Agfa, like I used a long time ago in Europe. So I happened to shake the cans, and noticed that some of them rattled, like they didn't contain film. You know me, I don't mess around, so I opened the can on top. Inside I found a bunch of Leica film cassettes containing old nitrate still picture negatives. I opened one and the film was OK, processed and sharp. Weird pictures of some sort of construction stuff and military people: I saw a few swastikas, so I knew it was German from the war. Since it was nitrate I carefully closed the can and resealed it with new tape. Then I opened the other cans, and found a bunch of thirty-five millimeter footage and an old diary, written in German, with lots of technical drawings and math."

"Wow, Harry, let's look at the pictures, where do you think they came from?" Keith's curiosity was aroused, and his technical background made him curious about the diary and its drawings.

"And I can read German, at least I could in school, so I'd love to look at the diary," Jessica added.

"Good, but let me continue. I was trying to figure out who would have sent this stuff to me and why. It didn't make sense, so I tried to think of anyone I knew who might be connected with Germany from the war years and especially the two people who knew about the camera. In the thirties I shot a bunch of background plates in the mountains and forests of Bavaria. Sometimes we would hire an open car and drive down a street while shooting to the side, then to the rear, and then to the front. When this film got back to Hollywood, they projected it onto a screen behind some actors who were sitting in a car on a stage, or maybe walking down a sidewalk. The projector and the camera were interlocked electrically so that when the projector's shutter opened, the camera opened and made an exposure. Simple 1920 technology, but it worked. If I got the lighting just right in my shots, viewers would think the actors were actually travelling down the same street I was. I had a long list of particular shots that we had to find and shoot, and not just daytime exteriors, but nights and mountains and all sorts of stuff to match some scriptwriter's dreams of what Germany should look like. They loved it whenever I got German signs or unusual architecture in the frame: then the audience was sure to know the actors were in

Germany."

"I hired a young assistant in Bavaria, a sharp guy on the way up, even though he wore a Nazi armband and a brown shirt. I called him Fritz, but that probably wasn't his real name and since I paid him in cash there were no records. His politics didn't bother me, and occasionally his uniform was useful when we needed to arrange a shot, to get a little cooperation from the locals. I'd shoot anything and go anywhere, and in those days I didn't know much about governments or what they were up to. So one day Fritz comes running from the phone in a panic and tells me that we've got to drop our assignment and jump in the car. We were shooting plates for a film Twentieth was making and the money was very good, and we were behind due to the weather, so I was hesitant. The way he talked, we didn't have a minute to waste, something important was about to happen and our cameras were needed immediately. I let him talk me into it and we rushed off down the Autobahn. As we drove he told me it was really important, we were going to help Leni Riefenstahl out of a bind. I knew she was a great director and camerawoman, and I had seen some of her propaganda stuff in German theaters, so I figured she had hordes of assistants and helpers: she was a major name, maybe the best film-maker in Germany, so how could the two of us be important to her?"

Keith and Jessica relaxed. Both had spent many evenings listening to Harry reminisce about the old days when he traveled the world for Hollywood studios, shooting film that provided exotic backgrounds for scenes made on stages in Hollywood. Harry, along with cameras, film, and assistants, had been all over the world in the years before the Second World War. The couple knew that Harry was beginning a long story which would eventually end with a connection to the interesting box outside his front door.

Keith and Jessica were both in the film business, she as a wardrobe mistress and he as a sound mixer and writer. They had just finished making the first full-length feature film Keith had ever written, a low-budget comedy about crazy transplant doctors and two-hundred-year-old senior citizens who grew their own replacement body parts on a secret farm. After finishing the film a bunch of doctors, who were the financial backers of the effort, had locked up the negative so it would never be seen by the public. It had been a terrible let-down for Keith, but the project had brought Jessica and Keith together. As their relationship developed he had discovered that she was far more than a wardrobe person, she was

9

a brilliant painter as well as some sort of psychic with a wide range of personal problems, most of which he didn't understand. Harry's story continued.

"Soon we were shooting a street riot as Leni shouted directions and moved us around. Her crew had been arrested and it was pretty clear that we weren't supposed to be doing this, but we shot it anyway running from cover to cover. She was a fantastic director, she knew exactly what I saw through the lens, and it felt like she was working through me, moving my hands and eyes as we shot. Two big things happened that day. The most important was that Fritz saved my life. He was the bravest guy I've ever met, really strong, not just physically but mentally. He stood right in front of me as a guy with a Lugar was about to wipe us out and just stared at the guy, daring him to pull the trigger. Maybe it was Fritz's uniform, but I think it was some sort of mental power he projected from his eyes. Fritz didn't say anything, he just stood like a rock protecting me. While this was happening I could see Leni out of the corner of my eye: she had her hand-held Arriflex and was shooting the confrontation, oblivious to her own danger. At the end of the day I gave Leni all the film I'd shot and she turned to me with the most beautiful smile then handed me her Arriflex and told me to keep it as a souvenir of a job well done. That's the special camera the caller asked about and her initials are engraved inside. It's an early prototype of the cameras you use today."

Jessica was fascinated, "I've seen Leni's **OLYMPIA**, her beautiful film about the 1936 Berlin Olympics and **TRIUMPH OF THE WILL**, her famous propaganda film. It was so effective that after seeing it I wanted to sign-up, to be a German patriot, even though I know what eventually happened: it was so powerful, the music and the marching and all the healthy young people. What fantastic camerawork and direction. I never thought that I would meet someone who had actually worked with her."

"And she was a great actress too. She competed against Marlene Dietrich for the best roles in the early thirties, but then Marlene left Germany to became a rich Hollywood star, while Leni stayed behind, helping her country through the war."

Keith enjoyed the story, but he wanted to see the diary. "So how does this relate to the film cans? Did Leni send them to you?"

"No, I think she died ages ago, but Fritz is somehow connected."

"Maybe it was Fritz calling from Germany?"

"No, at least I don't think so, now just let me finish. This morning, about an hour ago, I had a second phone call from the foreign voice: he said that he was calling from Warm Springs and asked if the box had arrived OK. Then he said that I would know how important the box was."

"What else did he say, I mean, how did he know about the camera?"

"There were odd noises and then the line went dead, something happened, and he didn't call back. You two could drive up to Warm Springs, in Nevada, maybe a day away. You could find out more, and I've got a feeling that you'd better go quickly, that we don't have much time."

"You want us to jump in the car and take off, just like that, right now?"

"Yes, and take a camera with you. Get some footage of the area after you talk with the guy. Maybe we can spin together an interesting documentary combining new footage with the old stuff. Wait 'til you see the footage that was in the cans, it was shot in a huge underground laboratory during the war."

Jessica jumped up, excited to see Keith coming back to life, "I've got a full tank, and food for picnics. Keith, why don't you find some maps and a camera while I pack: we can be on the road in less than an hour."

"Harry, you're coming with us aren't you?"

"No, I'm too old for adventures like this, but I'll loan you an Arri and some film: they're in my car, and I have a Nevada map with Warm Springs marked. It's just a little place, you'll find the guy easily."

"Ooops, I just remembered that we're supposed to visit David to see one of the sets for his new TV series this afternoon."

"I'll pack the car, we can leave for Nevada from the lot after we've seen David."

An Hour later they drove through the gates of the faded old Paramount studio on Gower Street in Hollywood and headed for stage five. David, Keith's best friend and the director of their first real movie, was standing in the middle of a deserted pink bedroom set. The walls were plywood flats, behind which lights and odd equipment sat motionless in the dark shadows. David was walking around imagining the action when the cast and crew arrived, when lights, people, and action would breathe life into this scene.

Jessica hugged David in greeting and looked around, "David what is this supposed to be? Who could possibly sleep in a bedroom like this?"

"People don't sleep here, they screw, this is a setting for a porno parody, not a real bedroom!"

Keith knew it wasn't real but had to laugh at the excessive chintz and the numerous phallic symbols and mirrors. "David, why don't you have a condom dispenser next to the bed, you could get some cash from Trojans if you put it in close-up, and the comedy possibilities are endless, like when they argue over which size the guy should use, or when they don't have a quarter to put in the machine."

"Why don't you get off your ass and come over here and help me. This place sucks and I could use a smartass to liven things up."

Jessica didn't know what David was shooting, but obviously Keith did. "So what's happening here? Why the sex?"

"On Jessica, I've gone down in the world. First making Keith's film about crazy doctors, and now this, a satire on the porno film business, and for TV, not even for the big screen."

Spunky slowly walked in from a dark corner and joined the others. She looked like a teenage girl, though she was a bit over twenty. Her sexy revealing clothes, her come-to-me smile, her soft long blond hair, her slutty appearance and demeanor, masked a serious actress on the way up who knew exactly what she was doing. She had been a star in Keith's film and had latched onto David, her best chance at an E-ticket ride to stardom. The two couples were close in spite of many differences.

12

"So what happens here," Jessica asked.

"Have you ever read that book about how to write sex scenes in novels? The main idea is that the really interesting scenes have problems and don't work out like the reader expects."

Spunky interjected, "Like with Judge Julie in our film when we see she's really a transvestite with a huge erection."

"This is much tamer than that. It's all played for laughs, with nerds encountering bimbos who can't remember to collect their money, or who can't get zippers undone," David added.

"Since it's TV, can you show anything, I mean like people with their clothes off, or at least in their underwear?"

"The best I can say is that they're paying me to be here. My real problem is that people will look at this when they ask 'what have you directed lately?' I've got to find a way to make this come alive, to breathe some form of artistic integrity into it or my career is over."

Jessica thought for a moment, then smiled at David, "David, have you read about Gladstone, Prime Minister of England in Victorian times? Although he was religious and proper he used to wander the streets of London late at night to find prostitutes. Then he brought them home and fed them and tried to convince them to give up their evil ways and go to church. He got in a lot of trouble, but he was so sincere that it worked, no sex at all. You could take a serious slant on all this stuff and come out to defend the girls, reach out to them, help them, dump the comedy and make a real statement. Get the audience involved, get them to help these girls instead of shunning them. They're tragic, they're the daughters of the parents in your audience, it can ring true, the people will love you for it, and tune in to the next episode."

Spunky hugged Jessica, "David, why not, put in some serious scenes to contrast against the comedy, go for sympathy instead of sex with these poor creatures, and let Jessica and me tell you what's it really like on the streets, with drunken bums who can hardly get their pants off."

Keith smiled, "You don't have to make it dull, maybe you can have a fight between girl and a drunk, clothes come off, audience sees some skin and gets excited, they struggle, sexy close-ups pass by, and then she throws him through the window. Next day he's in court with a sleezy lawyer trying to sue her."

Spunky interjected, "And she's treated like she's guilty when he was trying to rape her."

"But the judge's a woman and he's in the slammer!" Keith said.

"David, you've got a real hit on your hands, and I'll throw the bastard through the window for you," Spunky screamed in delight.

"Holy cow, I thought I was directing a stupid sitcom."

"Seriously David, for these girls, this wasn't their first career choice, it was the last, and they're miserable behind the rouge, tight clothes and falsies. You can take their side against the world and really make a difference." Jessica quietly implored.

"And it can be a lot of fun too, you can blend the laughs and the pathos and create something memorable."

"But in the meantime, Keith and I have to go, we're heading to Nevada to help Harry with a problem. We'll be back in a few days to see how you're doing with your new script."

"I want to see the dailies when Spunky heaves the John through the window, and the court scene the next day!"

As Jessica and Keith walked away, she turned back to David, "And don't forget the argument over the condom machine, all guys think they need the extra large size."

Spunky laughed as Keith and Jessica walked through the door into the sunlight.

Chapter 2
Nevada

"Jessica, this is a chance to see how fast your car will go: there's no speed limit in Nevada on rural roads."

"Good, you can drive the California part, then I'll drive in Nevada."

"No way!"

Keith drove the black Mercedes 380SE four-door sedan east toward Las Vegas. His old VW bug, part of his life before Jessica, was spending more and more time in the back of the garage. Jessica's car was only a year old, but it had been almost completely rebuilt after she had run it off Mulholland Drive in a drunken stupor late one night. She claimed that a tree had jumped in front of her, but they both knew the sad truth. Jessica had a bad alcohol problem which they were struggling to control.

Traffic was heavy, and everyone was going nine miles an hour over the speed limit in the belief that they were just below the threshold where an unmarked car would turn out to be a cop. Keith paid little attention to his driving, keeping his speed just low enough to avoid a ticket as his mind wandered. The roadside scenery was featureless desert interrupted by advertisements, cactus and trash. A good time for quiet thinking. Jessica slept on the seat beside Keith. When he glanced at her peaceful face, he slowed, checked traffic, and drove a little more cautiously. She was real, lovely, and his. As Keith thought over his situation, he began to realize that it was time to work hard and fade his memories of Kristin, doctors, transplants and what might have been and instead focus on putting his life back together.

Keith smiled to himself when he thought of the events of the past year. Although the result of finally shooting a feature film that he had written was not a box office hit, he had learned a tremendous amount in the process. Already David was working again and Keith had received, but ignored, several enquiries about writing projects. In addition, he could always work on sound tracks as he was a good sound mixer, combining

15

aesthetic sensibilities with technical mastery. It was time to do something to continue to make his reputation or his place would be taken by others who were on the way up and his name would be forgotten. Keith and David were minor celebrities as they had made what was rumored to be an excellent but very peculiar low budget film which almost nobody had seen. The stories about their film were probably better than the actuality, but in a year they would be forgotten unless he hurried back to work. Keith knew that he was an interesting commodity, a person who could attract meetings and questions, but unless he added to his resume he would soon be history. He wondered if Harry's film cans held the beginning of an unusual documentary or maybe a war flick. Maybe he could combine this train of thought with Harry's exciting life story and create an unusual action-adventure or spy-thriller. The possibilities began to look promising. Keith had been interested in film-making since childhood, and both of his parents had been screen actors. Movies were in his blood, and he knew it was time to get back to work, to start breathing life into what could become his first real hit.

While these thoughts raced through his mind, he skirted Las Vegas on the west side then headed north on I-95 for Tonopah where they would spend the night. It was exciting to finally be on the open road away from traffic and cities. No one else seemed to be headed this way, yet it was the major north-south road connecting Reno and Vegas. Nevada claimed to have the loneliest roads in the nation, though they were well-paved and maintained, courtesy of money from gambling taxes. As Keith slowly pressed the throttle down, the 3.8 liter V8 easily powered the car to eighty, then ninety, then one hundred. A solid German car made for safely cruising the Autobahns all day. He didn't dare go faster though the car was willing: top speed was at least 140.

Jessica awoke and noticed the speedometer. "Where are we? Hey, it's my turn to drive."

"We're north of Vegas, on 95, just coming into Indian Springs, but be careful when you drive. I saw an Open Range sign warning that livestock isn't fenced, and I've seen a few burros or donkeys standing on the edge of the road."

"Nevada has wild horses too, and the burros are from prospectors years ago. Look, there's a tumbleweed blowing across the road. Too bad we don't have a tape of the Sons Of The Pioneers singing *Tumbling Tumbleweed*. All I can remember is part of the chorus, '*see them tumbling down, pledging their love to the ground, lonely but free I'll be found, drifting along with the tumbling tumbleweeds*'. The music has sad violins, quiet whistling and the sound of a horse walking slowly. It's a moody piece from the old west, just like the lonesome scenery here."

"I don't know the song, but I saw something more modern, a billboard advertising a brothel. Nevada's got everything! Want to stop and see what it's like?"

"In your dreams. But stop if you see one advertising young men, now that could be fun."

"Somehow I don't think that's part of the attraction. Good thing I filled the tank in Vegas. I haven't seen a working gas station since, just abandoned ruins."

"Why didn't you wake me?"

"You were sleeping, so I stopped quietly, I didn't want to disturb your dreams."

"Maybe I would have liked to pee, or get a drink or something."

"Sorry, I'll stop at the next place that's open, or wherever you want."

"Keep driving, I want to sketch the scenery as the sun goes down. It's so beautiful out here in a strange empty ancient sort of way. The jagged cuts running up the hills, the snow on top, the bare rock and the lack of trees and brush. Look at the mountains on the left, they could have been just like that a million years ago, unmarked by human civilization. And the air is so crisp. I'll bet we can see a hundred miles."

"I wish we had looked at Harry's stuff before we left. I've been thinking of what the cans might contain, and what we could do with it."

"We'll be home tomorrow night, and who knows, we might learn lots from Fritz's friend or whoever sent them, and it's fun to be away from the city, to get out here and see something new."

"But we don't even know what we're looking for, I mean, we don't even have a name or a description, or anything solid to go on."

"So relax and see what happens: this is an adventure, not a scientific expedition. Imagine if you were in the audience watching a movie of us. Would there be tense violins, warning the audience that we were in danger, or would they see a cut with happy rabbits scampering around the desert and hear birds singing? In a film we can push the audience's expectations around, but this is reality so we don't have a clue what will happen next."

They arrived in Tonopah after dark and were glad to see restaurants, gas stations, and motels on the main street, which was also highway-95. The only signs of life they had seen on the drive north from Vegas were in the nearly abandoned towns of Goldfield and Beatty: not much civilization considering they had driven over two hundred and fifty miles on a major highway. Tonopah's main attractions, other than twenty-four hour gas and food, seemed to be a huge outdoor mining museum and the county courthouse: the center of law and order for a hundred miles in all directions.

They walked into the Silver Nugget Saloon across from their Best Western motel: lots of bright lights and slot machines, but also restaurant tables and solid food. Keith looked around as they sat at a corner table near the windows. "Jessica, I've got an odd feeling, sort of like maybe we don't belong here."

"We've been in hundreds of places like this, solid rural American food. What's on your mind? It looks normal to me."

"Everyone is wearing either flashy fake western wear or else they're real workers coming in from a hard day on the road. There's nobody like us here. I mean, look at our clothes, they're ironed, clean, and simple, no sequins or ribbons and bows and no grease or filth."

"Hey, I wonder if one of your brothels is upstairs. Maybe these guys are dressed for that and those flashy girls are the hookers! Now relax and look at the menu. I'm going to start with a large glass of wine, or maybe two."

While they waited for their food, a weather-beaten old man in faded work clothes came over to their table and addressed Keith, "Welcome to Tonopah stranger, where're you from?"

"L.A. We're just here for the night."

"I saw you drive up in that fancy car. We don't get many celebrities up here, so I thought I'd ask for your autographs."

Jessica could sense that something wasn't quite right about the old man and their conversation, but couldn't put her finger on exactly what was troubling her sensitive side. She remained silent but apprehensive as Keith continued.

"Sorry, but we're not important, we just work in the film business, we're not stars."

"Well, you look like you could be, so that's why I asked. Where're you headed, why visit Tonopah?"

"We're going to Warm Springs tomorrow morning to find someone."

"Really, now that's odd. What's his name? You sure he lives there?"

"We don't know exactly, but Warm Springs doesn't look like a big place on the map, and he's an old guy, probably German or European."

Jessica started kicking Keith under the table, but he didn't understand what she was trying to communicate.

"That's not much of a description and it can be mighty dangerous around the springs. You should take a guide."

Keith was about to accept his offer when Jessica interrupted, "I don't think so, at least, not yet. If we don't find what we're looking for, then we'll come back and ask for help."

The man paused for a moment, then turned and walked away with a smile, "You'll be back, unless that is, you get hurt out there."

After the man walked away, Jessica whispered to Keith, "Why did you tell him what we're up to? He was bad news: I could feel it."

"How can you be sure of that, and anyhow, what's the harm, we might need a guide since we don't know what we're looking for."

During the night Jessica worried about their encounter with the old man. She had felt something vaguely unfriendly about him: not a feeling she could put in words, but a premonition that kept digging into her thoughts. Keith was oblivious to her concern: his world was limited to things he could see and touch.

The next morning dawned cool and clear. A light dry snow had fallen overnight, but the clouds were gone, leaving a crystal clear deep blue sky and a breeze that blew traces of snow from the roads. The temperature was in the thirties as they loaded the car and headed east on highway six. Warm Springs was only sixty miles away, located at the intersection where highway six joins Nevada-375. Keith read in a motel brochure that N-375 was known locally as *The Extraterrestrial Highway* because it passed the northern edge of Groom Air Force Base. Some people believed that the government stored captured alien space ships as well as their strange passengers at Area-51, the most secret part of this Base. There were lots of reports from N-375 of strange sightings in the air, especially at night. Nevada really did have everything.

They drove the two-lane blacktop up to McKinney Tanks Summit, listed at 6391 feet on a bullet-riddled sign. From here they could see great distances in all directions. Looking northeast they saw their road going down from the summit like a thin black ribbon. It went straight across an empty valley and up the other side, at least forty miles distant on the map. There were no other vehicles in sight.

After crossing the valley they drove over Warm Springs summit, then cruised slowly down the east side of the range, expecting to see the town of Warm Springs at the bottom of the grade. They had seen only one other car on the road all morning and it had been headed the other way. Jessica broke the silence, "Look, there's the intersection but I don't see the town. Where is it?"

"The sign back there said we were headed for Warm Springs, but I don't see anything."

They slowed and approached the intersection. Jessica spotted a few ruins. "Is that ruined old motel all that's left of the town? How could someone phone Harry from here. This place is dead, it's a ghost town."

"Maybe the phone call was a hoax, and the caller was in Germany or who knows where and we've just wasted a few tanks of gas. That old guy last night must have thought we were nuts coming here searching for a living person."

"Let's check out the remains of the motel, and shoot some footage for Harry. Maybe he'll have a good laugh if nothing else."

"Waste of film, but I'd like to look around since we're here. Look out for snakes."

"They're in hibernation." Jessica's curiosity overcame her

forebodings: deep inside, she knew that they shouldn't be here, but the inner feeling wasn't strong enough to stop her from having a quick look.

They parked in what had once been the driveway of the WARM SPRINGS RESORT, stopping at a rusty steel wire rope that blocked the road, with a battered and shot-up NO TRESPASSING sign. Weeds and cactus grew everywhere, even through cracks in the old concrete driveway. Without a thought they hopped over the cable and walked to the front door, dodging cactus spikes and sagebrush. Most of the building's paint was gone and the motel's bone-dry gray twisted boards were falling apart. Rough slabs criss-crossed the old windows and doors. The place had been boarded-up and abandoned long ago.

"Let's walk all the way around and see if there's any way someone could have called from here," Jessica suggested.

"Impossible, they're no telephone wires, or electric wires for that matter, nearby."

"We should have been smarter: we could have called the phone company and asked for information in Warm Springs, then we might have had some idea if the place at least existed."

"I figured that it was a town, with people, I mean I didn't think it was just an abandoned motel in the middle of nowhere."

Behind the motel they came to a fissure in the rocks where steaming hot water flowed naturally from the ground into a series of smooth stone pools. Jessica reached down and felt the water. "It's just the right temperature: we could climb in for a quick soak."

"We don't have bathing suits, and besides, we're looking for Fritz's friend."

Jessica unzipped her jacket, "Come on, take your clothes off, nobody can see us back here. Live a little, take a chance, let's get together in the warm water."

"Maybe next time. Let's finish checking out this place."

Jessica dropped her jacket to the ground and pulled her sweater up over her head, "Don't be so serious, put your arms around me, let me take your pants off, you're getting excited, I can see it, let's get in."

"This is crazy, we don't have towels to dry off or robes or anything."

Keith picked up her sweater and her jacket then wrapped his arms around Jessica, "I love you, but I don't want to do this right now. Maybe after we've finished our search and shot Harry's film? We can bring some extra clothes over from the car and hop in then. OK?"

Jessica sensually pulled her sweater slowly over her body, "You do like looking at my body, and you're all excited. Maybe it's time for a quickie in the back seat of the car?"

After an hour of exploring and fooling around as well as a few encounters with cactus, they went back to the car for the tripod and camera.

"I'll set up a shot where I can focus on the highway signs, then pan to the old motel. Maybe you can be in the shot, sketching the ruins?"

Jessica opened her sketch pad and instinctively moved to a spot where she could draw a three-quarter view of the front of the old motel and the remains of its sign. Keith loaded the camera with Harry's black and white film, checked the light, then worked to find a location for the tripod. He knew that Harry would view the film critically, even though he, Keith, had no claim to camera expertise. He could load and operate the camera with technical competence, but he had limited skill in the aesthetics of cinematography.

Jessica shouted as she pointed, "Why not move over there, out in the open past that bush, then you can slowly pan across it to reveal the barren scenery, then the highway signs, then the motel and me. It'll tell the whole story in one slow pan. Make it good and you can run it behind the main title of your next big hit."

"Thanks, I can do that, and it will save film." Keith picked up the tripod and camera and walked toward the spot Jessica had suggested. She was fully engaged in sketching with a black pen and a few colored pencils, a gifted expert working quickly with her tools. Keith arranged his shot and started to roll his first take. Suddenly a loud noise disturbed the dead quiet.

"What was that? A truck or maybe an explosion?"

"It sounded far away. Can you see anything?"

"No, but I screwed up my first take."

"Something's wrong, it's time to leave."

"Let me shoot the scene again: just keep sketching. You look perfect."

"Hurry up."

Keith ran the shot again and as he finished they heard more loud noises, then the unmistakable sound of a ricochet as a bullet glanced off a nearby rock and kicked up dust near Jessica.

"Holy shit, someone's shooting at us."

They ran for the car and in what seemed like seconds, were sailing down the road as fast as possible. After a few miles Keith pulled onto the shoulder and stopped.

"What happened back there? Who would want to shoot at us?"

"Look at the map. The MM Mine and the AB Mine are up on the mountain behind the motel. Maybe a guy up there thought we were suspicious."

"I thought those were abandoned mining claims, the state's covered with old mines, and besides, we weren't doing anything."

"We were in a fancy big-city car, dressed in bright parkas, trespassing, and making a movie of their old motel. From their viewpoint, maybe we needed scaring off."

"Aren't you glad we're not swimming naked in the pool right now. Maybe they saw you start to take your clothes off through a telescope?"

"Let's go up the road a little: there's a landing strip on the map about eight miles north-east of Warm Springs. Perhaps someone there knows who lives here."

"I wonder how far from the motel people consider that they're living in Warm Springs? Maybe people for twenty miles in all directions say that they live in Warm Springs, since it's the only town around here that's on the map."

"More like fifty miles in all directions."

"The next town, or more likely ruin, on the map is Currant, and it's got to be seventy miles from Warm Springs."

In the end, they couldn't find the landing strip, though they passed many unmarked dirt roads leading across the desert into the barren mountains. Finally they stopped and turned back.

"At least we saw phone lines so maybe people are living out here far from the paved road. Perhaps a few of the mines are still active, but how can that relate to Harry and his film cans?"

"Too bad we didn't bring binoculars."

"And an airplane. We'll never find anything from the road."

"Hey, speaking of airplanes, anyone living out here could have a two-way radio instead of a phone, so maybe the guys shooting at us were warned by a radio message from that creep we met last night."

"Why would they want to shoot at us or scare us off: we're harmless."

"Could be related to Harry's box and the guy who called: maybe the box did come from here, and the gunshots are related to it."

"It's time to go home. We're not safe here, but let's stop for a minute at the crest of the next hill so I can make a good sketch of the view. I want to capture the feeling of space, the huge distances, the clear air, I can see so far, it's fantastic. We can call Harry when we go back through Tonopah, and you can check-out the mining museum."

"Hey, could you add an alien spaceship from Groom Air Force base to your drawing, as a contrast to the primitive scenery?"

Jessica didn't reply: she knew that Keith's artistic sense wasn't his strong suit. They pulled off the road at Warm Springs Summit. Keith wandered around the hilltop killing time as Jessica made several sketches of the view in different directions. Far away he saw something glittering in the sky: slowly it grew in size and Keith recognized it as a small airplane. He watched it casually, and noticed that it was coming their way. "Jessica, turn around and look at that little plane: it's coming our way."

"In a minute, I'm busy. Is it an alien spaceship?"

"Of course not, but I can't see the fuselage or the tail, so it must be pointed directly toward us. It's getting closer and closer, must be going fast, take a look. Holy cow, duck behind the car!"

All of a sudden the plane was upon them, its engine screaming just a few feet overhead. Wind from the plane kicked up clouds of dust and scattered debris as Keith hid behind a rock. He was sure that he had felt the heat of the plane's exhaust and his ears were ringing. Jessica starred after the plane in disbelief as it disappeared over the desert.

"Are you OK? That pilot must be nuts."

"OK. How about you?"

"Glad I was sketching instead of painting, there's crap all over my pad."

"I've never seen a plane like that."

"Too bad we didn't shoot some film: would've been much more interesting than footage of a deserted motel!"

"Damn, did you see it well enough to draw an outline? That was no everyday Cessna."

They stopped quickly in Tonopah, just enough for gas and a snack, then headed back to L.A. with memories, exposed film, and several beautiful but dusty sketches.

Vergangenheit

CHAPTER 3
INSIDE THE CANS

When they returned home late that night they found a phone message from Harry inviting them to Angela's house in the morning. Keith fretted over the invitation. On the one hand his curiosity about the contents of Fritz's cans and his desire to tell Harry about their Nevada adventures burned strongly, but his emotional side tensed when he thought of being close to living pieces of Kristin's body. Jessica held his hand tightly as they replayed Harry's invitation.

"You can do it Keith, just stay close to me so I can protect you from your feelings."

"How can you do that?"

"Maybe I'll tickle you or do something unexpected. Maybe I'll take my clothes off if you start to think of Kristin. Stick close because as long as you're holding my hand or touching me you'll be fine. You'll be inside my aura."

"I know you're teasing, but you do have a beautiful body. I don't see..."

He was interrupted by Jessica who wrapped her arms around him, pressing her body to his with a long slow kiss that melted into bed and sex. Just before going to sleep Jessica asked, "Sometime, when you're not so sensitive about Kristin, I want to ask you about Kristin's soft body. That night when I first entered your house, when I walked around her room and ran my hands over her clothes, especially her underclothes, I could almost feel the ghost of her body with my hands. She was so close, like we were intimate girlfriends, cuddling together telling secrets. Then on Christmas Eve she came to me again as I bathed then put on her clothes. She kissed me and told me to go to you, that she wanted to live with you through my body and it was time."

"I'm not sure how to answer, I mean your bodies are much alike, and you fit her clothes perfectly. Remember the time you dressed up to impress the lawyers in her most expensive dress and we laughed about how good the fit was. I don't know what else to say, except that I am very lucky to have found you."

Jessica smiled to herself as a warm feeling flowed over her like a moist tropical wave: she knew again that she was partially real, and partially a ghost from the past, warm and wet, wrapped in the arms of the man she loved. She hugged Keith tightly then snuggled closer into his arms and fell asleep.

After breakfast they drove to Angela and Harry's white wood-paneled house in Beverly Hills. From the road it was all shrubs, flowers and manicured trees, but behind the wrought iron gate was a beautiful house and a secret garden, a garden that held special memories for Keith and Angela. Harry had lived here since the thirties, along with many artifacts collected from almost the beginnings of the film industry.

Angela worked as an Assistant Director, the person in charge of keeping things moving and on schedule. In her younger days she had been an actress, then as her youth faded she had moved behind the camera, taking advantage of extensive contacts in the industry as well as a deep understanding of how it all worked. On the set, Angela was a fast and very efficient A.D. with no tolerance for slackers. Keith had been extremely lucky to hire such an experienced person to manage the shooting of his el-cheapo film, but he had known nothing of her medical history until her disastrous party on Christmas Day. Jessica held his arm as they carried Harry's camera and tripod to the front door.

"Remember what I said, just stick close and you won't have any problems."

Harry greeted them, then Angela appeared, moving very slowly with visible trepidation as she looked into Keith's eyes. Keith cast a glance at Jessica's calm face as she squeezed his arm, then smiled at Angela. "Sorry I made such a mess at your Christmas party. I was so surprised, I don't know what happened, I lost control. Your house was so beautiful, everything was perfect, then I collapsed. I don't know what to say."

Angela moved closer to Keith and Jessica as Harry joined them, "How about a cup of strong coffee while I run the projector. I know you're dying to see the old footage, and nothing we can say will change all the emotional stuff: let's skip the talk and cut to the chase."

"Dad, you're so excited, but just wait a minute. Keith, Jessica, welcome home: I miss you so much, please don't stay away any more.

I know we can work this out together much better than if we're apart." Angela wrapped her arms around both Keith and Jessica as she started to cry.

"Let's see the movies Harry, and how about a shot of whiskey in the coffee," Keith added, ignoring for the moment Jessica's tendency to drink too much: he knew that this was not going to be an ordinary day in any sense of the word, and was relieved that he had his emotions under control.

They moved to the comfortable chairs and couches in the living room, a room with blackout shades to darken the windows and a hidden projection booth, as well as a roll-down movie screen. This wasn't nearly as fancy a screening room as that found in some Hollywood homes, but it worked and allowed Harry and Angela to screen all manner of footage for guests and themselves.

"Make yourselves comfortable and get ready. The cans only contained ten minutes of film and some of it's hard to see, so we'll run it a few times. I don't know what we're watching but it is very strange, almost like science fiction but shot like a newsreel, pure documentary stuff with no story. I know I don't have the pieces in the right order: I just had everything printed then spliced it onto one reel."

Harry's excitement was contagious as everyone focused on the screen and the lights dimmed. His description was indeed correct. Most of the scratchy, high-contrast black and white footage showed scenes in what appeared to be a laboratory or mechanical workshop. Men in different kinds of German military uniforms were prominent in many of the shots. Usually the men were watching the operation of odd pieces of equipment. People in rags moved around cautiously in the out of focus background . Detail in the dark shadows was hard to see. Some of the scenes showed electronic equipment, panels covered with lights, meters and switches. The whole business could have been shot on a set from a Flash Gordon sci-fi movie from the thirties, except that it seemed to be authentic and un-edited. The main piece of equipment, which appeared in almost all the laboratory shots, seemed to be a kind of big round motor which occasionally rose from the floor. It was perhaps ten feet in diameter and a few feet tall, covered with wires and pipes. Steel cables constrained it from moving too far, but sometimes it rose from the floor with a quick jerk, straining its cables and spewing smoke and sparks, while the observers jumped back quickly in fear that perhaps it was out of control. In one shot the machine lurched sideways toward the camera and knocked it over while the camera was still running. The best piece of footage was extremely tantalizing even though it lasted less than a minute. In this sequence a bearded man in a dirty white lab coat sat on top of the motor operating controls while the motor moved up and down, then back and forth: he appeared to be flying the motor very small distances with complete control. No other people were in this sequence: the man and the motor were alone.

The relatively orderly scenes with the motor were in sharp contrast to a group of night exteriors made in a small town. Perhaps a bombing raid was in progress: searchlights scanned the sky, explosions rocked the camera, and fires burned everywhere as people and vehicles ran past the camera in fear. One of the scenes showed enormous steel doors cut in a hillside: perhaps the entrance to a huge cave or tunnel. Wreckage was burning against the doors.

Keith jumped up with an idea, "Harry, in each scene with the big motor it's slightly different, like they're building it or refining it, but you've got the shots all mixed up and out of sequence. Let's edit the film scraps and put them in order, to show the gradual evolution and construction of the big motor, then end with the guy sitting on top and flying it. At least then it would make sense, kind of a short story."

"What are the still pictures like? Do they give more detail," Jessica wondered.

"They're more of the same, but some of them are outdoors with the motor in a bigger space so it could move around, and there're lots of shots in small towns and woods, kind of like snapshots of the local area, and a bunch of after-the-bombing stuff that's grim."

"Do you recognize any of the men or their faces? Is Fritz in any of the shots?"

"Not as near as I can tell, but then he could have been taking the photos and shooting the film."

"I'd like to look at the German diary and see if I can read it. Maybe that will tell us what we've been watching."

"Harry, how can we be sure this footage is not faked in some way: it could be special effects shot on a stage with grips pulling ropes in the background to make the motor move around. We do phony stuff like that all the time."

"I had the same question so I took the original negative to an old friend at CFI and asked him what he thought. Just by running the original negative through his fingers, he could tell that the perforations on one side are distorted slightly, while those on the other edge are smooth. What this means is that the film was shot by a cheap camera that pulled the film on only one side, maybe with just a single claw. If this were studio footage, or fake stuff composited in an optical house, a proper camera with two or four perforation pull-down would have been used so that the film wouldn't be damaged by the camera. What this means is that whatever else we can say about the footage, it is most likely film of something actually happening in front of a simple camera."

"And you said the still photos show the same flying gizmo, but in different settings. It's like these are all records of the development of some sort of machine that actually existed."

"Let's put the stills and the pieces of film in chronological sequence, and match the stills to the footage. Then we can get a better idea of what happened."

"Jessica, here's the diary, see if you can read the German and the handwriting. I've got a big magnifying glass to help with the small print. I couldn't make anything out of it. Even the dates are weird."

"And wait 'til you see our movie of Warm Springs, when the guys started shooting at us."

"What! Who shot at you? Is he on the film?"

"While Jessica reads, I'll tell about our trip to Nevada. There's just one roll of film, and the end is messed up since I forgot to turn the camera off as we ran for the car when the guy started shooting."

Keith explained what had happened in Nevada while Jessica sat at a table with a bright light pouring over the diary. After a while, Jessica turned to the others with frustration, "Damn this thing is not written in German, it's in some other language, mixed with German. Maybe it's Polish or Czech with German words here and there. Do you have an atlas or a map of Central Europe? There are names which may be cities, so perhaps we can learn something by seeing where they are, and there are tons of abbreviations and technical terms that make no sense."

Harry and Keith used the rest of the day to splice the film into an approximation of a chronological sequence detailing the development of the machine. Then they started to match the still pictures to the film.

Jessica and Angela drove to the UCLA library and checked-out maps, atlases, history books and dictionaries. Like the excellent student that she had been in years past, Jessica made meticulous notes of her progress with the dairy. She had been the youngest woman to receive a PhD in Art History from the Sorbonne in Paris and had excellent academic credentials, though she usually hid them from strangers. Angela and Jessica had been friends for years even though Angela at forty-one seemed almost as old as Jessica's distant parents. Jessica and Angela had shared adventures and Angela had introduced Keith and Jessica to each other. Angela and Jessica had been as close as sisters, covering for each other in times of trouble.

In the past Jessica had maintained four separate identities and groups of friends: the academic from a rich family, the struggling painter, the grungy motion picture wardrobe mistress, and a mysterious psychic who gave unusual performances while in a trance. In her academic persona she studied alone, a brilliant conscientious student, a professor's dream switching from English to Latin to French in mid-sentence. As a painter she also worked alone, painting and sketching furiously as an impressionist rather than as a literal artist. [The previous book in this series, **SENIORS HAVE IT TOUGH**, describes her adventures in Hollywood, where she worked in the shadows designing, fitting, and repairing costumes for actors and actresses.] Jessica had psychic gifts, went into trances to contact the dead, suffered delusions, and made predictions. To men, Jessica had appeared asexual, spending much of her free time with very old people who would never approach her body: she never dated, though she occasionally went to wild parties with Angela, but as an observer rather than a participant.

Jessica had met Keith in a casual conversation at a coffee urn on the first day of the shooting of his bizarre film. As he had walked away she had a blinding vision where in a flash she had seen their future life together flying through her brain at high speed, all the way to their death in each other's arms. At the time she had thought it a ridiculous mental aberration: he was a nobody far from her circles, and they had just met, but something about him dug into her subconscious and wouldn't let go. Slowly he had broken through her mental barriers under circumstances which neither really understood. He was now an intimate part of each of her personalities, linking and weaving them together, aware of secrets that she had never shared with anyone: at times he held her life in his hands.

After a long day of research and film editing, dinner found them all around the table sharing their discoveries. Jessica began.

"Most of the towns and places mentioned in the diary are in

Poland, in the southwest corner near Germany: actually this part of Poland used to be part of Germany, but my history's a bit fuzzy. All the villages are clustered together. As a start, we need to find books that describe what happened there during the war. We've got shots of bombing and villages burning: we should be able to nail down the locations accurately, maybe from military records, and eventually we'll be able to read the book: it's in Polish and I've found some words and phrases in a Polish dictionary already."

"We've got the machine's construction footage in order. We'll run the new version after dinner. In the early shots there are wires and pipes leading off-camera from the machine, but as the work progresses these are slowly removed and the machine is more and more on its own, just tethered to constrain its movement."

"Like a wild animal."

"Right, and in some of the exterior shots, the Leica photographs, the machine is inside a group of concrete pillars, but with lots of slack in the ropes."

"In one of the shots it's flying ten feet off the ground: wish we had footage of that test. The machine could be the guts of a primitive flying saucer, but without a shiny metal skin."

"Hey I just realized something about the diary. Scattered around the book there is a little symbol, just on some pages, but now its meaning is obvious. The symbol represents a camera on a tripod, and I'll bet it indicates times when film was shot."

"Let's go to Poland and look for the ruins of the lab and see if it's still there."

"That's not so easy, and what about Nevada, we ought to figure out how the box came to be here and if there's a connection to Warm Springs, and why someone shot at us."

"I've an aunt in Germany, on my father's side, who's Polish: I'll bet she could translate the diary and tell us what it was like in Poland during the war. She escaped to the west after the Russians moved in. We could hop over to see her easily: I spent a few days with her when I studied in Paris."

Late that night Keith and Jessica went home, their heads buzzing with half-formed ideas and conjectures. As they walked through the front door, they found an air freight envelope that had been pushed through the mail slot. Jessica opened it quickly: she saw that it was from an art gallery in Carmel which displayed a few of her paintings.

"Keith, look at this, it's a check, they sold one of my Houdini paintings, the one with you and Houdini floating in the clouds. Remember, I sketched it the night you came to my show at The Magic Castle and I summoned his ghost."

"Holy cow, that's a lot of money for a piece of canvas with a little abstract paint and ink. Shouldn't I get something for being one of the models."

Jessica kissed him lightly, "Well you did get me, aren't I softer and warmer than a check? The painting was an impression, a vision in my head, not a literal description of you: nobody but the two of us knows who the subjects were."

"Well, you did entitle it *Houdini's Ghost Passing By*, so people have some idea of what's happening."

"I wonder if I will ever do another séance as successful as that one: it's the only time I really contacted his spirit and he was so close. I could feel it in the room with us, and you were so sad that night. Maybe there was a connection, our first date, Houdini's appearance, and my best show."

"And your ethereal white dress was so beautiful: you looked like an angel coming down from the clouds to visit me. Then you went home and drank a whole bottle of Scotch while you sketched frantically 'til dawn. I couldn't believe it when you told me."

"Hey, it paid off, here's the check, and those sketches are some of the best I've ever made. Tell you what, this money will cover our trip to Europe, and while we're there I want to visit Houdini's birthplace in Hungary: I sort of owe him for this check in an odd way."

"Maybe you should stay home and paint: you could be making a fortune if you sold a painting every month."

"I have over a hundred paintings scattered around: you've looked at them. How come none of them has brought a check flying through the door? I'm lucky if a few sales each year pay for the paint and canvas."

"And your sketchbooks are covered with ideas you haven't painted.

In Nevada you must have made a dozen more that need to be painted."

"Someday maybe, but not tonight. What I am going to paint next relates to the diary. I have a feeling about it, I can almost see the man, and I know it's a man and not a woman, writing. I can feel his pen in my hand as he wrote each word. I can feel his presence when I hold the diary in my hands. I can almost feel his hands on mine. He wants to tell us something, but I don't know what. Maybe I can sketch or paint his thoughts even if I can't put them in words."

They went to bed in each other's arms and Keith soon fell asleep but Jessica remained awake ruminating over psychic ideas. She had just finished reading **MIND REACH**, a book about scientific experiments involving remote viewing. Subjects had been asked if they could visualize an unspecified remote location where another scientist was standing. Jessica thought to herself, "I wonder if I can train Keith to become more sensitive. In the book scientists found that everybody has at least a little psychic ability. I'm good at it, so perhaps I can teach Keith, maybe without him even knowing that it's happening. Maybe I'm attracted to him because he's really sensitive but his skills haven't been developed. We could have fun if this works."

Vergangenheit

CHAPTER 4
RESEARCH

Keith awoke early and started shaking Jessica, "Jessica, I've got it all figured out, it all makes sense, we're headed back to Nevada."

"Let me see, I'll bet you had a wet dream and want to go back to Nevada to check out a real brothel."

"No dammit, be serious, just listen for a minute."

Jessica pressed her partially dressed body against Keith's pajamas and kissed him as she pulled his shorts off.

"I am serious, lie down. You can pretend we're in a brothel if you want. What do you think it would be like? Tell me about it. Is there a mirror on the ceiling?"

"Six months ago you froze if I touched your body, you held hands with old men, you shivered when I put my arms around you. You're so different now, so sexually active, I can hardly get away from you."

"I've got a lot of ground to make up, and don't tell me you aren't enjoying every minute we're in bed together."

"OK, but first, let me tell you my idea. The machine that we've seen in Harry's pictures is a secret technology for a flying saucer or flying machine of some kind. After the war all that stuff was scooped up by the army and hidden at secret bases in the US. Werner Von Braun, rockets to the moon, ICBMs and all that are just the visible part: there's tons that hasn't seen the light of day because it's still secret, too advanced, or maybe just becoming practical."

"So?"

"Fritz's machine is in that category. We've seen it flying, just a crude prototype. The modern version is out in Nevada at Groom Air Force Base and Area 51, and when they fly it around, people think they're seeing UFOs, when really they're seeing the latest incarnation of Fritz's old machine."

"That's a bit of a stretch, even for you, and how does that relate to the diary and the guy shooting at us?"

"Somebody stole Fritz's box of stuff from the secret base and sent it to Harry, and now other crooks are trying to get it back, and maybe the feds will be on the trail, and the Russians too. It all fits, and if I'm right, we're going be in big trouble because we shouldn't have this stuff."

"That's just a theory that fits the few facts that we have. They're lots of facts that we don't have, lots of leads that could point in other directions."

"But what if I'm right, we could be in deep Bandini."

"If you are right, and that's a really big if, then the first thing we should do is make a copy of all the material and vault it far away from Harry's house. Actually to do this correctly, we should vault the originals and make copies for study. I don't want to take the original of the diary over to Germany to show my father's cousin. Now stop talking and pay attention to my body."

In a moment they were in bed, their clothes on the floor, hugging and kissing, stroking each other, wrapped in pleasure and anticipation. They climaxed in minutes. Afterwards, as they relaxed and their breathing returned to normal, Keith hugged Jessica tenderly and asked, "Sometimes I get the feeling that you hesitate, that you almost push me away, just as I'm about to enter: it's almost like you change your mind at the last instant, even though you're so excited right up until then."

Jessica shivered and involuntarily pressed her fingernails into Keith's flesh as she hugged his body tightly. "It's hard Keith. I want you so much, I want to be part of you, to join our bodies together, but, but well, when I feel your cock pressing on me, about to work its way inside, I can't help it, but I remember that night on the alter with my hands and feet tied down and that big harry monster on top of me and I want to push you away. Then the memory passes and I enjoy you. I'm sorry, I didn't think you noticed."

"If there's anything I can do to make it easier, to make your memories go away, please tell me. I'd do anything for you."

"Just stick close to me, hold my hand when we're together, hug me and kiss me whenever you get the chance. I'm getting better, it just takes time."

Later that morning they were sitting with Harry and Angela discussing Keith's interpretation of the box. The only point of complete agreement was that the material might be valuable, and in that case, copying it was a smart idea.

Then they screened an overnight print of the hundred feet of film that Keith had exposed in Nevada. Harry liked the shot and they were all puzzled by the shooting at the ending. Angela was sitting closest to the screen and noticed an odd bit of detail.

"Dad, would you run it again, slowly if you can. Everyone, look carefully at the hillside behind the motel, about half way up the hill, there's a glint of metal in the sun, or at least that's what it looked like to me."

"Maybe it's the shooter?"

The picture ran through slowly, though Harry couldn't stop it at the area in question because the projector's bright arc lamp would burn a hole in the film if it stopped moving.

"Harry, I saw it too, but I don't think it's a gun. Let's put the film on your editing table and examine it carefully."

"This reminds me of Antonioni's movie *BLOWUP*, where the hero discovers that a murder or something strange happened in the background of a still picture he shot with a Nikon."

"The secret to that film was sexy Vanessa Redgrave trying to recover the negative while distracting the photographer: what a body."

Close examination of the Nevada film revealed that the glint was from what appeared to be an antenna, and the antenna was quite visible once they knew where it was.

"The antenna fits perfectly with my UFO scenario. The exterior of the motel is just camouflage. Inside is a modern operation with radios. The guy we met in Tonopah is part of a network of lookouts who are watching for suspicious characters who ask about Warm Springs."

"Keith, don't go off the deep end. Let's spend today looking at the diary and the still pictures and the other stuff that was in the box. Meanwhile the negatives can all be copied and we can order big prints of the stills."

"OK, we've just scratched the surface, and going back to Nevada without a better understanding of everything would be pointless."

"And dangerous."

"It might be much smarter to go over to Europe and get my father's cousin to translate the diary. Then we'll know a lot more about what happened and what we've been seeing."

"And it could be that what you two saw in Nevada has no relation to the box: the phone call could have come from anywhere, as could have the box. For all we know it's been sitting in someone's attic right here in L.A. for decades and they finally decided to get rid of it."

"Wait a minute, here's a whole different take on the situation." Angela stood and paced the room as she exclaimed, "Maybe the box did come from Nevada, but the guy who sent it to us is in trouble, he needs our help. His call was cut short: something happened. He could be worried, he could have shot at you because he thought that you were trouble rather than friends. The creep in the restaurant could be his friend, or even the sender himself, or the enemy. Maybe I could go over with dad and find out a bit more?"

Nobody spoke for a while. There were too many possibilities, too many unknowns. Keith picked up the diary, "If it's all right with everyone, I'd like to look through the diary, at the math and drawings and see if any of it makes sense to me. Maybe I can at least find out something about the science involved."

"Good, you do that while I contact my father's cousin in Paderborn. Then I want to find out how to get visas and train tickets to Hungary and Poland."

Keith had a B.S. degree in Electrical Engineering, so his university studies had included a considerable amount of math and physics. As he prepared to examine the diary he thought that understanding physics from forty years ago should not be hard. The math and the basic equations from those years were still valid and the intervening time had only added new layers of detail on top of the old ideas. Keith curled up in a comfortable chair with a fresh cup of coffee, a notebook, and the diary and began to look for math and physics among the Polish words.

Harry collected all the negatives of both the movies and the stills and left to visit his friends at Hollywood laboratories. He would have copies made of everything, then place the originals in a secure fireproof film vault where they would not be disturbed for a long time.

Angela and Jessica headed for their favorite travel agent to investigate the realities of traveling to Central Europe behind the iron curtain. The idea of travel to Nevada by anyone was shelved for the moment.

Keith's coffee grew cold as he poured over the diary. Although he couldn't read Polish, and the cramped fine handwriting in which it was written proved difficult to parse, he could detect a few scientific passages, and he began to note the appearance of the "camera" symbols that Jessica had seen, which probably indicated days on which film was shot. Keith puzzled over the book: how to approach it scientifically? How to begin to understand what it contained? As a start he began to write down unusual words that might be references to particular scientific effects which he could investigate, effects which were totally unknown to Keith, but which seemed to be important to the author. Repulsine appeared often, as did words such as Schauberger, Klimator, Repulsator, Podkletnov, Gerlach, Hilgenberg, and Bio-condenser. He also started a list of what appeared to be place names, such as Waldenberg, Leubus, and Ludwikowice.

As a break from the strange words, Keith studied the various sketches and drawings. Often a page would contain an elaborate diagram, a blend of plumbing layouts, chemical formulae, and electrical schematics. Then the opposite page would contain graphs and tables of what he assumed was experimental data related to the diagram. The paper was thin and Keith began to realize that the diary contained hundreds of pages. Many of the pages were pure text in very small handwriting. It would take Jessica's cousin a long time to read all this, let alone translate it into words he might someday understand. Keith's recording background suggested to him that he should take a tape recorder and a large amount of tape. He would record the cousin reading each sentence first in Polish, then in translation, hopefully in English rather than in German. If this were combined with an orderly scheme for referencing page numbers, it might all make sense eventually.

Keith was overwhelmed by the diary, so he shifted his attention to the photographs. Perhaps these would be easier to understand. And what about the reality in the films: what about the guy sitting on the machine actually flying it. Neither the visible mechanisms nor the diary entries related to any technology known to Keith. If the machine relied on a kind of jet engine, like the Messerschmitt jet fighters that the Germans developed during the war, there would be smoke and fire, and the machine would never be running indoors. Other than one piece of footage, featuring smoke and sparks perhaps from an electrical short, there was no evidence of fire or exhaust from the machine. And if the machine were instead a kind of electric motor, how to account for the exterior stills showing the machine off the ground flying by itself without power wires?

Keith decided to examine the still pictures carefully with a magnifying glass: perhaps he could gain a vague understanding of how the machine operated by studying the images. The whole process frustrated, but fascinated Keith. If he hadn't already seen footage of the thing actually flying, he wouldn't have been nearly as excited. And his vague thoughts about UFOs and Nevada were still alive: he might be looking at the raw beginnings of a completely new technology.

Angela and Jessica drove first to Jessica's childhood home which her parents still owned, but rarely visited. They preferred to travel, spending a month here and then there in foreign hotels and apartments with friends from their childhoods in Europe. Their absence had left Jessica to grow up by herself with a succession of nannies and boarding schools. The large old stone house in Hancock Park was home only to a housekeeper who doubled as a secretary, forwarding mail and paying bills. Their neighborhood had once been the most fashionable part of Los Angeles. Iron gates stood at the entrance to the four block area off Beverly Boulevard. When the huge houses had been built among the trees and gardens this was far from downtown, half-way to the ocean. Now the city and its traffic, noise and smog sprawled in all directions, and the fancy homes were just a reminder of what had once been a grand area. Jessica opened the heavy wooden front door for Angela.

"I'll just be a few minutes, I want to grab my diaries, photo albums and music cassettes from France to show Keith, and there's a bunch of stuff about cousin Gerta as well as pictures of her."

"What's her connection to your father?"

"Their family had a big estate way over in what was then far eastern Poland, east of Wilno, almost in Russia, for hundreds of years. An almost purely rural area in those days: dirt roads, huge estates, virgin forests, almost medieval. But the map of that area's been changed many times by invaders and wars. Wilno is currently part of Lithuania and it's been renamed Vilnius. Poland first appeared as a country about a thousand years ago, but then it completely disappeared in 1795 when the Prussians, Russians, and Austrians carved it into three pieces and gobbled them up. Napoleon brought Poland back together for a few years, but then he lost it.

Finally in 1918 Poland reappeared as an independent nation after World War I. But Poland had to fight for its existence almost immediately when the Russians attacked in 1919. By 1921 the Poles had completely trashed the Russians and were a solid and secure nation at last."

"My father's father, my Polish grandfather, managed to convert some of the estate into cash and jewelry in the thirties and bailed out for America with my father, leaving the others behind. Grandfather was one of the few who saw Hitler and Stalin coming and headed for the exit while he could. He bought this house in thirty-five, so my father grew up here, from age ten. My mother, Virginie, is a war refugee from France, so they had a lot in common."

"I'll bet the people your grandfather left behind were pissed that he took the money and ran."

"He was the oldest, and in charge of the family. His brother, Gregorz, was younger and interested in science, so he didn't want to run the estate either, so their sister was left in charge. Gerta is her daughter, and she can talk for hours about how unfair it all was. My father's version is that the others didn't want to go: they thought grandfather was nuts to leave such a huge beautiful piece of productive land, not to mention the fancy house and all the servants. For the first time in ages Poland was an independent country so the Poles thought that everything was looking up and that the future would be great. Man were they wrong."

"Still it must have been hard for any of them to leave their ancestral home, perhaps forever, and set out for an entirely new and different place half way around the world."

"Grandfather was sharp, and his degrees were from Heidelberg, so he knew a lot about the world and about the Germans of that era in particular. It wasn't as though he was a backward peasant, though most of the people on his land looked like they were living in the Middle Ages. That picture over the mantel is a painting of the estate they left behind."

"Geez, that's a huge pile, no wonder the others wanted to stay: it looks so solid, like it would be there forever."

"The site of the estate, near Lyntupy, is now part of Belarus because the Soviets stole the eastern half of Poland in thirty-nine. About a third of the Polish people were killed in World War Two and that big beautiful house is now a Russian army base: it's so sad: I wish I could do something to get it back."

"I don't know what to say, but let me help you carry this stuff: why so many French recordings?"

"I love the old songs, especially the ones from the twenties and thirties and one of them keeps running through my head at odd times."

Meanwhile Keith walked from his home in Westwood to the UCLA library, notebook in hand. The half-hour walk gave him a chance to think over his immediate task as well as larger issues. He realized that as far as making a hit movie was concerned, any semi-realistic bogus science that he dreamed up would work to explain the old equipment. However, Fritz's footage was real and Keith wanted to understand how the machine had actually worked. He could sink his teeth into this aspect of the project and make solid progress, whereas Nevada, the strange voice on Harry's phone, and the gunshots were subjects that might never be fully understood.

Keith took his collection of unusual diary words straight to the card catalog and started looking to see if any of the words were listed. This was a quick and easy first step, especially since the UCLA library was huge. After many dead ends he struck a gold mine, a series of publications from the twenties and thirties by and/or about Viktor Schauberger. Unfortunately they all appeared to be in German except for one small book, which he immediately requested.

The book, entitled **IMPLOSION**, described a partially biological and partially physics-oriented process for the creation of vast amounts of low-cost energy, using a special kind of water, Edelwasser, as a fuel. The drawings showed peculiar machines one of which was called a Repulsator, a word which appeared in Fritz's diary quite often. It seemed to be a turban-snail-like conical cylindrical structure, sort of like a rolled-up cornucopia. The book was hard to follow, jumping from discussions of dowsing for underground water to chemical formulae and vague conjectures on the auras surrounding living beings, animals and plants. The book implied that water, or at least special kinds of water, was somehow alive and energetic. Keith smiled to himself and thought of Jessica's statement that her aura would protect him from his emotions: pure baloney to his way of thinking, but perhaps she could make something of this book. Keith recalled times when he had seen Jessica make impossible predictions that did come true, though he knew that such things shouldn't work. One thing he did know was that she believed deeply in the existence of the spirit world, in things that had no relation to science as he understood it, and here, in this book, were more of these peculiar ideas. Keith read until it was time to go to

Harry's for dinner.

On the way home from the film labs, Harry had stopped to visit an old friend, an Austrian doctor who had been an officer in the German army before escaping to the west. Harry knew that Doctor Von Arlberg was a treasure-house of knowledge about the war and especially about scientific discoveries made in Germany. When Harry told him about the diary and the old footage, the doctor eagerly led Harry to his library and dug out a book from the fifties entitled **_HITLER'S HIDDEN WEAPONS_**. He opened it to a page showing blurry photos of German flying saucers in action against British airplanes. Harry couldn't wait to show the book to Keith.

After dinner Keith and Jessica went home exhausted and confused. Keith had the doctor's book as well as Schauberger's to read and study. Jessica held the diary tightly, trying to feel psychic echoes of its author.

"Keith, do you mind if I just curl up in a corner by myself and focus all my concentration on the writing in this book? I can't tell you why, but I feel connected to it. My hands want to sketch or paint, but I don't know what, and maybe I'll stay up all night with it. Sometimes my best ideas come when I'm really tired, just before dawn, when there's a hint of light glowing in the east."

Keith smiled and hugged Jessica. "Let me know if I can help and whatever happens, please don't jump in your car and go for a drive, OK?"

"I'm over that, though I'll probably have a few drinks while thinking about the diary. Besides, now I have a live-in chauffeur to keep me out of trouble with the cops."

Although Keith didn't notice, Jessica had tensed hard, then shuddered slightly as she remembered the night when she had driven her car into a tree. He had no idea about the other things that had happened that night, or that she had hit the tree on purpose.

Jessica stretched, breathed deeply, then poured herself a large drink and curled up in a comfortable chair next to her paints, sketch books, and canvases. Time to focus on the task at hand and try to forget the past. Keith turned out most of the lights, then placed a warm woolen blanket over her softly breathing body. She smiled, then closed her eyes as she hugged the diary tightly to her breast, focusing all her attention on its author.

Vergangenheit

"See you in the morning. Watch out for flying saucers!"

Keith climbed into bed and started to read, carefully studying the factual portions of the Nazi war secrets book and looking at the photos. Immediately he recognized the shots made inside the huge underground factories where the V-2 and V-1 rockets were built while Allied planes dropped bombs overhead. Harry's footage fit perfectly with the book's photos: the film could have been shot in any one of the underground locations in the book: the factories were inside gigantic tunnels hollowed out under mountains. Finding corroboration, at least for the places shown in Harry's footage, added a touch of believability to the project. Maybe the flying machine they had seen in operation had really existed long ago, but its secret had been lost. By eleven Keith was sound asleep and Jessica was either in a trance or sleeping peacefully.

In the early hours of the morning he jumped awake as he heard screaming and loud noises from the living room. He found Jessica struggling with the blanket and her chair as furniture crashed around her entranced body. Her eyes were closed. She hugged the diary with one arm as she fought invisible enemies with the other. Keith rushed to her side, wrapped his arms around her and tried to awaken her from a nightmare. She kicked, scratched and fought as hard as she could giving no quarter, but would not relinquish the book. Her nails dug into his arms, she scratched, and gasped from the exertion, she pushed and shoved as hard as she could, trying to escape his embrace. Gradually the struggle faded as Jessica opened her eyes and returned to reality. Keith had been through this before and knew that she believed that horrible wild spirits could possess her mind while she slept. Sometimes she stayed awake all night to avoid a particularly nasty visitation.

"Keith, it was so real, I was trapped underground and the freezing water was rising around my waist and I had to get out with the book and save it no matter what happened and everybody was pushing and shoving, tearing at my clothes, trying to get through a hole in the ceiling. It was awful."

Her breath was still coming in short bursts and he could feel her heart furiously beating against his chest: she was soaked in perspiration. Keith noticed brightly-colored abstract paintings and sketches scattered on the floor, and the clock: it was almost dawn. "You're coming to bed now, to sleep in my arms."

"Keith I saw it all, the place where the machine lived, the other people, hundreds of dead bodies all over, everything. The guy we saw on the machine in the film, he wrote the diary, he invented the flying machine and it worked, then he flew away on it and left me behind with the book as the tunnel exploded. I have to save his diary, it's so important. He wants it back. He needs it now."

Vergangenheit

CHAPTER 5

BAD NEWS

Keith awoke and looked at the clock: almost noon and Jessica was still asleep, resting from her encounter with the spirit world. On the way to the kitchen, Keith noticed an envelope that had been slipped under the front door, a small envelope with just a few words on the outside, "Wait 'til you see the video." He opened the envelope and nearly fainted in disbelief at the photograph it contained. A grainy low-angle shot looking up at Jessica's partially-naked body. She was holding the cock of an ugly tattooed man as he leered at her. Keith recognized her skimpy white dress: he had only seen her wear it once, and that was the night of her car accident when she had come to his house, bruised, bloody and completely drunk, long past midnight.

In the distance he heard Jessica, "Keith it's so late, how about skipping breakfast and going out for lunch?"

Keith pocketed the envelope and the photo and fought to regain his composure as Jessica approached. She wasn't wearing much and the contrast between the sight of her body and the photo unnerved him: he could hardly speak.

"Keith, is something wrong? You look kinda weird. Are you sick? What happened?"

"Nothing, I'm alright. Just confused. My imagination got the best of me."

Keith couldn't take his eyes off Jessica's body, as his mind blended the photo over the reality in front of him. The photo made no sense. In the time before their marriage and in particular, the night of the car accident, Jessica was so afraid of men that she froze whenever Keith had tried to kiss her. Even holding hands was almost forbidden so they had had a completely platonic relationship, though Keith had tried often to overcome her fear of men. Once, Jessica tried to hire an actress to give Keith a good time in bed since she couldn't please him herself. How could the frigid and platonic Jessica be the person in the photograph?

"Keith, say something, your eyes, you're staring at my body like there's something wrong with it. What is it?"

She moved to Keith and started to put her arms around him, but he turned away. He couldn't face her, but he didn't know what else to do. Then it hit him, maybe the photo was a fake? He turned back.

"Jessica, I'm sorry, I didn't mean to turn away from you, I'm so mixed up, just hug me. Don't ask why. Don't talk. You're so wonderful. I need you, I love you."

The phone rang and rang but they didn't answer it. Later the phone rang again and Jessica answered. The color drained from her face as she stared at the phone without saying a word. Keith heard a rough male voice, "Honey, did you like the picture? I'll send another, with some wet action."

Keith took the picture from his pocket, showed it to Jessica, then lit a match and burned it to ashes. He hugged her trembling body tightly as he whispered, "You're in trouble Jessica. Tell me what really happened that night. Let me help, I'll do anything for you."

After a long pause, she whispered through her tears, "What I told you was true, I just didn't tell you everything, I couldn't, it was so disgusting. I tried to kill myself by driving into a tree, but the damn tree broke."

"So the picture, I mean, it's not a fake, that's you?"

"I paid them ten grand to kill the . . . . . the perp who was about to get out of jail, but they teased me and said that money wasn't enough. To seal the deal I needed to make a screen test, a little porno footage for their archives. I was so scared, the creep's spirit was taunting me over and over, it wouldn't let go. I told the killers I'd do anything to get rid of it, and so I did."

"And now they're blackmailing you with the film they shot that night?"

"I've been sending a thousand a month, but they want more, and they tracked down my parent's address in Europe and are going to send them the film if I don't cooperate: you'll get a copy too, and maybe some of our friends are in for a treat when they open their mail."

Jessica cried as Keith pieced together the situation from what he knew of her past. When Jessica was fifteen years old and just beginning to explore her psychic powers she had been victimized by a fake wizard who raped her as part of a virgin sacrifice on a candlelit alter in the woods. A mythological scene, but one that was horribly real for Jessica. She had been drugged before she had realized what was happening. Her parents hired lawyers and detectives, tracked the guy down, and sent him to jail. To Jessica the trial was just as bad as the sacrifice. The lawyers kept asking for more detail and the perp blamed her for the whole thing saying that she had entranced him. People smirked when she tried to explain her view of the spirit world: she was treated like a teenage lunatic. After the trial she escaped into her studies, transferring her anger to her parents, whom she rarely saw after that.

Then last autumn she had a vision where she learned that her attacker was to be released from jail early for good behavior. His spirit invaded her head with detailed threats of revenge. The fear his threats engendered was so real that she had hired killers from Van Nuys who worked in the porn industry to murder the perp as soon as he was set free. They cut him apart and sent her a gruesome souvenir as proof of his death. She had felt his spirit die in horrible pain. The episode should have been over, but it wasn't.

"Jessica, we'll solve this somehow. Maybe the video isn't so bad: we could call their bluff and stop sending money?"

"No, don't ever think that. It's as graphic as any porno you can imagine, maybe worse because I was drunk and they had to force me to do things."

"We must know someone who can help, who can shut this down once and for all."

"I don't dare tell a soul, and I wouldn't have told you, but now you know. I was crazy with worry. I thought you would leave me if you saw the film. I'm so ashamed, I'm so unclean."

"Jessica, you're the most wonderful person in the world, and together we're going to beat this. Remember, you once saw a vision of our future and we were still together at the end, so you see, there's no way that I can leave you: we are destined to be together forever."

"But what are we going to do?"

"We'll tell Angela about the blackmail, but not about the perp and the murder, and ask for help. She knows a lot of shady people and owes me a big favor: those scumbags won't have a chance."

"What about the perp's murder? What if they threaten to tell the cops I paid for it? What then?"

"Where's the proof? I'll bet you paid in cash. There's nothing to connect you to the perp's death, and the murderers don't want the law asking questions either. If they say the video connects you, you can say you made it for fun, or even better, you can say that they paid you to make it. The law can't touch you, but let's not run the risk of bringing other people into that part of the story, OK?"

"But what can we say about the video, why I made it? Angela knows me really well, she'll know in an instant that I'm not telling the whole story, that I would never have done that willingly."

"Let's tell them that one night you made a big mistake and drank some booze that was laced with drugs that drove you wild. You can't remember anything, you blacked out, and then this video appeared and you've been paying to keep it secret ever since."

A few hours later they had brought Angela and Harry into their confidence and turned over the names of the blackmailers. Angela encouraged Keith and Jessica to leave town for a while and focus on the mysterious inventor and his diary.

CHAPTER 6

A TRIP TO EUROPE

In pouring rain under a lead-gray German sky Keith and Jessica drove their rented VW east on the Autobahn from Frankfurt. Trucks blasted their windshield with filthy gray water as they passed at top speed, then cut back in front of the little car with a few quick blinks of their turn signals and a blast of diesel smoke. Keith was completely focused on driving carefully in dense fast traffic while Jessica poured over maps under the glow of a flashlight.

"Dammit Keith, you should have turned at the last exit, when I told you to."

"There was no time, that truck was right on my ass, you've got to figure out the turns sooner."

"Take the next exit no matter what it says, just slow down right now, take the exit, go round and make a U-turn, or else I'll drive."

"No chance, you're didn't get any sleep on the plane, you're mad as hell that we're going to see your parents, and besides I can't read the German instructions."

"I'm not mad, it's just a stupid idea seeing them, we should be going straight to Gerta's instead of wandering all over Europe."

"Look, they've never met the guy who married their only child. Of course they'd like to have us visit, and I'd like to meet them. What's the harm in that?"

"They're terrible, and it's a big waste of time going to some damn resort in the middle of nowhere."

"Marienbad's a cool place, even if we're going at the wrong time of year. I want to see if it looks like it did in Alain Resnais's film: I've seen **LAST YEAR IN MARIENBAD** four times and I still can't figure out what's going on. Even the title is misleading."

53

"The film wasn't shot in Marienbad, I looked it up, so you can forget that, and the Hollywood subtitles don't begin to translate the nuances in the French dialog so it's no wonder you didn't understand the story. We're going to a dumpy old spa hotel which will probably be mostly empty and over-priced because of the location."

"Well, it will be interesting crossing the border into Czechoslovakia, and traveling behind the iron curtain. I'll bet it's still 1920 over there."

They made the U-turn, found the correct road, and continued for the rest of the day in a tense silence.

Every hotel in Marienbad seemed to be an old spa with ads for healing mineral waters. It had been a popular place for rich people in the eighteen hundreds when it was part of Austria. Eight o'clock that night found them standing nervously at the entrance to the formal dining room of a once-elegant Victorian-era hotel, the Czech name of which Keith could not pronounce. Keith looked around: the elaborate crystal chandeliers were covered with glowing wax candles, though he suspected they were very good electric imitations. The sea of white table cloths displayed glittering silver and crystal, but there were almost no customers: such a beautiful room for so few people. The Head Waiter approached and led them through an inconspicuous door on the far side.

Ladislas and Virginie were seated at a round table with four places in a small elegant private dining room. As the door opened, Ladislas stood up, moved to his wife's chair, and helped her slowly rise as Keith and Jessica entered. Keith noticed that Virginie was holding her husband's arm tightly and that she stood with difficulty: then he saw a walking cane beside her place at the table. Virginie was beautiful with shoulder length black hair, a soft intelligent French face, and a trim figure in a slightly-formal black dress complemented by a single strand of pearls. Keith was surprised at her close resemblance to Jessica: what a lovely pair of women. Ladislas was tall, at least as tall as Keith, and his hair was just beginning to turn gray. He moved with a smooth casual grace, completely at home in the surroundings. For a moment Keith thought that he was looking at Captain Von Trapp from the film version of **THE SOUND OF MUSIC**, then he smiled to himself and realized that perhaps being in a beautiful part of pre-war Austria had played a trick on his mind: this was not Christopher Plummer playing an Austrian noble, this was the real thing in the real setting. As Keith looked around the room he saw windows with sheer white curtains, flowers on several small pedestals, and a serving table covered with food and plates. Overhead a chandelier provided dim soft light, so as to not overpower the four candles on their table. Keith felt out of place in his wrinkled travel clothes.

"Welcome to Marienbad Keith. How nice of you to come so far to visit us. I'm Virginie and this is my husband Ladislas."

Keith smiled and reached to shake Ladislas's free hand. He wasn't sure if he was supposed to hug Virginie or kiss both of her cheeks or shake her hand. "Thanks, I've been looking forward to meeting you."

On impulse Keith bowed to Virginie and kissed her hand. "Oh my, what a polite young man. Jessica, I don't know how long it's been since anyone greeted me by kissing my hand, and he's so handsome. We're going to be good friends." Keith blushed slightly but knew that he had done the right thing as Jessica remained silent and tense.

"Please sit down. You must be tired after the long drive, and we've had a busy day too," Ladislas said as he seated his wife.

Jessica's annoyance almost rose to the surface, but she contained it, smiled perfunctorily and seated herself before Keith could move to help her. "Yes, it must be tiring playing cards all day at the Casino."

"Actually we've been working at a nearby orphanage teaching English and sewing to the children since before breakfast. That's the main reason we come here," Ladislas replied.

"And there's a slim chance that the mineral waters will help my legs, so I soak them every night after dinner."

"Why do you come to the orphanage here, I mean, it's a long way to come to teach, though the kids must be grateful," Keith asked.

Jessica glared at Keith, annoyed that he was showing interest in her parents instead of in her, but before she could think of a sarcastic comment, Virginie answered. "The family that started this orphanage are old friends, and we've contributed what we could to its operation over the years, but what's really needed are modern teachers, people who can bring them language, math, and useful skills."

"We take turns with other volunteers. This is our month to teach every day." Ladislas turned to Jessica, "The children are much more interesting than the casino."

Ladislas wished that somehow he could rejoin the family ties that they had shared before Jessica's trial. When Jessica had been young the family had been close, travelling, laughing and playing together as one being. In those days Jessica had occasionally mentioned strange dreams and thoughts, but they didn't seem unusual for a little girl with an active imagination. But when she passed through puberty a change began to come over her, and a curtain or gauze descended on their family relationships. He and Virginie talked with psychiatrists and psychologists, but in the end decided to let Jessica follow her own lead, doing the things that she felt she must do. She began to drift away, saying strange things, reading unusual books and playing with odd people. This wasn't a real problem and they were still a family until the attack. After that it was impossible to talk with Jessica or interact in any way. It was almost as though she blamed her parents for what happened instead of her crazy friends and weird ideas.

Keith could feel the tension between Jessica and her parents. The bad feelings were so strong that they were almost visible. He wondered how he could defuse the situation, and he had never seen Jessica in such a foul mood. Perhaps flattery was the best place to start: things couldn't be much worse.

"My parents were killed in a car accident when they were driving home after a wild party with drugs and too much drinking. They threw their lives away. I miss them very much." Keith turned toward Jessica, "But now I've found a new family, a family with the most wonderful daughter, my lovely wife Jessica. I know the four of us can become the best of friends, much more than friends, a whole family together again."

A tear rolled down Virginie's cheek, "Thank you Keith, that would make me the happiest person in the world. We can't replace your parents but you must consider yourself our son."

"Why don't you two join us tomorrow? Come help us teach. You don't need to understand Czech, you can talk to the kids in English, just be patient. And Jessica, you could paint or draw with them, they love bright colors and some of their drawings are amazing. We walk over about seven-thirty and have breakfast in the midst of a hundred smiling faces," Ladislas suggested.

Jessica had already drained the cut-crystal glass of champagne near her plate and was almost through the refill that the silent waiter had provided. She churned inside, annoyed by her misjudgment of her parents' activities, pleased by Keith's flattery, but uncertain what to do next. Keith broke into her thoughts.

"We haven't eaten since before noon, so is it alright if we start?

56

The food looks great, and I know Jessica's famished."

Ladislas said something in Czech to the waiter and nodded toward Jessica. Breads, hor d'heurves, and salads moved from the sideboard to the table. "Please begin. The kitchen can make anything so if there's something special that you would like, let me know and I'll order it. Keith, don't be bashful, eat as much as you can or the staff will think we aren't enjoying ourselves."

As the meal progressed gingerly with tentative small talk about tomorrow's activity and their travels, Jessica noticed that while the glasses of the others were often refilled, hers was never touched by the waiter. After yet another round of three but not four refills, she threw her napkin on the table, jumped up and walked quickly from the room, muttering "I hope the bar has better service."

Keith rose immediately and followed, "Please excuse us. Jessica's just tired, she'll be OK in the morning, tonight's been really hard for her."

Keith found Jessica in the almost empty ancient dark paneled bar with a glass of champagne and sat down beside her. "I'm sorry Jessica, I never should have made you come here."

"You had to meet them sometime; it's just so damn awkward. They think they're doing the right thing by cutting off my booze, but why can't I have at least as much as they do, or you?"

"I don't know the whole story, or even part of it, but they can't be all bad if they had you as a daughter."

"We'll be out of here soon, so let's just make the best of it, OK?"

"May I order you some food? Would you like to leave here first thing in the morning before seeing them again?"

"Thanks, I already asked for a plate of fruit and cheese, and now that you're here we'll get a whole bottle of champagne and relax."

"You seemed surprised that they were here to help in the orphanage."

"I'm out of touch with them, and then I say the most stupid things."

"It will pass, and meanwhile we're about to have a great adventure. I'm working on a great project and finally pushing Kristin and all that into the background. You've saved my life Jessica, and I'll never forget it."

They kissed, "You're worth saving." Jessica smiled then laughed, "Hey, I just had an idea, maybe a long shot, but I think my parents know some film people in the European scene, so maybe you can talk with them about it. They could be useful as you get to know them better."

In the morning they met Virginie and Ladislas on the marble steps at the front of the hotel: both were wearing casual inexpensive clothes, indistinguishable from local people doing their morning errands. Although Virginie walked with difficulty and held her husband's arm tightly, she held her head up and smiled as though nothing was amiss. The weather had changed, the sun was out and the city glowed in a cool freshly-washed breeze. They walked in a park along the tree-lined river which flowed through the center of town. The first leaves of spring were budding on the trees.

"Keith, you are probably wondering what is wrong with my legs, but you are too polite to ask so I'll tell you. I was born in 1925, as was Ladislas, but while he was raised on a farm with abundant food, I was not as fortunate. My parents lost everything in the Great War, so my mother had little to eat while she was pregnant with me, and as a girl I didn't have much food either, so the bones and joints in my legs didn't develop properly. My first really wonderful meal didn't happen until 1944, when I met Ladislas at UCLA and he took me home for a veritable feast."

"I can understand why you want to help the kids at the orphanage," Keith replied.

"Yes, one thing we and our friends are able to do is to see that the children have plenty of food: they can't develop if they are hungry all the time," Ladislas added.

"You mentioned that you are going to visit Gerta so that she can translate an old Polish book, but surely you must have other plans while you are in Europe?"

Keith paused before answering in hopes that Jessica would join the conversation but she remained quiet, so he answered. "While Gerta works on the book we're going to visit Houdini's birthplace in Budapest and some old war ruins that I want to see for a script I'm writing."

"Let's not talk about Houdini, it wouldn't interest you," Jessica quickly added while trying to think of a way to turn the conversation, but it was too late.

"I don't know about Houdini, but there is much to see in Budapest," Ladislas replied.

"Jessica's interested in Houdini's spirit. She summoned him one night during a séance. I couldn't believe it, but I was there and Houdini really appeared. Jessica's amazing, as I'm sure you know."

Jessica grabbed Keith's hand and started to drag him back toward the hotel. "Just shut up, will you, that's not something we talk about, so drop it."

Before Jessica and Keith had a chance to move, Ladislas put his arm around her shoulders. "Jessica, please don't go, it's all right, we know much more than you realize and we love you so much."

The four stood close together in silence for a moment beside the rushing water, Jessica holding Keith's hand while her father comforted her. Virginie gently rubbed her back, then whispered to Jessica, "We made mistakes, we didn't understand your world, but now we know a little. My grandmother, your great grandmother Andresha, also had the gift: we talked with her about it last month just before she died. I wish you had been there. I never knew anything about her interest in spirits, people just don't talk about such things; most don't believe it's real."

"What did she say? Did you tell her about me?"

"Yes, she was fascinated, and I so wished that I knew more about what you've done, what you've seen. She wanted to meet you, but she died too quickly."

"Did she die on February seventeenth?"

"Yes, that's right, in Bordeaux, around dawn."

"I met her spirit that night, but I didn't know who it was. Such a lovely experience. Why didn't we get together before she crossed over: if only I had known sooner? Why didn't you tell me?"

"It happened too fast. We drove all night, and when we reached her she was already dying. We talked for a few hours then she was gone, oh Jessica, we've been so wrong. Can you forgive us?"

Keith sensed a change in Jessica and squeezed her hand then released it. An invisible barrier between Jessica and her parents had melted. She turned to her mother and hugged her tightly as they both cried.

Keith took Ladislas aside, "I don't quite know how to say this, but I need to warn you about something that I hope doesn't happen. You may receive dreadful photos or even a video involving Jessica. She's being blackmailed. It's all a terrible mistake, but I think we have it under control. She is very worried about it: she didn't realize how much you love her. Please don't ever mention the pictures if you see them."

"You're visit has changed things. We've treated Jessica badly because we thought she hated us: too many harsh words were spoken on both sides. That is over. I hope you can stay a few days so that we can begin to make amends."

"Thanks, thank you very much. Lots of exciting things have happened in her world and in mine and we want to know more about what you've been doing."

A week later Keith and Jessica drove into the modern German city of Paderborn and went straight to the hospital where Jessica's Aunt Gerta was a Neurosurgeon. While Marienbad had been old, crumbling and lacking the comforts of the western world, Paderborn, in spite of extensive bomb damage during the war, was fresh, busy, modern and on the way up. After they waited in the spotless antiseptic lobby for over an hour, Gerta, clad in a green gown with a face mask dangling loosely around her neck, walked briskly into the room and headed for Jessica.

"Wie gehts Jessica, and you must be Keith, hello. I'm busy but I can spare you a few minutes for coffee. You are now married Jessica, what are you going to do with all your education and study? Is it to be taught to your children or wasted, and Keith, what are you trying to accomplish? Where is your life going?"

Keith was not prepared for the barrage of serious questions that flowed naturally from Gerta, but Jessica had the advantage of having been through Gerta's brusque style of conversation before, so she grabbed control by replying with a question. "How is your germ containment initiative? Have you reduced the number of patients dying from disease contracted in your hospital?"

"So, you remember our last conversation. Yes and No. Even in America you have ninety thousand people a year dying from germs caught while staying in hospitals, not to mention the million or more that are saved after being infected by the doctors who are supposed to be curing them. Now we have the latest alcohol disinfection stations in almost every room so doctors have no excuse not to sterilize their hands between patients. But still, even more than a hundred years after the Hungarian Doctor Sammelweiss and Doctor Lister, and with all the modern antiseptic equipment, we have cross-contamination from patient to patient by overworked staff. It's a burden, but we are working to become better, not quite perfect yet, but closer and closer. And now, what about you? What are you doing here?"

The trio had walked into a coffee shop that was part of the hospital, a clean white room with antiseptic surfaces and furniture, but friendly: the aroma of excellent fresh coffee filled the air near the heavily laden pastry cart.

"Aunt Gerta, we need your help in translating a diary written in Polish during the war."

"We have film footage showing the author and a mysterious flying machine as well as his laboratory diary, but we don't understand it," Keith added.

"Why come here? Surely there are Poles in America who could read it. I am too busy for such a trivial project."

"But you were there during the war, you know what it was like, you know the nuances, your translation would be so much more realistic than a straight literal reading," Keith replied.

"And you told me that I could come to you if I ever needed help, or if I wanted to know more about family history, about what happened in the old days."

"Not now. Later we'll talk about what it was like being a young girl in Poland, how our family was killed one by one by the Russians, but please don't ask. You two have no idea, absolutely no conception of what it was like to live in a country ruled by military thugs, to grovel for necessities, to be afraid of being raped every time you walked to the market, or by a teacher in school."

"Why didn't you escape with Ladislas and his father before the war started?" As soon as Keith said this he realized that he had made a colossal error. Gerta stared at him in disbelief.

"Mein Gott! Do you think we were invited to go with them, to share the money they stole from the family? What has Jessica told you to make you ask such a question?"

"Please, I'm so sorry Gerta, I mean Doctor, it just came out. I'm logical, I figured that people in Poland would have looked at the map and seen Stalin and Hitler coming, and run for their lives."

"Believe me Keith, it was not obvious to those of us who were there, and we received no invitation to come to California until it was much too late. Virginie was lucky to escape from Vichy France, but many others died trying to get out, and your country was not as welcoming to refugees as it appears in your history books."

"Please forgive Keith, Aunt Gerta. He doesn't know much about us, and for that matter, I don't know a lot either, and as you realize, my knowledge of the past is colored because it came from Ladislas, not from you and the rest of the family. We want to understand, to know more, but it's hard to even know what to ask."

"We will have dinner tonight and talk further. Perhaps you can help someone who deserves a break. A Polish patient of mine is recovering. He cannot go back to work for weeks, maybe months, so he has nothing to do, and he needs money: he's here on a temporary visa, a guest worker. We will ask him to do the translation and you will pay him well, perhaps with some of the money Ladislas's father took from the family."

Gerta's visit ended abruptly with an emergency call over the public address system, so Keith and Jessica were on their own. Keith was relieved that their visit had ended in the coffee shop and that they hadn't been forced to wander around the hospital with Gerta as she did her rounds: his memories of Kristin and his visits to her in the UCLA hospital were still fresh. In addition, the conversation between Jessica and Gerta about virulent hospital germs and patient deaths raised new doubts in his mind. It had never occurred to him that perhaps Kristin's death was caused by germs passed by the very doctors who were working to save her, and that this was the basis of the hospital's secrecy concerning details of her death.

They walked downhill to the quiet park surrounding the peaceful clear springs that form the headwaters of the river Pader, then wandered around the old cathedral area amidst ruins dating back to Charlemagne in 800 AD. This had been his capital, the city where he had received Pope Leo the Third and where he was crowned the first Holy Roman Emperor. Although Jessica was interested in the history and the old buildings, Keith was more curious about the puzzle of the three rabbits: "can you draw three rabbits with only three ears so that it appears that each rabbit has two?" The reason for his interest was that there was just such a drawing in a sixteenth-century stained glass window in the Paderborn cathedral, and it did appear that each rabbit had two ears, though there were only three ears in the window. Copies of this drawing, which shows three rabbits running after each other in a tight circle, "die drei Hassen", appear on tee shirts, flags, and many other things in Paderborn: the local football team is called the Paderborn Rabbits.

That evening they met Gerta for dinner at a little country inn near her home. Heavy wooden tables, old sepia photographs of neighborhood farm scenes on clean whitewashed stone walls, and a warm friendly staff created an ambience that hadn't changed in decades. Gerta began to explain some of her family history to Keith.

"There were two brothers and a sister, and they inherited the estate, all the workers, and thousands of acres in eastern Poland after their parents died in 1920. Of course Ladislas's father as the eldest had the real control, and the others were there because he allowed it, at least that's how it seemed. Ladislas's father, your grandfather Jessica, was just finishing up at Heidelberg so he came home and took charge. His younger brother Gregorz stayed in school, but in Berlin. Gregorz was a disaster for the family. He was brilliant as a child, first in everything, especially science. But instead of coming home to help manage the estate after your grandfather left for California, he buried himself in research and joined the Nazis: he never returned to Poland. I have no idea what happened to him, we never heard a peep. Perhaps he wrote to California, but I never heard about it. He might have had children, or died in an air raid, or on the Eastern Front: no one knows. Your grandfather, Jessica as you know, headed for California in thirty-four, so that left only mother at home, and she had a five year old daughter, me, to take care of as well. She did her best, but she had no chance to go to university, or much of anything else. I was born in 1929, just as the rest of the world settled into depression, but that was far removed from us, that is until Stalin's soldiers arrived when I was nine and started raping the women and killing the men."

"Sitting here in this cozy German restaurant, looking around at the people here, it's hard to imagine them starting a war and attacking all their neighbors," Keith wondered.

"Of course people like this didn't attack anyone, it was their idiotic leaders and politicians who dragged them into it."

"Gerta, you're a doctor, a neurosurgeon, you know how people's brains work, why do they follow such crazy leaders, why did they let themselves be led into such a disaster?"

"I just don't know, it makes no sense to us sitting here, but when you talk to the old people, the ones who were there, who were in the Hitler Youth, in the SS, in the Luftwaffe, they say that it just happened, that it seemed like the right thing to do at the time. They wanted to get even with the villains who had crushed their country in the Great War. I know it's wrong, but it's what they say, and perhaps our task, mine as well as yours, is to see that nothing like that happens again."

"What's that big book in your bag Aunt Gerta?"

"It's photographs from the old days: I want to show both of you what it was like. One of the few things that Ladislas did for me, and I was only five at the time, was to give me a Zeiss Ikonta-C six-by-nine folding camera and a book on how to use it. That was just before he left for California. It was a wonderful camera and it folded up into a small and concealable package but it had a few quirks. At first I only used ortho film because the camera had a red window on the back to see the exposure number. If I loaded it with panchromatic film, like you use today, the red window would let in enough light to fog the film, at least in bright light: eventually I made a little cover to go over the peep hole so I could use the latest films. That camera got me into medical school, or rather the pictures I made with it did. And its instruction book was how I learned to read German, parsing it out with a dictionary and mother's help. Maybe I had a crush on Ladislas as he was four years older than me and seemed so handsome as he set out to explore the world. He told me to take lots of pictures and mail some to him so that he could see how the estate was doing."

"How did my father's camera get you into med school? I've never heard about that."

"Well, what would you think if you saw a grubby little girl playing with a simple camera? Of course, you would ignore her, and assume that she was playing with a piece of junk that didn't work. You would never imagine that she was quietly taking very good photographs, then developing them herself in a modern darkroom at home. I realized quite early that I could become almost invisible if I dressed in peasant's clothes, put dirt on my face, and kept to the shadows. It was like being a private eye or a secret reporter, and the large six by nine negatives allowed me to make very sharp and highly-detailed prints of interesting subjects."

As Gerta talked she had removed a battered old camera from her purse and casually played with it on the table.

"For example, look at this camera, a Zeiss Super Ikonta four, made twenty-five years ago. It's the last descendant of my old pre-war six-by-nine. These cameras have been eclipsed by modern and more flexible equipment, but they still take great pictures."

"I take photographs too, but with a 35mm Leica," Keith interjected.

"What do you like to photograph? What time of day is the most interesting to you?" Gerta asked as she played with her camera.

"I like night photography in available darkness: I've got an F one point two Noctilux and lots of fast panchromatic film that can be push processed to ASA sixteen hundred."

"I wish I had had an outfit like that in the old days, and actually, in the wards, I use a Leica now if I need color pictures for medical records."

"Do you ever take pictures just for fun?" Jessica asked.

"As a matter of fact, I just made three photos of the two of you illuminated by candlelight on fast grainy Royal-X pan film while we have been talking. I'll make you a set of prints next time I'm in my darkroom."

"Wow you're really good! Did you become a spy, or a newspaper reporter after the war?"

"Let's just say that I managed to take a few valuable shots and use them to convince the right people to place me in good schools. During and after the war life behind the iron curtain was turbulent, crazy with no order, but there were opportunities for those who moved fast. I bought this camera the day I graduated from medical school in Leipzig. Then, with a big dose of luck, I crossed into West Germany and I've almost never looked back."

"I can't wait to tell father what a valuable present he gave you all those years ago."

"Ladislas's a very nice man, I mean, it's hard to put it in words, but I'm glad to have him for a father-in-law, he's so kind, so involved in helping other people. Do you ever see him?"

"No, that's not my impression, but what I mean is that our paths diverged and I don't feel that I have anything in common with him, even though we're first cousins."

"We were just with him, and Virginie, in Marienbad where they were working in an orphanage. We helped a bit, and we'll have a chance to do more next year."

"Are any of our Polish relatives still alive, your brothers and sisters, other cousins? Do you see any of them," Jessica asked.

"Very few survived. I hear a bit from one cousin in Russia, and another in Poland at Christmas, but we're part of history now, almost gone. So Jessica, it's time for you to have lots of children and carry the family into the next century. Are you pregnant yet, and if not, why? Keith seems virile, you two should be as busy as the Paderborn rabbits, resurrecting our family!"

With this Gerta raised her glass of Rhine wine in a toast to the future, and signaled an end to talking about the past.

Twenty-four hours later Keith and Jessica were bundled in warm coats, hats, and gloves as they wandered the streets of Paderborn. Keith stopped at a bookstore window, "Hey this shop has English books: let's take a peek and get warm at the same time."

"OK, perhaps they have French books too: I'd like to see what's popular in France, and look, they have a wine bar."

As Keith wandered through the English books, he came upon a dusty photography book, a red-jacketed **LEICA MANUAL**. It was old so he carefully looked for the printing date and found that it had been published in 1939, just as the war was starting. He thought to himself, "This book is about the kind of camera Fritz would have used, exactly. One of these cameras could have made the images in Harry's box. Fritz might even have had a copy of this book."

Five minutes later they were sitting in the wine bar as Keith intensely poured over the pages while Jessica pretended to explore a copy of Le Monde, and enjoyed a large carafe of red wine. Jessica thought to herself, "He's so intense on this old book, he feels it, he's disappeared into the pages."

"Jessica, when I look at these old pictures, like this one of snow falling on German businessmen in heavy dark overcoats as they hurry home under the street lamps, I can feel the camera in my hand, a Leica IIIb with a fast 50mm lens and a shade to keep snow off the lens. I'm cold, I'm there, I know what the exposure is. My feet are freezing in the snow and I can feel the slush on the sidewalk through my thin shoes. I compose the shot then shift my eye to the rangefinder and set the focus, then click the shutter. I can almost hear the Christmas carol, *In The Bleak Midwinter*, as the snow falls on these people. How can a simple old black and white photo like this turn me on, take me there, make me the photographer, when I don't even know where this is?"

"How old is the camera, the equipment, in your book?"

"Fritz could have had a camera like this in 1939, he could have made these shots, these cameras were the last series before the war started."

"Maybe it's a message from the past, stop! Don't argue, just listen. Maybe somehow you were drawn to this book, to these images, and now your emotions are catching up. You see the images, you feel that you're the photographer, you know this stuff, you live it and breathe it, and now echoes from the past are drifting into your consciousness. Tell me about the other pictures in the book. Tell me how the camera feels in your hand when you move the controls. Is the focus ring stiff? Do you take a few shots at different exposures to be sure you've got it or do you move on to the next opportunity? You are the photographer in Germany as the war was starting. Smell the smoke from the coal fires, feel the excitement. Are you a Nazi or an ordinary citizen, or Jewish, fearing for your life?"

"Jessica, what's in that wine you've been drinking? This is just an old photography manual, but I do wish I had one of these cameras. I'd like to step back in time, to travel in the slow lane, to compose carefully, to work to make each shot count when film was expensive and rare."

"Don't talk, just let your imagination take control. Pick up the camera, how many exposures are left? How dim is the light? Hold still, you can nail the exposure if your freezing hands don't shake the camera. Hold your breath while you make the shot. You're there, you're living in 1939, your thin coat isn't warm enough, you're hungry, this shot will pay for dinner, so be careful, make it count. . . . . ."

Vergangenheit

Keith awakened and shook himself into consciousness as a waiter touched his arm. "What happened? He looked around, the wine bar was closing, Jessica's wine carafe was empty, and she was asleep in her chair. Suddenly it came to him: she hypnotized me, and in public, right in front of all these people."

As they walked home Jessica hugged Keith tightly and smiled to herself. She knew that Keith was becoming more sensitive to the spirits, he was moving into her world, he just needed training and steering, they would live together forever.

CHAPTER 7

BUDAPEST AND BEYOND

Two days later Gerta's patient, Gregor Ponczki, was busy translating a copy of the old diary page by page and Keith and Jessica were on a train headed to Budapest via Munich and Vienna to visit Houdini's birth place. Their change of trains at dusk in Vienna marked a transition from a familiar world into another that was totally foreign. Vienna was a piece of the western world that poked far into Eastern Europe. The Viennese railroad station is shaped like a large 'L', with modern electrified trains on one leg and ancient coal-powered steam trains on the other: a junction of technologies across a hundred years. The electric trains were headed to Western cities like Rome, Paris and Geneva but the destination boards next to the steam trains were lists of cities that Keith barely knew existed. A few of the trains ended in Moscow, but most of the destinations were off Keith's mental map.

They were apprehensive but excited as they looked in the windows of the ancient steam train that they would ride later that night. It was already in the station, with a large black engine hissing and smoking at the front though departure was many hours away. The passenger seats were bare wood and there was a pot-belly stove and a box of coal at one end of each car for heat. A few people were already on board, huddled against the cold near the stove. Jessica bought a canvas bag and stuffed it with bread, chocolate and fruit in case their train ran into trouble. On the map, Budapest was only a few hundred kilometers distant, but their slow train was scheduled to take over eight hours for the journey as it meandered through small cities along the way.

At nine they boarded the train after wandering through the station and the nearby streets in the cold for hours. As Keith looked around their almost empty old coach, he thought of the footage of the scientist, his invention, and of the world Gerta had known as a child. This very car could have carried the scientist on secret journeys: he might have visited Vienna and walked on the same train platforms they had trod today. He must have heard the same steam engine noises, the grunting of the injector pump forcing water into the boiler, the whine of the small electric generator powering the headlamp, the constant hissing as steam escaped through leaks. These would have been part of his everyday life, along with the aroma of coal burning, not just in steam engines, but in every house and factory, providing heat and power. It was not an unpleasant smell, just something that Keith and Jessica rarely encountered in the western world.

"Jessica, can you sense anything of the past here? Did our inventor pass through this station, or ride in this car?"

"It's a nice thought but I really don't know: I'll bet this car and the track underneath us are old enough for it to have happened. This is like stepping into a history book. If you do make a film about his story, let's include a night journey on this train: it's perfect, so much could have happened in this car, on these seats. Think of all the people who could have sat here, maybe smiling, excited about where they were going, or crying and afraid that they were on their last journey."

At exactly midnight the train rolled slowly out of the station. At first, they were too excited to sleep and stared out the window at the lights of Vienna passing by. The seats were hard cold wood but when Keith complained Jessica reminded him of an old quotation, "an adventure is just inconvenience and discomfort correctly imagined."

They awoke as the train rolled through the Hungarian countryside, and into the Budapest suburbs. It was time for a breakfast of coffee, hot chocolate, and pastries in the splendid old world cafe next to the Budapest train station.

As they ate crisp hard rolls and butter Jessica explained a little bit about Houdini's time in Budapest. "Houdini was born right here, March 24 1874, and we're going out to the house where he was born. He came to America at age four, but he told people that he was born in Appleton, Wisconsin after he changed his name. His father was a Jewish Rabi who left Hungary because of persecution: Houdini's real name was Ehrich Weiss, and he died on Halloween night, 1926, in Detroit. The story is that he let someone punch him hard during a show in Montreal to demonstrate how well he could control his stomach muscles. A few days later he came down with appendicitis because of that punch. I've seen all five of the silent films he made: he was great, and someday I'm going to visit the Houdini museum in Scranton Pennsylvania."

"I didn't realize you knew so much about his life, but how do you know exactly where he was born? I mean, that was a hundred years ago, and there've been wars and new streets, and lots of changes, not to mention all the bomb damage and ruins we saw from the train."

Jessica paused, then answered defensively, "I've got some notes and a map. Maybe we'll get lucky." The apprehension in Jessica's voice was only partially caused by doubts about her directions to Houdini's house, plans which were based on an old newspaper story she had found in the UCLA archives. Underlying this worry was a dim but unmistakable fear about what would happen if the map were indeed correct. What would she sense and feel at the site? Would his spirit live in the old home, would it contact her, would it be scary or nice? Would it be glad to meet her after their contact last year, or would it be mad that she was invading its space?

As soon as they had checked into a hotel near the station, Jessica collected her pencils and pens, her sketchbook, and her maps and notes and headed for the front door. Keith started reading a guidebook and studying tourist maps as Jessica talked to cab drivers, seeking one who knew a bit of English or French. Keith could tell that their taxi driver was surprised when Jessica showed him her map and where she wanted to go, but the driver didn't complain as the meter ticked off the long drive out through the suburbs, through neighborhoods that once had been separate towns. They went north, following the slow-moving wide Danube river for almost an hour, then turned away from it on a rough little road that wound through an area of ruined buildings and disorderly clumps of old bricks. Weeds grew everywhere and there were no street signs or people about. Keith began to worry that they would never find a taxi to take them back to their hotel once they started walking around. The car stopped in the middle of a small street and the driver pointed to the spot which Jessica had marked on her map. She climbed slowly from the cab and started to wander around the ruins with her eyes half closed. Keith wondered how to get the driver to come back to collect them later. At the last minute, he remembered something he had seen when working on a film location a few years back. He tore a fifty-dollar bill diagonally in half and gave one half to the driver, then pointed to his watch, four hours hence. The driver understood completely and drove away with a big smile.

There were no house numbers or street names and Keith's logical self began to wonder if they were anywhere near Jessica's chosen location, or the actual house of Houdini's birth. She seemed puzzled as she silently walked among the weeds, the remains of foundations and old cellars, the few standing walls and their hollow windows, their doorways to nowhere. Old bricks, blackened pieces of bricks, bits of concrete, isolated chimneys, were all that was left of an old abandoned blitzed-out neighborhood where people had once lived before the war. Keith put a lens on his camera and looked for interesting subjects to photograph. He knew that Jessica was in her own world with no interest in conversation. Eventually he sat down on cold stone steps that had once led to a doorway and started to write in his notebook, using an old fountain pen that had belonged to his father. These ruins might be, with lots of imagination, what the neighborhood above the inventor's underground workshop looked like today, forty years after the bombing. He began to dream, to imagine that the secret tunnels and workshops were under his feet right here, just waiting to be discovered. He shot photographs of a ruined house and fantasized that amidst the rubble was a secret entrance to the tunnels underground. It could be true, at least in a film, and writing down his thoughts and imaginings made the time pass quickly. In his mind, he could connect these scenes from today, in a cinematic sense, to the inventor's footage of bombs falling, people running away, fiery buildings burning brightly in the night forty years earlier. It would work, especially if the new footage was shot at night, with a bit of fog and confusion.

The ruins were quiet, no vehicles, no birds or insect noises disturbed the silence. A silent breeze drifted dust along the street. Keith listened intently as he heard something in the distance. Then he knew instinctively that he sound was Jessica, crying her heart out. As he looked around, he saw her far away sitting on the ground in a corner of what had once been a small brick house: what a sad but beautiful scene, her soft body resting on the hard rubble of war-time destruction. Against his better judgment he quietly shot photographs of Jessica and her surroundings, grateful that his Leica had a quiet shutter with a very soft click. More than once this had enabled Keith to take pictures in situations where cameras were not to be used. As he walked over to comfort her, he saw her sketch pad, open but with only a few scratches on the tear-stained page and her pen case scattered on the ground nearby. Keith gently massaged her back, though he knew that there was little he could say or do to ease her pain. Perhaps she had found the right place, or she had realized that her quest was impossible. Either way it was so sad.

That night she awoke shaking violently and cried herself back to sleep several times but Jessica couldn't tell Keith what she felt: it was beyond words in any language that she knew. All she could do was to hug him tightly as she shuddered in pain.

One day in the future Keith would have his film developed and see an odd fuzzy area in the pictures he had taken of Jessica amidst the ruins. She would cry out, exclaiming that the negative showed Houdini's ghost hovering over her, but Harry would counter that it was an optical effect caused by sunlight hitting the lens at an odd angle. Keith didn't argue either point.

As soon as she awoke the next morning Jessica wanted out. No visits to tourist attractions like the mummified right arm of St Stephen, the protector of the city, at the gigantic hilltop cathedral, or to the opera house or to the beautiful parliament buildings. She was done with Budapest and ready for something else, and the sooner the better. Keith opened his collection of maps and notes on the mines and tunnels mentioned in the diary, rented a car, and they were off without a moment's hesitation.

Vergangenheit

CHAPTER 8

SEARCHING FOR THE OLD LAB

Once they cleared the traffic and narrow streets of Budapest in their rented black VW Jetta, the drive was easy and scenic, but slow. The largest Hungarian roads were what at home Keith might call two-lane-blacktops, but here they were major highways, often filled with creeping old trucks belching black smoke from what Keith thought must be poorly refined fuel. They headed north along the Danube following the old trade route through Dunakeszi and Vac to Esztergom.

Leaving Hungary was easy as they drove through the beautiful old city of Esztergom, once the capital of Hungary, then onto the bridge over the Danube to Sturovo in Czechoslovakia. As they entered Czech customs, a well-armed customs agent motioned them to the side of the road, to a holding area, while the rest of traffic passed through. Keith was annoyed, why were they stopping? The guard starting asking questions in a language that Keith presumed was Czech, but which he didn't understand. Jessica answered the guard in French, then English, then German. When she started to speak German, the guard looked surprised, then opened the driver's door and motioned them out as he yelled something to another officer.

The second guard addressed Jessica in English, "You will not speak German here, and if you want to visit our country, you won't speak it anywhere else, understand?"

"Yes, I'm sorry, I just wasn't sure what language we might both know. Would you rather converse in French?"

"That won't be necessary as you're probably American or British, aren't you?"

"American, just tourists passing through," Keith answered.

The guard pointed to the rear of the car, "Customs inspection, please open your car."

Keith started to protest, but Jessica touched his arm, then smiled at the guards, "Of course, we've got nothing to hide."

The inspection was quick and perfunctory until a guard lifted

75

Vergangenheit

Keith's backpack and noticed how heavy it felt. Without asking, he opened it revealing Keith's Leica M4 camera and three lenses, as well as his Arriflex 16S movie camera, lenses, battery and rolls of film.

"This is not tourist equipment. What is the real purpose of your visit?"

"We work in Hollywood and are on vacation. For us, this is tourist equipment, stuff we use every day. Most of this gear is ten or twenty years old, it's not fancy by professional standards."

"Maybe, but it is expensive, like your car, and not something we see very often."

Jessica sensed that the guards were uncertain, that perhaps they just needed a reason to let them go, "We're only passing through on our way to Poland from Budapest and thought it would be nice to see a bit of Czechoslovakia instead of going around through Germany. You have a lovely country and this is our first chance to see it, and perhaps bring back a few pretty pictures to show our friends."

Keith added, "Jessica's an artist and she's wanted to see your country for a long time. I just point the camera where she tells me."

Passports were stamped, hands were shaken, and soon they were on the road north toward Notra and Trencin, driving through lovely and primitive agricultural areas, little villages, small roads passing occasional ruined old castles and churches.

"I had no idea we had rented an expensive car until that guard commented on it."

"Me either, I'm sure glad we don't have my car, or we'd still be back at the border."

"Next time we'd better get a Trabant, maybe an old one, so that we'll blend in better."

"They wouldn't rent one to us because we look too rich and used an American Express card to pay."

"I bet with cash we could buy an old Trabant for what this VW cost to rent for a week."

"Relax. Let's stop in the next village and buy local cheese, bread, beer, and sausage then go for a walk on the old streets. It'll be fun trying your guidebook phrases in the grocery store, and maybe you can take a few tourist snaps while I sketch."

"Good plan. Depending on how we go, it's only three or four hundred miles up to the border. We can stay on little roads and skip the big cities, the smoky trucks and see the countryside."

They stopped just outside Martin, on the Turiec river, and their picnic among the ruins of an old monastery led to a long walk, sunset photography, and a pleasant though rustic night at a small hostel next to a rural café. The next day saw them through Zilina, Olomouc, Kralove and Turnov. Here Jessica insisted that they detour onto a small road to Semily and the ruins of an old castle overlooking the river Jizera. The castle had once been an artist colony about which Jessica had read. The interior woodwork and walls in the surviving rooms had been decorated by artists at least a hundred years ago. Jessica particularly loved one room whose walls were faded light green. Faux gold molding divided the walls into panels, and each panel held a woodland scene painted right onto the wall. Trees, leaves, a fox smiling at the viewer, birds singing on a branch, an elf-like creature, all perhaps representing "A Midsummer Night's Dream". The whole room was like this, with the patina of age around the ancient door hardware and the creaky furniture. In one corner stood a ceramic stove, covered in white tiles with blue patterns. This stove was an Austrian invention providing heat for the room. Unlike pot-bellied stoves and heaters that Keith had seen, this was different: no chimney and no opening to insert fuel or light a fire. Eventually Keith wandered into the adjoining hallway and discovered an access door through which a coal fire could be started in the stove. The chimney went up through the wall which was at least a yard thick.

"When we get home, I want to paint something like this, maybe on the walls of our dining room. I wish we could pack up this whole room and take it back: it's perfect."

"At least we'll have photos and your sketches, and hey, maybe you can work with a set-builder to install molding and fake doorways to get the effect, though we'd never get this ceramic stove home."

"I think ceramic stoves were built right into rooms at least a hundred years ago when people discovered that they didn't have to live with soot and smoke messing up their homes."

"And it must have been nice to have servants who carried the coal and tended the fire out in the hallway instead of coming into your bedroom unannounced."

"I still like lying on a rug and looking at the glow of a fire in a fireplace. Remember the rainy night in front of your fireplace when you tried to get my clothes off after we came home from the movies?"

"Yes, and you pushed me away and told me find a more cooperative girl friend."

Later they sat in a café with notes and maps, planning their trip across the frontier into Poland.

"Keith, you let me do all the planning for visiting Houdini, while you planned our visit to the inventor's old lab. So what happens next? Where are we going tomorrow when we cross into Poland?"

"Houdini was easier because you knew where he was born. I've made a list of every place mentioned in the diary, at least what I thought were the names of towns and places. Then I tried to mark them on a Polish map I ordered from the Polish Embassy in New York. Half of these places aren't on the map they sent. Then I looked into the old *MICHILIN GUIDE BLEU* to Poland that your grandfather bought in 1934, the one we found in your father's library. The maps in the *GUIDE* are a lot more useful because many of the names have been changed since the war. Our whole area was once part of Germany, now it's in Poland, and it's really close to the Czech border, so the names are a mess."

"So where are we going?"

"Here's the list of names and a copy of the map where I marked everything I could identify. The good thing is that all these places are in an area about fifty miles across, so the lab is somewhere among these towns and cities: Walim, Gluszyca, the Gros Rosen Concentration Camp, Jedlina, Jugow, Swierki, Kolce, Jelenia Gora, Luban, Nowa Sol, Nowa Ruda, Gontowa, Walderberg, Waldenburg (Walbrzych), Ludwigsdorf (Ludwikowice), Najdłuższy, Ksiaz, Gluszyca, Rzeczka, Sowie, Wlodzickie, Milkow, Wlodyka, Osowka."

"Too bad we don't have the translation of the diary and more detailed information."

"I think we should go to the middle of the area, check into a hotel, then drive around looking for old mines and ruins. We'll buy local maps, or find a guide, or a helper once we're there. I'd like to start in Walbrzych, which used to be called Waldenburg, because it looks like a good-sized city, at least it was in 1934. We can probably get a good map with more detail at the train station."

"That works fine in the West, but I have a feeling that maps and information on old secret installations are not available here. This was a major factory area during the war since it was beyond the range of our bombers until we re-captured France, so the Guide Bleu may not be too useful. The Germans changed everything here during the war."

"We can visit the tourist information kiosk, or a bookstore, or something, you'll see. I'll bet the Hotel Metropole is just like in the guide."

"Yes, with coal fires in every room, gas lights on the walls and no running water: all the conveniences of a hotel that was already ancient in 1934."

"You're going to love it, an adventure not an inconvenience, as you reminded me on the train in Vienna."

Jessica was pleasantly surprised that the old guidebook was accurate enough to get them through the streets of Walbrzych to the hotel, and that the hotel looked to be in good shape and quite nice. It was one of the few buildings that had been scrubbed. Most of the city was coated in gray slime caused by coal smoke and dust from the nearby mines.

The train station was near the hotel, as shown on Keith's 1934 map, but inside there were no maps or western newspapers for sale. Keith was surprised at how few travelers were in the large station, and at the trash-covered tracks that hadn't been used in ages. Jessica estimated that only a quarter of the station was actually in-use, probably because geographies and borders had changed since it had been built. In addition, she suspected that passenger travel was restricted by permits and a lack of money. The only passenger train they saw consisted of a small steam engine and two unpainted wooden coaches.

Keith and Jessica were dressed in what they thought were inconspicuous clothes which they had bought in Marienbad while working in the orphanage. Their coats, though dark gray and cheaply-made, were clean, which separated them from most of the other people on the street. This became obvious when a lady stopped Jessica in the train station and asked, in English, where she had bought her coat, as she knew that Jessica must be a visitor, and perhaps one who would sell it for the right price.

Keith took the opportunity to ask the lady about bookstores and where they might buy local maps, but at the mention of maps, the lady tensed and hurried away without a word.

After lunch they started exploring the local roads. "Keith, I'm wondering what happens when we pull into one of these little coal-mining towns on your list. What do we do? Do we dig a hole looking for an old tunnel, or ask everyone we meet if they've seen one or what?"

"I just thought we'd drive around and see if we could find the entrance to the old tunnels, and ask people, especially old people, where they are."

"I think most of the people who were alive then are gone. The Germans who had lived here for ages moved west as fast as their feet would carry them or were sent to Siberia when the borders were re-drawn after the war. Then the Commies moved everyone else around: the people we'll meet are all new-comers to the area who don't know anything about wartime events."

After waiting half an hour to fill the VW tank they spent the next day driving on almost every road in the surrounding countryside. First they went west to Jalena Gora, then south to Lubawka, east to Nova Ruda, and north to Strzegom. It became obvious that this was a futile exercise as the roads that looked promising were blocked by either a large concrete rusty barbed wire barrier or a very clear entrance-forbidden sign. They could see dozens of mine shafts heading underground in some of the valleys and on the hillsides. The inventor's underground lab could be anywhere around here. Piles of mining equipment, tailings and old buildings littered the landscape, and railroad tracks, some abandoned and some in use, ran every which way. A few aspects were modern but most was old, dilapidated, and rusty. From what Keith had read, the mines extended for miles in all directions making their task impossibly complex. In addition it seemed that police and soldiers were patrolling everywhere, all heavily armed.

By accident, near the town of Rogoznica, they came upon the remains of the Gross Rosen Concentration Camp, a grim prison that supplied thousands of slave laborers to underground projects in the area. Some of the stone walls, which had been built by prisoners, were still standing. Keith read on the memorial plaque that at least 40,000 of them died here during the war. "Keith, please don't take any pictures, this is a bad place, they're so many spirits floating around, I can't stand it, let's go."

But in Kamlenna Gora they had a break. "Look Jessica, I'll bet that's a mining museum, or at least it was, isn't it?"

"You're right, that's what the old German sign says."

"Come on, these guys will know all about underground stuff."

They entered a dilapidated soot-stained concrete building which appeared to be deserted. The lights were off, but the door had been open. The walls were covered with faded maps and sepia photographs of miners and mining. Tables held samples of different kinds of coal and rusty old tools.

"Jessica, look over here, a wooden scale model of the underground parts of a mine. You can see all the tunnels and shafts. If we could find one of these with the lab, we'd be in business."

"Even if we did, it could be flooded and inaccessible: remember my dream about escaping while water rushed past my legs as I carried the diary to safety."

An old man in a dirty gray lab coat entered the room and approached the couple, "Wie Gehts?"

Jessica answered in German, "Hello, is this your museum?"

"Yes, though not many people come here and I of all people can't afford electricity for the lights or coal for heating it."

"I'm sorry, but why do you put it that way, I mean about the electricity?"

"Oh, a long time ago I worked in a huge power plant burning tons of coal every hour, providing electricity for cities in all directions. In those days it was never dark or cold around here, but that's history now."

"Was your plant next to a coal mine?"

"Yes, the coal came out of the mine and right into the yard, then we sent electricity everywhere. What brings you to my humble museum?"

"We're looking for a special place, one of the underground factories that the Germans built during the war."

"There were dozens here, but most are flooded and the rest were destroyed by the Russians. All that is history, it's gone now."

Keith knew enough German to follow the conversation, and on impulse he removed a pad from his pocket and drew a picture of the huge round test stand where the inventor had flown his machine outdoors. He added a stick figure to show the scale, to show how big the structure was. When the old man saw the sketch he exclaimed, "That was near my power plant! I can tell you exactly where it is, though you can't go there because it's a closed military area."

"Wow, can you tell us about it, we're really curious."

"First, tell me why you want to know, where did you hear about this?"

Keith thought quickly, then Jessica translated, "My father's uncle worked near this round thing, whatever it is, during the war. He was a Polish prisoner and my father has a sketch like this that he made before he died. I thought that since we're in the area we'd try to visit and take a picture for my father."

Jessica could tell that the old man didn't quite believe them, but she sensed that he would love to talk about it anyway. "Could we buy you a beer or lunch or something while you tell us about it, and why it was near your plant. Did you help built this thing?"

"Oh no prisoners built it and it was top secret, walled off from everyone, but after the war the walls fell away and I saw it clearly. My plant was built in 1925, solid German equipment, wonderfully strong, it ran without stopping and we kept it in perfect order. Then in 1941 things began to change. The valley leading to the mine was covered over with a roof, and the roof was then planted in brush and grass. I never saw it, but I heard that from the air the whole valley was invisible. My power plant at one end was the only thing that showed, and it had been there a long time. Then under the roof a big train yard was built next to the mine, a place where trains could be hidden during the day. Workers arrived from Gross-Rosen and started expanding the mine. Judging by the rock that came out on the trains they did a lot of digging. I was never allowed inside and I really didn't want to know. I just kept my plant running. I did notice that we kept sending more and more electricity into the mine. We had meters on the power lines in the switchyard, so I could tell how much power went to different areas. One thing for sure, we were never allowed to cut off power to the mine, so in emergencies, during bombing raids or heavy snow, when we had to cut back, we kept the mine running no matter what."

"Is your plant still running? Could we visit it?"

"No, the Russians disassembled it around 1960 and took the equipment away. Today there's not much left of what used to be Poland."

"Do you think the military authorities would give us permission to visit the site? I mean, it's forty years old and probably falling apart, so it couldn't be very secret anymore?"

"I doubt it, and I wouldn't try unless you can think up a very convincing story of why you want to see it. Your structure and the remains of my old power plant are outside of Ludwigsdorf, which is now called Ludwikowice.   From that village, follow the railroad east four and a half kilometers, then you will see a big set of abandoned points where track used to run up to the mine. If you walk up the old roadbed you'll come to a series of security fences, that is, if the guards don't shoot you first. I wouldn't go near the place, it's far too dangerous."

A uniformed man entered the museum and the old man began to converse with him in Polish, ignoring Jessica and Keith. Jessica took Keith's hand and motioned him toward the door. As they left she turned to the old man, smiled, bowed, and thanked him formally in German.

As soon as they were in the car, Keith reached for his maps, but Jessica stopped him, "Keith drive, drive in any direction but get away from here. We can study the maps later."

"Why, who was that guy?"

"Some kind of cop or military official, not a person we want to talk to."

"Look at the map, let's cruise through Ludwigsdorf and see if it has a hotel, and if it does, we can move there or someplace close by. Maybe we'll get lucky and find a way to the lab. We're so close."

Late in the afternoon they moved into Ibeza, a comfortable guest house with a restaurant on the ground floor, in the middle of the old part of Ludwigsdorf, a small town of twenty-five hundred. The town had been a busy manufacturing center during the war. Now it was surrounded by the ruins of military factories and logging operations. In addition there was a candle factory, a mini-zoo, and a few tourist hostels for people who wanted to hike in the mountains which surrounded the town. After a snack

Keith and Jessica walked the streets, becoming acquainted with the town and wondering what it was like forty years ago, when their inventor had worked a few miles away as bombs rained from the sky. The sun had just gone down and the weather was turning cold.

Suddenly Jessica had an idea, "I've got it Keith, I know how we can get into the old mines and maybe the lab!"

"How?"

"Teens! They're curious, they go around blocked roads, they explore forbidden places, and they can always use extra cash. One of them is bound to know how to get into the old tunnels."

"They also love to play tricks on foreigners and deal in half-truths."

"Got a better idea?"

"We could hire a guide, a history buff or a museum person?"

"And where will we find one?"

"Well, actually I haven't seen many museums or tourist bureaus, around here."

"But I saw a few kids hanging out near the train station, over on the side by the abandoned tracks."

With trepidation they approached several teens in threadbare clothes smoking cigarettes standing in the shadows behind the station. The kids looked tough, but Jessica realized that they were just poor and wary of strangers. She approached them casually in German but was quickly interrupted in English.

"You're American, so why are you trying to speak German?"

"Sorry, I didn't realize you were so well educated." Jessica was startled, but Keith jumped in with his story before she could continue.

"We're trying to hire a local guide, or several guides, who know where the old tunnels from the war are hidden and how to get to them."

"Hire, as in paying cash, American dollars?"

"One of my distant relatives died around here in an underground factory during the war and we promised his mother we'd try to find it and take a few pictures."

"We thought we'd just drive there but all the interesting roads seem to be blocked by cops," Jessica added.

"Welcome to our socialist paradise: everybody owns everything, but nobody can go anywhere or do anything without permission. I take it you haven't tried to get permission to go down into the tunnels?"

"No, who should we ask?"

"Forget it, he's teasing, you could never get permission to go where we can take you," a tough young girl interjected.

"So tell us more. What sort of tunnel are you looking for? Why here? Why not in Germany?"

"During the war there were secret underground factories and laboratories around here because bombers couldn't come this far until France was liberated. My uncle was in a laboratory deep underground near Ludwigsdorf, in a secret valley, which contained a power plant. The tunnel had a big steel entrance door to protect it during bombings and a railway line. The most distinctive feature was that just outside the tunnel there was some sort of round concrete structure, a ring with vertical columns, like a little Stonehenge, at least that's how he described it in an old letter. Have you ever seen anything like that?"

"This is going to cost you plenty. What you want to see is called the Ludwikowice Klodzkie: it's dangerous around there, definitely off limits. It's near an army base, and soldiers wander all over even though there's nothing but ruins to see. How much can you pay?"

"You mean you actually know how to get us there?"

"It's a long walk, and we'll go at night, but we can get there given the right incentive."

"Could we get there at dawn when there's a bit of light so I can take a few pictures without flash."

"Definitely without flash. You don't want to be shot, and we're not going to jail."

"My name's Keith and this is Jessica. We've got a rented VW but we could all cram inside, if all three of you want to come."

"Sure, we'll all go. I'm Hans, this is Johan, and she's Lilly."

"Great. If we gave you a bunch of dollars, won't that be suspicious and get you in trouble? I've got some Hungarian Forints, Polish Zlotys, and German Deutchmarks if that would be better."

"Mixed currencies are fine, as long as the total is right: how about four, no five hundred dollars, and we guarantee to get you to the Klodzkie in faint daylight?"

Memories from Keith's days in the fast-moving world of film-making popped into his head: he had been in many situations just like this, where they needed something badly and there was only one person offering it for sale: the price was not negotiable. You either wanted it and paid, or you walked away. The idea of actually seeing the test-stand where the inventor had flown his machine outdoors trumped any consideration of cost or negotiation. Keith smiled, "Can we go tonight?"

Everyone smiled and Lilly asked, "We need warmer clothes for the long walk, how about a down payment so we can grab things before the shops close?"

"Would you also buy bread, cheese, and mineral water: picnic food that we could eat along the way?" Jessica asked.

Keith started to count out odd currencies from his multi-pocketed European wallet. "I've got at least a hundred dollars worth of East European currencies: what's your favorite?"

"Small bills in any currency are best, but we can use everything you've got: this is our lucky day."

"Ours too!" Keith added.

Jessica smiled, laughing quietly to herself at the way Keith had adopted her idea and merged it with his own. She half felt that they would never see these kids again, but knew that they would put the money to good use. She wished that she could watch them bargaining for warm clothes and food, while spending as little as possible of their windfall. As the kids started to leave, she pulled some money from her pocket, "Here, take this and buy especially good food for tonight, we're in for a great adventure, so let's celebrate."

"Wear your darkest warm clothes and boots: we'll need to walk about ten kilometers through the woods from where it's safe to park. See you here around midnight."

The kids faded away as Keith and Jessica walked toward their hotel wondering what they were getting into. Keith smiled, "Can you believe it! What if they actually show up and take us to the place where the machine was tested?"

"Keith, whatever you do, don't mention the inventor and the machine and our old photos. Your cover story is lame but adequate. We don't want to let anyone know what we know. We could be really close to the remains of the old lab, and maybe to secrets that have been buried for forty years. We wouldn't want to let others grab them and start asking questions."

Vergangenheit

CHAPTER 9

TUNNELING

Midnight found Keith and Jessica shivering in the damp cold air by the deserted train station watching their breath as it floated away in the faint light from the weak gas streetlamps. After half an hour two dark shapes appeared in the distance walking toward them: Hans and Lilly all in black, and each with a backpack. With few words they packed into the cramped Jetta. After driving carefully for half an hour on ever-smaller roads, they stopped deep in a forest, at a small dirt clearing. They started walking down an old path, a trail that had once been a single-lane road or driveway judging by the width of the cleared area between ancient trees. Talking was in nervous whispers. As they walked the kids shared out sausage, bread, chocolate, cheese: Jessica's money had indeed bought a feast.

The trail was long and cold, but not rough. The moonlight was sufficient to see outlines though occasionally Hans used a covered flashlight to point out a dangerous area or old fences that had to be crossed carefully.

Jessica had been munching chocolate and thinking that this was just a long walk in the woods on an old road: nothing too exciting or unusual. But her mood changed at the second barbed wire fence. It was ancient and sinister, especially the way the eight-foot high strands were arranged diagonally to cut anyone who tried to cross. The posts were angled toward them making it almost impossible to climb over. Fortunately a gap had been cut through the fence over in the woods, out of sight from anyone patrolling the road. Keith looked at the wire fences which were strung on rust-stained concrete fence posts, posts that were as solid and foreboding as the day they had been erected half a century ago. He thought to himself that there was something about concrete fence posts, and concrete utility poles, that looked sinister, in contrast to the wooden fence posts and utility poles common in America. In his logical mind, he knew that in Europe wood was too scarce to be used in fences, but the concrete substitutes, especially those with old rust stains, reminded him of photos of concentration camps and the darker aspects of history.

Near the car they had crossed over a low barbed wire fence, not too difficult, ancient and rusty, but not a real barrier. The second barbed wire fence they crossed was much larger, higher, denser, and stronger. However the worst part of their journey began after they crossed the second fence: faded old yellow caution signs began to appear on the side of the road.

The signs showed a person stepping on something that looked like a bomb exploding. When he asked about the signs, Hans told him that yes, some of the area was mined and that no, the mines had not been removed after the war, and that there were also traps and snares scattered in the woods. The third barbed wire fence was the most substantial and difficult to cross. Clearly whatever had been in this valley during the war had been extremely secret. It would have been impossible for unauthorized visitors to came here when the fences had been patrolled.

As the dawn began to lighten the eastern horizon Keith saw that they were walking along the side of a shallow valley. He could begin to make out the ruins of old factories indicating that once this had been an industrial area. Substantial trees now grew through roadways and the remains of buildings. This place had been abandoned for decades, perhaps since the war ended. Suddenly he recognized something from Harry's old still photos, the remains of a distinctive large building that had been in the background of several of the exterior shots. One of the walls that was still standing had an unusual round window near the top, and it was this feature that Keith remembered. The building had been huge, maybe a block long.

"What's that old building over there?"

"It's what's left of a dynamite factory, but there's not much inside: burned out in a bombing raid, and finished-off by the Ruskies after they took all the machinery. We don't have time to explore inside."

"Let me stop for a moment and take a time exposure by propping my camera against a tree. Maybe there's just enough light." Keith was glad that he had had the foresight to bring his fastest lens, a Noctilux, and very sensitive black and white film.

Jessica recognized the building too and realized that they must be very close to the old laboratory. She shuddered involuntarily, remembering the dream where she had been trapped in the tunnels rescuing the diary. She wondered if the dream was partially real, a blurry vision from the past that somehow had found its way into her mind. And if so, perhaps the laboratory was flooded and inaccessible. But her vision was only a dream, and she knew that it probably had been caused by looking too long at the old pictures.

The remains of railroad tracks ran among the buildings, though the steel rails had disappeared long ago. Lumps of coal were scattered randomly and there was a large pile near an old ruin which had an enormous chimney, perhaps the old power plant. They walked on, keeping to the shadows, with no conversation. Suddenly they saw it in the distance, a circle of huge vertical concrete columns topped by a heavy concrete ring. Keith froze, he couldn't believe his eyes. "Holy shit, we've found it."

Jessica squeezed Keith's hand. "Shhhh, be quiet and move slowly, just be patient, we can walk right up to it."

Keith stopped to take pictures as the light improved and as they moved closer. He wanted to examine the structure, to look for traces of the old equipment, to take measurements and see the details. Jessica felt apprehensive, something about this place was bad, but she couldn't put her finger on the reason for her feelings. She liked the inventor and had grown attached to him after pouring over his book and imagining his world. But the reality now was very different: they were walking through the ruins of his life, maybe through a graveyard where thousands had died. The silence was eerie.

Keith felt the columns, maybe twenty feet high and several feet in diameter: they were huge and the surfaces were rough to the touch: strong posts quickly assembled. How exciting to be here, in the place where the machine had once been tethered as it flew above the ground. He almost started talking about his feelings, but then remembered Jessica's warning and remained silent.

Jessica stood off to the side pondering the structure, then instinctively started to draw quickly on her pocket sketch pad. Lilly looked over her shoulder, "Why are you drawing this, you've got photos?"

"Paintings and sketches are better, they capture the feelings, the mystery, the desolation. A painting can tell a story, it's not like a mechanical snapshot."

"You're good, you draw so fast without having to erase anything."

"This is a weird place isn't it. All these old ruins. Think of how many people must have been here to build all this stuff and to work with it when it was finished."

"They're all dead, blown-up or carted away: only ghosts around here now, and sometimes you can hear them screaming or crying. Wait 'til we go in the tunnel: I don't like it in there."

Hans looked at his watch, "Let's get moving if you want to see the tunnel: we need to be out of here in an hour or less."

He led the way around the ruins of another building then Keith saw a large rusted steel door cut into the hillside. The remains of a railroad track ran through it, so trains could have driven underground when the door was open. Although the door was burned and warped, there was a narrow entrance at the side. They squeezed through being careful not to cut themselves on the jagged steel edges. It was almost completely dark inside and Jessica noticed that it smelled old and earthy, kind of like a deep cave she had once explored. Their flashlights revealed a big tunnel stretching into the distance, maybe for miles. Parts of old rail cars were scattered here and there. Bits of rusted machinery lay in piles. Keith and Jessica looked for the laboratory but saw nothing like it.

"Is there just one long tunnel or are there others branching off?" Keith asked quietly.

"Who knows, this goes on forever, but all the good stuff has been removed. What are you looking for?"

"I don't know, I've never been a place like this. I've been in working mines, but they had normal equipment and lights and people. This is like a factory, but it's been trashed and just bits and pieces are left, hard to tell anything about how it worked or what they built here."

"They built guns and bombs and wartime stuff all over these hills in the old mines: whole bunch of slaves grinding it out until they croaked. It was insane. Cruel bastards ran the whole thing. There are skeletons and dead bodies farther down in the tunnel, but we don't have time to go there now."

Jessica flinched at these words, knowing from history books that the words were right, but they didn't match her picture of the inventor struggling with his machine. She worked hard to suppress the feelings of grief that began to overwhelm her. This was indeed a grim place and the psychic impact was beginning to tear at her heart.

Keith picked up an old notebook and several nuts and bolts. "Mind if I take a few souvenirs?"

"Take what you can carry, now let's get out of here before the sun comes up."

Before anyone knew what was happening, Jessica fell to the ground holding her head and crying. Keith realized that she was going into a trance and that she had lost control of her body: she was limp and shaking with emotion as she lay on the ground against a rusty steel barrel. The others were startled and impatient to leave.

"What's wrong with her?"

"She's sensitive, she can feel ghosts and spirits and sometimes they take over her body. Help me pick her up and get her out of here."

"Will she recover when we get outside?"

"Eventually. Let's go. I never should have brought her down here."

They carried Jessica to the door, looked around, then slipped outside and headed for the trail. She was heavy and groggy but they managed to half carry and half drag her along. Slowly she came back to life and struggled to walk, holding onto Keith for support. Everyone was silent, moving as quickly as possible away from the valley, anxious to escape.

As they neared the dynamite factory, Keith asked, "Let's stop, I only need two minutes and there's just enough light to shoot a little film."

"Film?" Hans asked as the group paused.

Keith dropped his backpack to the ground, pulled out his Arri 16, plugged it's cord into an eight volt battery, and began to shoot a slow pan of the area, hoping that his fastest lens, a Schneider 25mm f/1.4, would capture an exposure on the sensitive 7224 black and white film he had loaded before they left. He paned very slowly while leaning against a tree for stability, to cover the whole valley, especially the concrete test stand. He managed two passes and a closeup of the scene before the one hundred feet of film, almost three minutes of run-time, ran out .

"What are you doing, we've got to move before the sun comes up."

"OK. Let's try for a shot from up on the hillside on the way out."

"Move, now!"

They started walking fast as Jessica recovered. Keith wasn't allowed to stop for another shot. Just after they crossed the first barbed wire they heard a shot in the distance.

"Nine millimeter automatic, probably soldiers out for a morning walk shooting at birds or anything that moves in the woods," Hans whispered.

They walked faster as they heard another faraway shot.

When they reached the car a surprise was waiting, a bearded Hiker with a backpack was leaning against a nearby tree. The teens were startled and apparently didn't know this person. Conversation was in Polish, quiet Polish, as everyone seemed to know that they were in a forbidden area. Keith took Hans aside and whispered in his ear, "Should we offer him money to be quiet about this?"

"No, that would make him suspicious, what he wants is a ride back to town and a bite to eat."

"Do you want to squeeze him into the car?"

"No, he's not one of us, he's a Russian and we never give them anything. We're leaving and he's staying."

It felt good to be in the car heading back to town, even though they were exhausted from the hike and the tension. The teens talked among themselves in Polish, then Lilly asked, "Why was your uncle here, that is, what was he doing in that tunnel, and your movie camera, what are you up to, you're not tourists?"

"I don't know much about him. He was a scientist or engineer working in a factory. I'm sure he would much rather have been home or somewhere else."

"So he was a prisoner, not a soldier or SS?"

"He was a peaceful German and lived in Gorlitz before the war, but like lots of people he didn't have any choice as to what he did or where he worked. It must have been awful working underground like that."

"What happened to him after the war?"

"We think he died before it was over. His mother only has a few old letters, and now we can tell her a little about where he was at the end."

"Any idea what he was working on, what kind of weapons?"

"No, but I would like to explore the tunnels further and take more photographs. Is there any chance that I could hire you to take me back in a few days. I'd like to stay underground for a whole day, then come out at night when it's safe. We would have maybe twelve or fourteen hours to explore the tunnel."

"Don't do it Keith, that's a bad place and it'll get worse as you go further inside," Jessica said.

"I know you can't go back, but I could, the spirits don't bother me, and I could get some great photos deeper inside with a flash and some flares. You could drop us off at the clearing, take the car away, then come back for us in the middle of the night. Lilly could stay with you, so it would be simple. You wouldn't be scared at all."

"Keith, I don't want to lose you. You could be hurt or captured or fall down an old mine shaft and never be seen again."

"It's not that bad, it's just more of the same, a long tunnel with lots of worthless junk. There's no way he would get hurt as long as we were careful. Even rats don't live in there because there's no food for them," Hans replied.

"What about your German movie camera? Those things cost thousands of dollars, even old ones. I know because I took a film class and the school had one that was treated like it was made of gold. Are you a reporter? What're you going to write about this and about us?"

"I want to hear about your film class and what you studied. Jessica and I work on films too, but we're on holiday and we are definitely not reporters. Jessica's an artist and she'll paint a few scenes based on my photos and her sketches when we go home."

"You didn't answer the question about your movie camera," Hans replied.

"My sixteen millimeter Arriflex is twenty years old and it's worth about the same as my still camera. It's not all that valuable or special. I'm an engineer working in the movie industry. I like mechanical things, so when I had a chance to buy a decent movie camera I took it. Where we work people use much bigger and more complex film cameras, not little things like this."

"Tell us a bit about the Russian hiker. What was he doing there?" Jessica asked.

"Those creeps are all over the country, they act like they own everything and think we're their servants. He was probably lost."

Lilly added, "If we're lucky he'll wander off into the woods and step on a mine or fall into a trap, it would serve him right for being rude to us."

Keith asked, "Do you think we could round up supplies in a day or two and then go back, maybe tomorrow night?"

"Tell me exactly what you need, not food, but photographic equipment," Hans asked.

"First I'd like to get a big flash unit, as bright as possible and maybe a dozen or two dozen bulbs for it. We can flash inside the tunnel because nobody will see the light. And if possible, I'd like to get a bright flare so that we can light a scene in the tunnel for a minute or two of film. Maybe a red railway flare would work, but they're not very bright and they smoke a lot. I've seen bright white magnesium flares at home but I don't know where to get one around here."

"Flares, any kind of flares, aren't for sale but the military uses them on night maneuvers so they're around. We might be able to obtain one tonight. Money talks and I know a photographer with lots of gear who'd be glad to rent us whatever you want. We'll be discrete, and don't answer any questions if he asks where we're going."

"And let's take several flashlights, a bunch of batteries and a bit of food."

"I'll stay with you while they're gone. You can teach me about drawing and sketching: I'd love to know more and you're so good at it," Lilly said to Jessica.

"And I know a mining store where we can buy headlamps like the coal miners wear. That'll make walking around and seeing what we're doing a lot easier."

Jessica worried over the plan, seeking a way that the return to the tunnel could be avoided, "Maybe it's not safe to drive back into the woods? What if the Russian sees us again, won't he be suspicious and wonder what we're doing?"

"Don't worry, we'll go a different way, there're lots of old roads and trails leading into the valley. It's easy to become lost if you don't know the way, but we know, and the Russians don't."

Two days later Keith and Hans were inside the tunnel, each with a backpack loaded with supplies and food. They had entered at first light, having seen or heard nothing unusual on the way in via a different road.

"We've got at least twelve hours inside. How about walking fast as far as we can for maybe four or five hours, then coming back slowly looking at details and making pictures as the time allows," Keith suggested.

"Wow, we'll get really far if we do that, maybe to the other end. I've never been anywhere near it, but I've heard stories."

"Let's go. Whatever happens, let's stick together. This would be too creepy alone."

"That's for sure. I've heard that this place was built as a secret factory but originally there was a coal mine here, so there're side tunnels and bits of the old mine scattered around. Let's stick to the railroad tracks, so we can find our way out even if our lights crap out."

"Right, no going down into the old mine where we could get lost forever. Are there really skeletons and dead bodies up ahead? Did you ever see them?"

"I saw a skeleton dressed in old rags in a dark corner, but that's about it. I've never gone very far, so this is as much an adventure for me as it is for you."

"At the end of the war, this tunnel and the rooms off to the side must have been full of machinery and people, all sorts of stuff, but look around, there's just junk here and there. What happened?" Keith wondered aloud as they walked quickly down the center of the tunnel next to the main tracks.

"The Russians took everything of value and sent it to Moscow. They changed this area from an industrial sector with good jobs to a slum. When the Russians moved in, Germans who didn't make it across the border were sent to Siberia or worked to death. Then the Russians moved people like my parents in from the farms and put them to work in the mines, digging coal for Russia. Have you noticed that all the heavily-loaded coal trains are headed to the east? My father used to say that that life under the Nazis was much better."

"Hey, I just noticed something. Stop for a minute. Do you feel a faint cold breeze? It's almost imperceptible, but there's ventilation from other openings. At least we're not going to suffocate from bad air."

"Maybe this is a tunnel with an opening at the far end, like I've heard about."

"If so, let's approach it carefully, as we have no idea if it comes out near the army base you mentioned."

Keith and Hans walked quickly, stopping only to quickly peer down side shafts and doorways that they might explore later. So far there had been little of interest for Keith. Junk was scattered randomly, odd bits of rusty metal, lots of old papers, empty cans and bottles, bits of clothing. He knew that an archeologist could analyze this stuff and recreate life as it had once been in the tunnel, but Keith was interested in the inventor and the lab in which he had worked, and of that, they had seen nothing. Occasionally there were cave-ins blocking a side tunnel, or in some cases piles of rubble which might be hiding something, or which might just have been shoved out of the way by salvage crews. Keith looked wistfully at one of these piles and wondered if it was blocking the entrance to the old laboratory, but he had no way of knowing.

Keith found that walking was strange. His headlamp illuminated the area in front of him, but not at his sides, yet Keith's peripheral vision included things to the side, which were pitch black. He could turn his head and look to the side, but it was awkward, especially when walking quickly, focused on avoiding the junk underfoot. When he walked in normal light, he could see his surroundings but not here. It was something that miners and underground workers adapt to, but this was his first time and it was disorienting.

As they walked, he noticed regularly spaced lines and numbers on the wall every hundred meters or so.

"Hans, have you noticed those numbers on the wall, they seem to be in meters and they're decreasing. I bet they're the distance from the far end, a sort of addressing scheme so people could tell where they were in the tunnel."

"Orderly Germans at work. If you're right we're about eleven kilometers from the far end, and maybe one from where we entered. We're walking fast, so we'll be at the far end before four hours is up. At least we'll have plenty of warning as we approach it."

"What do you think about these huge piles of rubble, like that one over there. It looks to me like machines were used to push a bunch of rock and junk there on purpose, maybe to cover up the entrance to something they didn't want people to see."

"Perhaps. Could be almost anything, even a giant latrine or bottomless pit on the other side. Maybe we really don't want to know."

Keith had been thinking of the secret laboratory, not about poop, and the thought sent goose-bumps rippling down his spine. They walked fast and in silence, carefully noting their position at the hundred meter marks. Neither wanted to make extra noises or waste breath on small talk. To Keith the tunnel seemed endless, and the more he looked, the less likely he thought they would find the old laboratory. This went on for over an hour, but then he stopped in amazement.

"Look at that, a huge side tunnel with "Eintritt Verboten" painted right on the walls. We must be almost in the middle of the tunnel, at the most secure spot in the whole place. This side tunnel even has its own railway spur."

"Look down the tunnel where my flashlight is pointing, there's a monumental pile of rock closing it off. Whatever the Germans had down there is buried forever."

"It must have been very important: this is first place we've come to with any sort of warning sign forbidding people to enter."

"Maybe the Germans buried it themselves when they abandoned this place as the Ruskies moved in. Could be some good stuff behind this pile if we could climb around it, or it could be a big cave-in from the old coal mine."

Keith's mind was running at full speed: he felt that there was at least a chance that the laboratory was behind the pile, but then his logical side reminded him that it could also be just a dangerous area where the builders didn't want to lose any workmen.

"Let's go a bit further, then come back here, to meter sixty-one-hundred and explore carefully. This could be exciting, or just a dangerous area."

They continued for an hour more, to meter thirty-five-hundred, but if anything the tunnel was becoming small, dull, and empty. It seemed to be turning into an old railway tunnel, just big enough for a train, with not much room left over for factory workings. Keith looked at his watch.

"Let's go back to the middle and explore the forbidden area. I don't think the builders had a chance to expand the factory this far. Maybe this is just a place for trains to hide-out from bombers then escape out the far end."

"Great, I've been thinking the same, and I don't want to emerge into an army base, though if this tunnel continues straight, it wouldn't even be close to the soldiers."

As they turned to leave Keith's headlamp swept across the track. "Hey, stop for a minute and look at this."

"What's wrong?"

"Look at the rails, they're almost shiny on top, just a thin coating of rust."

"So?"

"A train has been through here recently, at least this far into the tunnel."

"But back up the tunnel where we came in, the old rail cars on the tracks are falling apart, they haven't moved in decades."

"I know, but maybe the far end of the tunnel is open and railroad people or the army park trains in here occasionally."

They turned around and Keith made a note of the farthest milepost they had reached. Then they walked away quickly. Keith had thought that they were alone in the tunnel, but now he began to worry that a train full of soldiers could appear at any time.

Back at the sixty-one hundred level they walked down the side tunnel with the big warning signs and scanned their flashlights over the rubble blocking it. This tunnel was almost as big, at least twenty feet in diameter, as the main tunnel, and the railway spur looked substantial as though it had been built to move lots of freight this way.

Keith used the rented flashgun, a big unit with a seven inch polished reflector that fired number twenty-two flash bulbs, to make an exposure of the tunnel and the rubble pile blocking it. While Keith calculated the exposure, based on his estimate of the distance to the pile and the power of the flash bulbs, Hans scampered up the pile, hoping to find that it didn't quite reach the ceiling so that he could sneak through to the other side. The big clear flash bulbs had a guide number of 320 when used with 100-speed film, but Keith was pushing his Tri-X film to 800, three stops faster, so the bulbs could theoretically light a huge area. Keith calculated that when he was standing 40 feet away from the pile, he could still shoot it at F-twenty-two. He wasn't sure about the distance or the quality of the bulbs so he made several different exposures. Whenever a bulb went off he caught a brief glimpse of the whole tunnel area around the pile and thought to himself, 'what an impressive place!'

"Damn, they filled this thing right up to the top, there's no way to get through to the other side because they used explosives to drop the ceiling down onto the rubble. It's incredibly solid and dangerous up here."

"I may be wrong, but it doesn't sound like something the Russians would bother to do. They took all the good stuff and left. Why would they seal one of the shafts after looting it?"

"You've got to be right, but if the Germans did this, they had to have a very good reason. I'll bet they didn't waste much time saving lives or protecting prisoners from collapsed or dangerous mine shafts."

Keith agreed: this was done by the Germans before the Ruskies ever entered the tunnel. The real question was why were the signs posted, and why was the blockage so solid. Questions that would gnaw at Keith for months to come. Keith carefully photographed a warning sign he had not noticed earlier: it said that anyone entering this area without permission would be shot on sight. More than ever he knew that this had to be the old lab, or at least something closely connected to it.

They retraced their steps toward the entrance, stopping to photograph interesting objects such as the remains of old rail cars, piles of clothing, indiscriminate heaps of junk. Along the way they passed underground rooms, both big and small, which had contained the workings of the old factory. Invariably the rooms contained lots of trash, but no equipment or signs of the old lab. A few rooms appeared to be crude dormitories with bunk beds stacked closely together: even the blankets were gone. They came to a large side shaft that was blocked, but when Hans climbed to the top of the rubble he saw that there was a space between the rubble and the ceiling.

"Keith, there's room to get through, to climb over the pile and into the side tunnel. Come on up."

"What can you see?"

"Nothing. Looking ahead there's just a long black tunnel. I don't know why it's blocked."

"Can't be important or they would have dropped the ceiling onto it."

"Maybe the Germans didn't have time to detonate the ceiling."

"Let's skip it for now, I'm tired and we have a long slog to get back to the car."

"I'll just try to scoot down the far side of the pile and see if there's anything interesting."

"No dammit, we've got to stick together: if you get hurt what am I supposed to do, leave you over there and call for help?"

"But what if there's some good stuff down here?"

"You can come back for it any time you want, meter seventy-five-hundred. It's not going anywhere."

There was no reply. Keith made a few shots straight down the tunnel with the big flash gun and a wide open lens, wondering how far the bulb would illuminate the tunnel. Fear entered his mind for the first time as he stood alone in the cold black silent tunnel. What if Hans didn't return, if he became trapped? Maybe it was time to leave, to return to Jessica and go home? How long should he wait? Dare he climb to the top of the rubble himself?

Miles away Jessica and Lilly huddled in a small hotel room wondering if the detective they had spotted was still in the hallway waiting for them, waiting to follow them to the tunnel tonight. Escaping without being seen was going to be tricky.

Back in the tunnel, Keith waited minutes that seemed like hours then he heard a loud scream from Hans and saw rubble moving as Hans scampered back through the hole at the top of the pile and slid down the near side, panting from exertion as he landed at Keith's feet.

"What happened? Why the scream?"

"There's a huge pile of corpses on the other side, hundreds of them, skeletons, skulls, clothes, it's horrible."

"We're lucky that Jessica isn't here. Let's head back to the entrance and shoot some film with the flare you brought. There's a good scene where those old rail cars are piled together. Then we can eat something while we wait for dark."

"What are you going to do with the movie film when you get home?"

"One of my best friends is an old Hollywood cameraman, maybe eighty years old, so the first thing I'm going to do is show it to him and tell him about the flare and the exposure I used and technical sorts of things. He loves to talk about cameras and difficult shots he made in the past. And since he sold me this camera, he's always curious to know what I've done with it. We'll have some laughs about what a poor cameraman I am when he runs the footage. And I'll show it to Jessica and our friends and tell them about our adventure."

They came to an area where semi-open railroad box cars were both on and off the track. Each car had a crude metal roof, a wooden floor, and side supports, but most of the side area was open, not enclosed. Some of the cars had barbed wire wrapped around the outside: perhaps these had been used for transporting prisoners. The ones beside the track were badly damaged, but the ones on the track weren't much better. Since they only had one flare Keith decided to put it behind the cars, then shoot footage from that side as well as a backlit version through the cars from the nearside, then as many other angles as possible. With luck he could get an exposure reading when the flare started burning and make a number of shots on the six minutes of film that he had brought.

"Hans, what's the writing on the flare say about how long it will burn?"

"It's in Russian, but I think it says ten minutes, but being Russian crap it might burn for only a minute. Better get your best shot first, then move around for other angles until it quits."

"OK, you stand over there and light it when I tell you, just hold it close to the ground for the first shot." Keith arranged this shot using a flashlight. He carried the camera battery in his backpack while he hand-held the camera.

"As soon as you get it burning, I'm going to take a light-meter reading, then start filming. After I get the shot I'll tell you to lift the flare up as high as you can next to the car, OK?"

"OK, the handle isn't very long, but I'll lift it as much as I can."

"Light it up, let's roll!"

Neither Hans or Keith had ever lit a military flare, so they were both startled when it ignited with an intense white light. Hans dropped it, but then moved it to the ground position they had agreed.

"Holy cow, that thing's bright, I can shoot this at F-eight."

Hans moved the flare as Keith filmed, both scurrying around the old cars. Part way through the second roll of film the flare fizzled out, leaving the tunnel in darkness. Smoke was everywhere, but a slight breeze drifted it slowly away toward the other end of the tunnel.

"Man, it's going to take a while for my eyes to recover, I hope you got the shot OK."

"Your flare was perfect, what a crazy scene I saw through the lens, especially in the smoke with the shafts of light cutting through the sides of the cars."

"Let's go back by the entrance and eat. It'll be time to leave soon."

While they were eating near the entrance, Keith heard something and felt a slight vibration. "Shhh, what's that? Do you hear it?"

"Shit, it's one of your trains, I bet they smelled the smoke from the flare when it drifted down the tunnel."

"Let's go, it's dark enough and we can wait up by the road instead of in here."

They moved quickly, keeping to the shadows as twilight faded into darkness. This path was longer than the one they had used on the first trip, and the fences were trickier to cross, but fear of discovery pushed them forward without a thought about how tired or sore their muscles were becoming. They reached the pickup area but the car hadn't arrived yet.

"We're at least an hour early. Would it be safest if we went into the woods a little way to wait for the car?"

"Right, we don't want to meet any hikers or others if they show up here."

"How can you tell where the traps and mines were planted?"

"Common sense. Think of the easiest place to walk from here, like that path going into the woods. That's the most dangerous, while the dense areas filled with brush are always safe."

Occasionally they heard a car or truck on the distant highway, but nothing on their little road. Nervous hours went by but the car didn't come. When it was two hours later than the agreed meeting time, Keith spoke, "I have a feeling that they aren't coming, that something happened to our plans. Would it be safe to hitch a ride back to town?"

"Maybe, but there aren't any cars on these roads in the middle of the night. Let's start walking and keep to the shadows."

"How long will it take?"

"We'll be home before daylight. I'm not worried about my feet as much as I'm worried about Lilly."

"What could have happened?"

"Two things. The Hiker could have told the cops about us so they might have put a tail on your car to see what we're up to."

"Then they would have followed us in here this morning."

"Maybe, maybe not: they don't get up very early if they don't have to."

"So what's the other idea?"

"When you first met us, we were three, Johan was with us, but he chickened out, he was afraid to come along. I gave him fifty dollars anyway so that he wouldn't be tempted to rat, but maybe he earned more by turning us in."

"Is he that unreliable a friend?"

"Things are tough here, or we never would have done this. We might have sold you a map of how to get here, but we never would have walked to the tunnel without a lot of money on the line."

"Is Lilly smart enough to spot the cops if they tried to follow the car?"

"That's not a problem, she's good, but if she saw the cop, then what?"

"Drive somewhere else then go back to the hotel for the night and wait for a safe time to come for us?"

Just before the first blush of light in the east their weary feet reached the hotel. The town was asleep, they saw nobody on the streets, nobody near the car which was parked in deep shadow behind the hotel. As they approached the car, Keith and Hans jumped as they heard Jessica whisper, "Keith over here, in the car."

Jessica and Lilly were in the car, whispering. "Keith, get in the car, we're leaving, I've got the suitcases, you can sleep while I drive."

"What happened?" Hans asked as Lilly moved out of the passenger seat and Keith through his backpack into the rear.

"Shhhh, later, Lilly will tell Hans and I'll tell you. Thanks for everything."

Jessica started the car with the headlights off, then drove slowly out of the parking lot and down the street, making as little noise or light as possible. Hans and Lilly faded into the darkness.

"Lilly saw someone following us today, so we went on a trip to Waldenburg for lunch, then came back. The car followed us all the way, so we knew it wasn't safe to come for you tonight. Lilly figured that Hans would make you walk home after a while, and I could sense that you were afraid and worried about us, but that you were on the way, so we quietly moved out, climbing down the fire escape, and waited for you. I gave Lilly most of the money I had, and a sketch to remember us by."

"What happens at the border? Maybe they'll be looking for us?"

"We'll be across the frontier and back in Czechoslovakia before the cops have their morning coffee and discover that we've gone missing. Then we'll head straight south to Brno and on to Austria and Vienna. We'll be driving past your favorite train station late this afternoon, it's only two hundred miles from here, but we're not stopping for anything but fuel."

"Great, I still have some food and we had adventures too. Wait until you see the footage!"

Vergangenheit

CHAPTER 10

PADERBORN AGAIN

Keith and Jessica quickly returned the rental car in Vienna and boarded a train for Munich, then another to Paderborn. They headed for the nearest phone and called Aunt Gerta. Keith wanted to know the best place to have his film processed and they both were anxious to hear how their translation was progressing. At the hospital they reached a nurse who was a close friend of Gerta's who told them that although Gerta was in surgery, she always took her film to Haus Dieterhof: she was certain they could find it in the phonebook. They arranged to talk with Gerta later and meet her for dinner.

In the phonebook Keith found that the lab was a block from the train station, a quick walk. They arrived at a large professional photo lab that looked a bit too commercial to handle film from an amateur. Keith and Jessica approached the front desk. The reception was cold and brusque, implying "we don't process tourist film here", but when they mentioned Doctor Gerta's name, the attitude changed instantly and they were suddenly the best of friends. Keith explained that he wanted his Tri-X processed at ASA-800, and that he would like contact sheets of the results. Things were looking up and Keith couldn't wait to see how his pictures with the giant flash bulbs had turned out. Unfortunately Paderborn didn't have a movie lab, so Keith decided to take his tunnel film home for processing.

That night they had dinner with Gerta and discovered that their translator was unexpectedly out of town, but that he was making good progress on the translation. Gerta was very curious about where the couple had been traveling, and what they had seen.

"Jessica, you are evasive, I can tell, you and Keith are up to something and it's more than just a translation and the need to process film."

"Keith, why don't we tell Gerta everything. Maybe she can help us solve a few riddles."

"Gerta, we're trying to solve a big puzzle and lots of the pieces are missing or held by people who shoot at us, so it's complex. Maybe we should begin at the beginning, if you want to hear the whole story?"

"Oh oh, this calls for another bottle of wine, and perhaps schnapps as well! Why don't you tell me first why you are trying to solve this mystery, then tell me the details, everything. And how does photography fit into the puzzle?"

Hours later, after many interruptions from Gerta, they had explained the whole thing, as well as how they had met during the filming of Keith's first motion picture, and all sorts of random photography and film-making details. Gerta loved the subject of Keith's film, a parody of the medical profession with outlandish scenes. Gerta was one hundred percent on their side, bubbling over with comments on how to explore secret Polish tunnels and outwit the local soldiers, nitwits, albeit armed nitwits, in her considered opinion. Whatever else happened, Keith and Jessica now had an ally in their quest. Gerta couldn't wait to see Keith's photos, and was full of advice on how they would photograph the tunnel next time, when she accompanied them. One of her suggestions was hilarious: she proposed that they make the army soldiers dig out the rubble blocking the secret tunnel! Keith fell out of his chair with laughter at the sheer audacity of the idea and rolled on the restaurant floor.

The next day they collected the film. Jessica was fascinated at the pictures made deep inside the tunnel. In spite of the photographic difficulties the pictures were mostly good and Gerta loved them.

"While we're waiting for the translator to return I'd like to drive over to Nordhausen and see the underground factories where the V-rockets were built. It's open to the public, with guided tours and lots of the machinery is intact. Want to come," Keith asked Jessica.

"More dead bodies and ghosts?"

"They've got electric lights, guides, and maps: all the ghosts are gone, but you don't have to go inside if you don't want to. You could stay in a cozy hotel and sketch or read while I do the tour. It's not a long drive, and we have two days to kill anyway."

"Why do you want to see another tunnel?"

"I want to see what it was like when all the gear was inside, when they were in operation. Our tunnel, at least the parts I've seen, is just a hollow shell, but I'd like to get more of a feel for what it was like when it was busy. The museum in Nordhausen has lots of books and pictures as well that I'd like to browse."

110

"You can look at Harry's old movies and see even more: what's so special about this?"

"I want to look at the construction of the tunnels themselves and maybe get some idea of what might be behind the rubble in the forbidden area of our tunnel. I'm curious and Nordhausen was one of the biggest underground facilities."

The next day Keith was part of a guided tour of the Mittelwerk Rocket Factory near Nordhausen. This site contained two huge parallel tunnels under the Harz Mountains with forty-seven galleries between the tunnels. Each of the huge tunnels was wide enough to fit two full size railroad lines side by side and each was as high as thirty feet in places. Originally the tunnels had been gypsum mines, but the war effort had enlarged the tunnels and added galleries between them filled with manufacturing equipment. The tunnels themselves were assembly lines for both V-1 and V-2 rockets as well as jet airplane engines and smaller rockets. The site manufactured 13,000 V-rockets and flying bombs in less than two years, an amazing feat given the constant bombing overhead.

As the guide led the group into the tunnels Keith focused his attention on the way the tunnels and the galleries were built. Here, most of the galleries were large, but not as big as the tunnels, and most of them ran directly from tunnel 'A' to tunnel 'B'. It was a perfect arrangement for mass-production: machine shops made sub-assemblies in the galleries, then attached these to rockets traveling on railroad assembly lines in the tunnels. He quickly realized that his Polish tunnel was very primitive by comparison, and that perhaps it was more of a research complex than a factory for full-scale production. Keith began to think about his number one tunnel problem, how to get into the laboratory behind the rubble in the Polish tunnel. Even if he could get a back-hoe or some other heavy equipment into the tunnel, moving the rubble would take a long time, with an ever-present danger of more of the ceiling falling on his head while he worked. As he wandered through one gallery looking at pieces of a V-2 rocket, he saw a little man-size tunnel which directly connected two galleries. Maybe the answer was here, just dig a small tunnel in the rock next to the rubble pile, just big enough to go around the rubble and into the area behind it. If his new tunnel were fairly high up on the wall, it would only need to go around the top of the rubble pile, where the pile wasn't too thick. An idea, but maybe not very practical.

In one gallery Keith noticed a hole near the ceiling and asked the guide about it. The guide replied that air vents had been cut into most of the galleries so that there was no danger of suffocation even when smoky processes like welding were being used. This set Keith to wondering if there might be vent shafts running through the Polish tunnel. As a first step, Keith could study his photos carefully. It had not occurred to him to look for air shafts while he was in the tunnel, even though he had felt breezes.

After the tour Keith visited the museum to study old pictures of the construction of the Mittelwerk complex. It looked like the main construction technique was blasting followed by rock removal on trains, working twenty-four hours of every day: not a solution to his problem.

As soon as they returned to Paderborn they had dinner with Gerta and the translator, Gregor Ponczki who was bubbling over with excitement. He had translated only part of the dairy as he had had to make several trips to a remote library to learn the meanings of obscure phrases that he had never heard before.

"The diary is a personal account by a great scientist describing the biggest discovery of his life. The excitement is palpable, it erupts from the page. Much of the diary is scientific data, but in between the cold facts are impressions and personal comments which reveal his excitement. I'm sorry that I haven't made more progress, but I've had to find scientific dictionaries to do justice to the material. I've made Xerox copies of each page, then added reference numbers to the copies so that my notes can be matched to the drawings. This book is too important for a rushed approach. I know you are anxious to read the whole book, but I also know Doctor Gerta would never forgive me if I did sloppy work."

"Have you found any references to his laboratory inside a Polish war-time tunnel," Keith asked.

"I scanned the book at first and most of it was written in difficult circumstances, which is probably what you mean. The beginning is a summary of his technical work before that time, then the bulk of the book is about his inventions when he was pressed to make discoveries as fast as possible with lots of workers at his disposal. He often comments that he wishes that he had associates of equal brilliance with whom to discuss ideas. He is very lonely, one brilliant person in the midst of an army of drones, forced to make progress that only he can appreciate. He is under two kinds of intense pressure. The external pressure comes from military people who demand progress on their terms or they will kill him, and the other pressure is from within, the pressure to explore an incredible scientific breakthrough that he has made. He has little sleep and works constantly. He is so excited and it shows on every page. I wish you could read Polish: Doctor Gerta will enjoy reading the original when she has time. I am excited as well and now that I have the right dictionaries progress will be swift. I will mail you the finished translation in chapters as it progresses."

Jessica turned to Gerta and began to talk quietly with deep emotion. "I don't know how to begin this Gerta but I must tell you something. I have a psychic sense, maybe a sixth or seventh sense that sometimes lets me feel or see into other worlds, to feel vibrations and messages which science says do not exist. It's not something I can control, rather I am its slave. It's like when you walk down a street and smell bread baking, you can't tell yourself not to smell the bread, it just happens: you cannot consciously control your sense of smell. For me the spirits are the same, they just come and go, and sometimes I have a bit of control, and other times I am completely overwhelmed as Keith can attest. I am telling you this because I have felt the spirit of the scientist who wrote this book. When I hug the diary, not the copy here, but the original with his own fingerprints, where he poured his life onto those pages, I can feel his presence and he is so worried that his discovery will be lost. He is troubled, he may be alive or dead, I can't tell, but he wants his diary, he needs it, and I don't know what to do. My feelings are so deep and so strong, but I'm trapped. He isn't behind the rubble in the tunnel, he isn't in the pages of the book, but he's out there and he needs us, he needs us to bring his discovery into the light. Please help me."

There was silence as everyone thought about Jessica's revelation. Keith knew exactly what she referred too, but the others were probably skeptical.

"Jessica really does have the gift, and it can be very painful. I trained as an engineer, a scientifically rational being, believing in nothing but that which could yield to repeatable scientific analysis. However I've seen her do things which are impossible. Jessica can see into the future as well as into the past in ways I cannot explain. She can do it, and her visions have saved lives. I have no explanation for what she sees, but I love her with all my heart. Please take this seriously."

"Jessica, you are not alone. I have seen others with similar gifts, and we rational beings, we who are trying to cure disease and injuries with primitive tools, are in their debt. You have a blessing, not a curse, and we will help you, don't worry," Gerta softly replied.

"Gerta, when we were with Jessica's parents we learned that Jessica's grandmother, Virginie's mother, also had similar gifts, but she just passed over. If only we had known sooner we could have visited her and maybe learned more," Keith added.

As the wine flowed late into the night, Keith described the psychic adventures he and Jessica had shared and Gerta told them of inexplicable scenes she had witnessed as a doctor: more than once Gerta had seen mysterious cures as well as illnesses and deaths. The more that Gerta practiced rational medicine, the more she became convinced that other realms of knowledge existed. Now perhaps there was a chance to explore them with Jessica as her guide.

CHAPTER 11

SEX WITH DAVID AND SPUNKY

Keith and Jessica flew home, glad to be among familiar surroundings and friends. After dropping his movie film for developing and printing at CFI, Keith went to visit David and see how his TV show was developing. He found him in a small cluttered office inside a trailer, an old portable office parked next to a stage. Keith knew immediately that David had come down in the world since not only was the office ridiculously small, but the air conditioner was broken as well.

"David is this really your office?" Keith asked.

"I'm not on the street yet, but close to it. My ratings are terrible, the show's a bust. The only thing saving me is that the producer is hot for the lead actress, so he's keeping it running."

"Hey, speaking of the street, why don't we add some excitement to your show and do some live scenes on the street? We could talk with hookers on Hollywood Boulevard and maybe shoot some stuff inside a club with pole dancers and table girls?"

"Are you nuts, they'd never allow it."

"Why not, I'll bet it's cheaper to do live video footage on location because there's no editing, no post-production to pay for. We could interweave the live stuff with commercials and set pieces you shot earlier."

"I've never done anything like that. What's the advantage?"

"Other than saving money, it will be spontaneous, we'll get publicity, it will be exciting because we won't know exactly what will happen. People will tune-in just to see these girls unrehearsed in their real-life surroundings. I bet nobody's done anything like this before. It'll be like reporting from a war zone, the rougher the better."

"We could pre-select the girls and coach them a bit, and girlie, I mean Veronica, can interview them in one of her hot outfits. She has to be in every scene or I'll be in trouble. She's the only thing keeping my paycheck coming."

"Look, we can work out what's supposed to happen during the whole show, get the existing footage and commercials cued-up, then go onto the street with a single hand-held camera and a small crew. You will be on the street directing, and your Assistant Director can be in the truck at the controls, cutting away to tape if anything goes wrong on the street. I'll be with you. We'll have a riot."

"Do you think we'll be allowed to do this, I mean with real hookers and dancers? What if a John shows up and tries to buy the girl, do we shoot the approach and the negotiation?"

"Don't ask permission, ask forgiveness afterwards. You aren't a big deal prime time show so people won't notice at first: we can sneak it in with a little technical help. Then when we have a big hit they won't dare cancel the live scenes."

"We can run a blurb across the bottom of the screen, 'Live from Hooker Lounge' or something."

"Right, and in that case, Hooker Lounge will let us in free for the publicity they'll get, so we won't need to pay location fees."

"What about unintended consequences, like street people yelling at us, and traffic noise. We won't have any control over what happens."

"Who cares? Street people may laugh and say funny things and they may look crazy but Veronica can play off them. Seriously though, we should do the first live broadcast indoors where we have a bit of control over the scene. Get the technical stuff down in a safe setting, then go for the street."

While Keith and David laughed and planned their first attempt at live TV, Jessica and Angela talked seriously on Angela's back porch. Jessica was nervous, almost in tears. "Dammit Angela, I wish you knew who the blackmailers sent the video tapes to before they died. I mean, my parents could be watching me screwing that guy right now."

"We messed up, but at least it's over. Your real friends will never mention it, they'll figure it's fake, that it could never really be you. And there's been no publicity about it, not a peep, so they didn't send it to the media. Have you heard anything?"

"Not a thing, but I worry, I mean, from now on whenever I see one of our friends I'm going to wonder if they've seen it."

"Can't you use your psychic sense to find out, to tell if they're looking at you in a funny way?"

"And if so, what do I say, do I blush and turn bright red because I know that they know but that they're too polite to say anything, I mean, it would almost be worse knowing. When they sent it to you, did you let Harry see it?"

"Of course not, I erased it then threw it in the trash. And the best thing was that there was no note or writing or anything, just the tape."

"Which papers had the picture of the dead guy? Did anyone mention it to you?"

"All the papers ran the shot for a day, then it was over, and nobody connected it to anything, just a bum out in the desert killed in an interesting way, lying beside the road. No clues, no nothing."

"Bet the TV shrinks had fun explaining that he suffocated because his cock was stuffed down his throat. Did they blame it on his girlfriend?"

"He did have an estranged wife who the cops interviewed: she said she wished she'd done it herself."

The next morning Keith collected a print of his tunnel film and headed to Harry's home. Harry took Keith's four rolls and started winding them onto one reel, trimming off the ends and splicing the good sections together with sixteen millimeter perforated tape: he was in his element, handling freshly exposed film, eager to see what it looked like on the screen. When he was done they had about ten minutes to screen.

Angela and Jessica were already in the living room drinking coffee as Jessica described their European adventures and showed Angela prints of Keith's still pictures. Soon Keith's movie was on the screen as Keith described what was happening as he shot it.

"Keith, this is really good footage: it's rough, the shadows are pitch black, the camera isn't steady, what I mean is that this film is alive, it makes me feel like I'm right there with you," Angela said.

"You did a very good job considering the circumstances, and especially in the tunnel with the flare around the old railway cars. I can smell the smoke, I couldn't have done any better, maybe not even as well," Harry added.

Angela jumped up and started pacing around the room with excitement, "Keith, this stuff, I know what you've got to do next. This film looks old, it's grainy black and white just like the footage from the wooden box. They could have been shot at the same time. Take this new film, get it blown-up to thirty-five millimeter, then intercut it with the old footage. You've got the beginnings of a great film here, I can see it coming together."

"But Angela, I'm nowhere with the script, I can't tell which pieces of this to put where or even begin to tell how it will all fit together."

"Doesn't matter. This footage is very interesting. Take it all into dad's cutting room and mess around with it, try different things, show it to us, let us give you suggestions, play with it. You'll begin to see your script coming together as you handle the film, I just know it will work. The footage will write the script, it's been done before."

"And I love some of the stills, and Harry's stills too. You can pan across them with a movie camera so that they become part of your film. You can also pan pages of the diary especially the scientific drawings and tables of numbers," Jessica added.

"You're a sound man, you know how to cut together a sound track with effects, German music, Hitler squawking in the background, explosions overhead, all that stuff. You'll make a great track to run against the visuals," Harry added.

"And then Keith you know what happens next? Next we show the finished effort to money people and get a contract, with a big upfront bonus. I already know who we'll invite to the screening, and I'll be your A.D. when we do the live action," Angela said as she continued to pace the room, a bundle of energy ready to jump into action. "Dad, please run the film again so we can give Keith ideas about how to cut this together."

Later, as they walked out the door Jessica kissed a bewildered Keith, "You know the best thing about this morning?"

"I'm not sure, so much is running through my head."

"The best thing is that you've come back to life, you're excited, you can't wait to get to work, we're all together again."

As soon as Keith was home he began to work. He knew one thing he could do immediately. He could collect ingredients for the sound track and review the resources already in hand. He poured through his collection of photograph records looking for odd sounds, old music, he even found a scratchy record of Nazi marching songs including '*Die Fahne Hoch*', '*The Horst Wessel Song*', and '*Deutchland Uber Alles*' with the Nazi verses. As he scrounged through boxes and boxes of 3M quarter inch recording tape looking for useful sound effects that he had recorded over the years, an idea came to him, now he knew how to assemble this short film.

In a flash Keith realized that he was really making a trailer, the short films shown in theaters to excite viewers and to get them to come to a movie. Trailers are normally two or three minutes long, and they are supposed to contain actual scenes from the movie being advertised. But trailers are just advertisements and they often contain scenes that aren't even in the film: the goal was simple, get people to pay to see the flick. Keith focused on making an advertisement for his new film, an advertisement that would run five to ten minutes with as much action and excitement as possible. The real movie would use this footage too, but in other ways, in ways that he had yet to envision.

The jewel in Keith's home was a well-worn Ampex two-track flat-bed tape recorder, a professional studio machine for editing and recording quarter-inch magnetic tape. Keith was an expert with splicing block, single-edge razor blade, and splicing tape. The first task was to transfer the useful bits from phono records and his own tape library to tape duplicates he could cut and splice every which way. The hours rolled by as he happily worked on the track. Harry was already at the lab ordering blowups of all the good parts of Keith's new footage and tomorrow they would pan some of the stills with one of Harry's thirty-five millimeter cameras. The project was off to a great start.

A week later Keith and David waited nervously for the start of their first live porno-TV segment, a five minute interview inside Hooker Lounge. It was semi-scripted, everyone knew what was supposed to happen, a safe introduction of a new idea. They had rehearsed and all was ready as a clock counted down. Veronica, the hostess of the show, stood next to a pole while a scantily-clad girl twirled overhead to music: she wore both the top and bottom of her bikini outfit so that the censors couldn't complain that she was naked. Her body was as covered as the girls in beach volleyball tournaments, but she moved in different ways.

The red light came on, Veronica started talking, emphasizing that this part of the show was live. The camera panned around the club, then up to the dancing girl. She slid down the pole then started playfully chatting with Veronica. So far it was all according to plan as Veronica asked her about her job and how she liked dancing while wearing only a g-string. What did she think of the guys in the audience?

"As long as I'm up there I ignore them, I just twirl around and do my stuff for half an hour then take a break. But when I'm down here it's different, the guys get excited about my body, they want to get close, to touch me, to feel my body next to theirs. I mean, look at David, your Director over there by the camera. There's a huge bulge in his pants right now. Hey cameraman, get a close-up of his pants, pan over to David, look at him blush!"

Keith ducked behind a table, afraid that he would be next. The audience in the club roared with laughter as the camera panned to David. Veronica and the girl walked over to David and the camera covered the three of them close together.

Veronica improvised, "David, you're human after all, isn't she a great dancer, what a nice body, hey, don't turn away, you're on television."

The girl rubbed against David as the audience cheered. Then she started to unbutton his shirt. "Come on, dance with me, you've got too many clothes on, let's strip! Veronica help me, he's coming up on the pole when we get his pants off."

Veronica couldn't resist the fun, "Come on David, I'll take my dress off if you drop your pants."

David lost his pants and his shirt, Veronica unzipped and dropped her dress to the floor, and the three of them danced to a sexy song as the audience laughed, chanted and cheered. Back in the truck the crew was roaring with laughter, letting the scene run, ignoring commercial breaks and their script until the song ended and David picked up his clothes to a great round of applause. Veronica carried on with the interview she had planned while the girl helped her dress, acting as though getting dressed on TV was a normal part of the show. Then she encouraged viewers to tune in next week when they would be live in another sexy location. What a TV show. Their ratings went through the roof.

When Keith came home that night he found that a package had arrived, a package from Germany with the first translated pages of the diary.

"Jessica, what do you make of this? Have you read this translation of the first part of the diary yet?"

"Yes, but I didn't understand most of it, and I suspect you won't either. Our inventor was involved in a branch of science that didn't reach the western world."

"I just scanned a bit and it reminded me of that book of Schauberger's that I read, stuff about living water and secret energy hidden in the landscape."

"The only thing that I know that even comes close is Orgone research, work Wilhelm Reich did with his Orgone Accumulator. He was arrested, and his books were banned, but you can find them in big libraries. He believed in Orgasmic Energy and everyone thought it was all about sex. After all, his first book in 1961 was entitled *Function Of The Orgasm.*"

"I remember, he built things that collected strange energy, then he fired the energy at clouds to cause rain, and sometimes it worked."

"But he got in trouble because he also claimed to be able to cure cancer, if sick people would climb into his accumulators. I think they got him for practicing medicine without a license or something similar."

"But how weird, I mean to ban and confiscate his books in America. There're lots of books by kooks in every bookstore. He must have been on to something big for the authorities to trash him so thoroughly."

"So, think of our inventor, making a flying saucer is pretty strange too, but he didn't even get a chance to have his writings published or to spread his ideas around. Somehow we have to help him."

"Jessica, Gerta and I were trained to believe only what we can see and touch and what can be proved in laboratories. We never learned the things you understand instinctively, the things you believe in so deeply. You need to teach me about your world, about the things I can't see, but which you know are there. Otherwise I'll never make sense of the inventor's diary."

"Start by reading *MIND REACH*, about remote viewing. Two normal Stanford physicists wrote the book, but they don't understand their own results, yet they saw things happen, and measured everything carefully and wrote it all down. They're part of your world, but they're investigating my world, and now they believe in it."

"If we work together we can figure out how to blend both worlds and begin to understand how the invention could fly. I mean, in the pictures it's a bunch of metal, pipes, and wires, stuff I should be able to understand, but in the diary we discover that the heart, the energy that powers it, comes from something completely foreign to my way of thinking, from Edelwasser and living energy, whatever that is."

In the days that followed Keith studied remote viewing and read **MIND REACH** twice. Here were two physicists watching as subjects visualized scenes they had never visited, miles away, sometimes across the country. And it seemed that everyone had at least some of this talent and could develop it with training. There were several key aspects to the phenomenon: first, distance didn't matter, far away scenes were just as easy as near ones; second, time could shift slightly, as the scene might be seen before or after something happened; third, electromagnetic shielding didn't affect the process, viewers could be inside a shielded metal room or outdoors, the results were the same.

Keith rushed to find Jessica, "Remote viewing, you're really sensitive, you must be great at this stuff, have you viewed the inside of the inventor's lab? What's it like now? Is there another door we could open? Can you walk around inside the lab and see what's there? Is it all ruined or is the stuff still OK?"

"I tried but no luck. Didn't you notice in the book that remote viewing comes in little flashes or inspirations, and it's hard to separate them from memory and imagination. Whenever I think of the lab, I see the pictures from Harry's box. My memories of those photos and movies blot out any remote viewing experience I might have. The memories are too strong. And now I see your pictures of the tunnels too."

"I missed that part of the book and when I tried remote viewing I couldn't tell if it was imagination or the real thing."

"Right, in the book they did controlled experiments, with feedback and analysis, to tell when it worked and when it didn't. If you visualize the inside of the lab, even if you could do it, you wouldn't know if it was real or if it was your imagination because we have no way of checking the accuracy. I see all sorts of images in my head all the time, and maybe you do too, but we don't know what they are. You imagine things, you make up crazy scenes and write them into screenplays or David's TV show, you visualize things that have never happened. Where do you get these ideas, these pictures in your head? Maybe they really exist somewhere or in the future or the past but we don't know."

"This is a lot more complex than I realized. You and I could do controlled experiments like in the book, it wouldn't be hard to arrange."

"I know. I'd like to develop your skills and measure mine, but it's too bad we can't apply them to something practical like finding an entrance to the lab."

"I don't think we can go back anyway, at least not while the soldiers and trains are around."

Whenever Keith had a free moment, or when lying awake in the middle of the night, he thought about his screenplay which involved the inventor, Harry's adventures travelling the world in the thirties, Fritz and Leni filming riots, WW2 bombing of underground labs, and the flying machine. He had lots of scenes but the backbone which would tie them together eluded him. He knew that although he had conflict, emotion, and exciting scenes, that somehow it didn't hang together. There was no unifying theme. Keith went for long solitary walks around the neighborhood, watched old movies with Jessica, and tried to breathe life into his story. So far it was just words on paper, it didn't leap off the page like his effort with crazy old people that they had filmed last year: there was a big difference and it frustrated Keith. It was always in the back of his mind, but he had less and less time to work on his script, though his advertising trailer for it was coming along well.

Keith's days were filled with tasks from the real world. He had agreed to be a member of David's writing team which meant four hours a day discussing ideas with the other team members, reviewing footage and reading reviews, and brain-storming new ideas, and of course he was supposed to come up with new ideas on his own and present them to the group. In reality this consumed eight hours a day, five days a week, just like a normal job, but it did pay well at least while they had a hit show on their hands. In addition translated diary pages arrived for analysis and he longed for time to explore remote viewing and ideas from Jessica's world. On top of all this, he and Jessica had been given an old apartment building as a wedding present, as a partial payback for psychic work she had done for an old real estate magnate. Now they discovered that it needed work, that tenants had to be found, plumbing had to be fixed, and a whole day could slip away as they worked the details.

Vergangenheit

CHAPTER 12

CHEMISTRY

One quiet Saturday night Keith and Jessica were home, happy to have quiet time together, reading translations of the diary and talking about what they might mean. "Jessica, look at this bit about the fuel and how it fast it evaporates and his struggle to make it more stable. The special double-walled fuel container he describes is just like that brass bottle that was in one of Harry's boxes. Maybe there's some fuel in it and we can get it analyzed at a chemistry lab."

"I wonder where we can find a place that could handle something so strange, so unusual. I mean, the fuel, at least as I understand it, isn't a normal chemical substance, it's alive somehow."

"UCLA's a few blocks away and Cal Tech's over in Pasadena, there must be world-class chemists around here who could look into this."

"But what will we tell them? Do we dare tell them anything about the inventor and the lab and the machine? Supposing it explodes when they place it in their analysis machine, or poisons the chemist who looks at it."

"We could find a research chemist and take him into our confidence, at least a little bit, and swear him to secrecy, it might work. I'll bet you have an academic contact who could steer us to someone, someone we could talk it over with."

"My contacts are in the School Of Art, but let me make a call, maybe one of them knows who we should visit as a start."

Sunday afternoon they were in the UCLA faculty lounge talking with a young chemistry professor, Mike Auerbach, about their request.

"The container is special and at least forty years old. The liquid that may be inside is a mysterious substance, a chemical compound, but one that's supposed to be alive in some way, but we don't know much more than that, and it might all have evaporated. We haven't dared to open it. It might be dangerous, or nothing, or it might not even be analyzable with normal equipment."

"I can analyze anything, it can't be that strange, I mean, chemicals

125

are chemicals. You've got me interested. If there's anything in your can, I'll take a little of it and run a few quick tests and we can take it from there."

They handed over the brass container. Although it was about the size of an overgrown one liter bottle, it was surprisingly heavy, as though it were solid metal.

Monday Keith went back to work with David's writing team, thankful that he had a new idea to present. It had occurred to him as he drove down Sunset Boulevard, past a litter-strewn dump identified as a Gentlemen's Club. As he told the rest of the team, "We can do a segment or maybe a whole show comparing and contrasting two different kinds of sluts. One kind only teases guys but never actually does anything with the customers. She's playing, laughing inside at the customers, and taking as much of their money as she can. She could even be a virgin, but she's a really good entertainer, maybe a dancer or singer who strips because it pays better. The other kind of sluts are hard-core hookers, who think the big money is made in bed. I have a feeling that the first kind actually makes more money with less work than the other kind, and then there's the whole medical side. The first kind doesn't get V.D. or beaten up by drunks."

His team loved the idea and spent the rest of the day laughing and fleshing it out, calling girls and asking if there really were two kinds of sluts. By evening they had roughed out a complete show and had schemed up two live segments, one for each kind of girl, which would cover a third of the running time: the rest of the show would be on-stage with girls, Veronica, and customers telling what they thought of the girls.

Dinner at home with Jessica was interrupted by a visit from Mike Auerbach and another man. Mike began, "This is Mr. Dowling from the FBI. My boss contacted him when our alarms went off."

"What alarm, what is this all about?"

"I put your container inside a sealed sterile chamber we use for analyzing weird things, substances which might be dangerous or poisonous. Then I used robotic manipulators to open it and remove a few drops for analysis. It's a most interesting violet-colored fluid by the way. I was moving along, doing my thing, when an alarm went off."

"A fire alarm?"

"No a radiation alarm. It never occurred to me that your sample might be radioactive so I didn't scan it first for radiation or try to x-ray it or anything like that. I'm a chemist, so I started doing a chemical analysis. Your stuff is quite radioactive, and I think the container is mostly lead so as to protect people who handle it. The alarm's never gone off before so we were all surprised, and that led to this. As I'm sure you know, highly-refined radioactive material is not quite legal without a pile of paperwork."

"You didn't tell Mr. Auerbach where you obtained this container, but now I need to know where you found it, and if there's any more where it came from. This is highly dangerous material, we can't leave it lying around where it might hurt someone."

Keith hardly knew what to say but he was annoyed, "It's the only sample we have, we don't know where it came from, and we'd like to have it back. It's ours, isn't it?"

Jessica added, "And Mike, you told us that you wouldn't tell anyone about this, that it was our secret."

"Look people, this material is not only dangerous, but from the little Mr Auerbach has told me about the composition it's probably a top secret compound that is or was part of a national defense project. There's no way you can have it back and keep it in your house. This needs to be locked up safely and investigated thoroughly, and you two may be in trouble with the law if this is stolen property."

Keith had spent all day with David's writing team and was on a creative roll. Crazy ideas were still popping into his head. "Wrong Mr. FBI. You can take Mike's analysis to all the secret defense labs and you won't find one that knows anything about it. We didn't steal this from anyone, we found it and it's ours. It came from outer space and we just want to know its exact composition. Take Mike's analysis. Go to your secret labs, ask them, I dare you. They won't know squat about it. Mike can keep the bottle in a safe place and analyze it while you check us out, but we want it back in thirty days."

Jessica asked, "Mike, what's in the violet liquid, what's so special besides it being radio-active?"

"It's fascinating, it's liquid, but most of the components are metals, and not just metals but very rare elements like Thorium, Lanthanum, Holmium, and Ytterbium, all from the Lanthanide Series of the Periodic Table. I've never seen anything like it. I've got a grad student researching in the library right now, this is neat, a great discovery, and thanks for letting us keep it for another month. Do you know anything else about it?"

Keith was about to say it was a fuel, but one look at Jessica told him to shut up. The men left, with Mr. Dowling scowling, "You can bet we will take the analysis to all the labs. This isn't over by a long shot."

After they left, Keith said, "Thanks for reminding me to be quiet. Maybe the best thing that just happened is that we learned that the inventor was really onto something special. If a modern chemistry prof can't figure out a substance made forty years ago, we have a fabulous discovery."

"I wonder if the violet liquid is alive in some way, not a way that Mike can analyze, but in a different dimension. Maybe it's a liquid form of orgone energy, or a whole new kind of substance?"

"Or the inventor's phrase, living energy, could have referred to radioactive substances, but in a different vocabulary. Perhaps in the original Polish the two terms are similar?"

"I'll write to Gerta and ask her what she thinks of the actual Polish words and the fuel references."

Keith spent the next morning with the writing team, then in the afternoon all the writers, David, and the crew assembled to film the staged portion of the next episode. Veronica talked to scantily-clad girls about tricks they had played on customers, about bad dates that hadn't worked out, about violence and abuse. The idea was to alternate interesting sexy and funny segments with serious stories of abuse and betrayal. Part of the show was supposed to make people laugh, part of it was designed to excite male viewers while staying just inside television boundaries, and the third part was a tear-jerker where girls who had been forced into the business were offered hope and escape. The show had a telephone number where girls could call in anonymously with their problems, and Veronica had started a charity where viewers could send contributions to help the troubled girls. Keith and David were surprised at the number of calls they received and at the money that had started flowing through Veronica's charity.

David's girlfriend Spunky watched from the shadows and talked quietly with Keith. She had been cast into the only sexy role in Keith's film and had thoroughly enjoyed teasing Keith and David during the shooting. "Keith, isn't it amazing how successful this show has become. I mean, who would have thought that we could even run this stuff on TV, and that people would watch it?"

"You're an expert, you know how well sex sells. We've just found a way to package it differently."

"Do you think I'm a slut, like the girls over there with Veronica?"

"No Spunky, at least not in my book. I think that you know exactly what you're doing when you put on a tight low-cut dress and parade around with your boobs showing. You're smart, you're turning guys on right and left and laughing at the same time. For you sex is all about fun, at least that's the impression I have, but I'm a guy and you turn me on too. The girls on our show aren't nearly as clever, or if they are, they've lost their way, so maybe we can help them. What I'm trying to say is that I think you play with sex, while they have to use it to earn a living."

"That's a good distinction, but don't tell anyone because I like guys to think I'm a bit slutty, that maybe they can get somewhere with me if they treat me nicely. Girls have to look out for themselves around here."

"You could catch anyone you wanted if you set your mind to it."

Spunky took Keith's hand and held it in hers, looking into his eyes. "I couldn't catch you now no matter how hard I tried. I could have grabbed you when you were broken up over Kristin's death, before Jessica moved into your bed, though I never would have guessed, I mean, about that part of her. Why did she do that?"

"Did you see a video, or some stills, is that what you're asking about?"

"It was wild. Even I've never done that."

"Spunky, please, please listen. She was drugged, she can't even remember most of it, and she tried to commit suicide when she realized what had happened. She's been blackmailed ever since, but it's over. Destroy the tape, don't ever mention it again, especially not to Jessica, OK?"

"You two have deep secrets, but you appear so happy and normal on the surface."

"You and David are our closest friends, but we can't talk about this, even with you, and yes, you could easily have caught me before Jessica did, but now you're in David's arms and the four of us are going to have lots of fun," Keith said as he squeezed her hand then let it go. For a long moment Spunky looked into Keith's eyes, then turned away.

"Who's that sexpot walking toward us? I don't think she's in the cast." Keith asked.

"Oh shit, that's Sarah-Jane, we used to be friends, but she disappeared. I wonder why she's limping?"

"She's waving to you and coming our way, I think I'll go talk with the other writers and let you two have some girl-time."

"Keith, thanks for telling me about Jessica, I'm so sorry."

"The girls over there aren't the only ones who've been forced into bad sexual experiences. Hey, here comes Jessica, I invited her over to see what we're up to, to prove that it wasn't a bunch of horny guys exploiting young chicks. Give her a hug, have a few laughs on us!"

Jessica, Spunky, and Sarah-Jane chatted at length then all three left the stage and didn't return. Keith hardly noticed since he and his team were busy constantly re-writing dialog to fit ideas that came to the cast, to David, and to themselves. The format of the show was loose, the atmosphere electric and creative, and new ideas flowed constantly. A very busy time for Keith.

When he arrived home he was surprised to find Sarah with Jessica. She was drying her hair and wearing one of Jessica's robes. He couldn't help but notice her large breasts which the robe didn't completely cover. Keith kissed Jessica and addressed Sarah, "Hi, I'm Keith, I saw you on the stage but I was too busy to say hello."

"I'm Sarah, and Jessica invited me to come here until I find a place to live."

Keith was pleasantly surprised, and turned on by her voluptuous body and soft coy voice, but curious as to why Jessica had done this.

"Don't get silly ideas Keith, Sarah is just visiting and sleeping in her own bed. I can read your mind, and we're both watching your expression as you admire her boobs."

"Girls know everything, so I'm sure that you can see that I'm imagining a threesome with you both, but you can also tell that I know it won't happen today, tonight, or ever, but you're both so attractive that I am excited."

"Hey, at least you're honest about it. Maybe Jessica will let you play with me sometime, but she's the boss around here, the one who counts, so don't get out of line Keith. Keep your pants on."

"Jessica, what's happening, why are you both teasing me turning me on and off with sly grins and flashes of skin."

"Relax and have a drink Keith, it's all right, you can get as excited as you want, we won't mind in the least, in fact we'll help you if you're nice to both of us. Sarah has had a rough time, she's hurt, she's broke, and she's in trouble, but she knows a lot about handling people. We can help her, and help ourselves at the same time. I've offered her a job as the manager of our building. She can live in that little unit in the back as soon as we get it fixed up. She'll take care of the tenants, call the painters, plumbers, and all the other maintenance folks. That'll give you more time to work on your project, and I've started painting again, working over my sketchbook, so I'd rather stop answering calls from the building myself."

"That's a great idea. I'm just surprised that you've invited such an attractive sexy young woman into our house to live with us for a while."

"I know where your heart lies, even if your body wants to be somewhere else now and then. You and David are spending a lot of time with hookers and sluts, but I don't mind, I really don't. I know you get excited about them, but you come home to me every night, that's the important part. If you really want to jump into Sarah's bed, go ahead, if it's all right with her, but don't lie about it. I understand you completely and I want you to have a good time, even if it hurts me to think about it."

"I don't ever want to hurt you, you know that. Not ever. I have to run now; remember, Harry's editor is coming over tonight to help us finish my trailer. I've got a million things to ask him, we're really close."

"When you come home, remember our bedroom is the one at the end of the hall, don't get lost."

"You two are having too much fun playing with me. Bye!"

Morning found Keith at a small recording studio, the kind of place normally rented by musicians and record companies. He had used it a few times before and knew that he could usually rent time in the morning because musicians were night-people. The studio had an eight-track recorder, a big mixing board, lots of odd effects, and several two-track machines. Late last night he had finished the film portion of his trailer so it was time to make a serious pass at the sound track. Normally motion picture sound tracks are mixed down (the process of blending many tracks into a single track) in a fancy studio, really a small theater, where the different elements of a sound track can be matched to the film while it plays on a big screen. Time in one of those places costs hundreds of dollars an hour, while this studio was cheap. Keith needed time to experiment quietly by himself, to discover how different combinations of sounds worked together. He had written an elaborate plan with the duration of each segment of the film noted. The first step was to copy bits and pieces of his own tapes to the eight-track machine, putting each piece in the right place in terms of running time. Then once the pieces were all on a ten minute roll of wide tape, he could play the big tape while fading the various sounds from the different tracks in and out. Each time he ran through the whole ten minutes of his trailer the result became a little better, a little more fluid and emotionally exciting. Keith was totally absorbed in his work and only stopped when the first musicians arrived late that afternoon. He left with a smile and a finished ten minute quarter-inch tape. Tonight he would play it alongside his film for their friends at Harry's. He could hardly wait to see their reactions.

When Keith arrived home he found Mike and Jessica talking about Mike's analysis of the fuel container.

"We were just talking about the violet liquid and where it might have originated. Mike's stumped, there's nothing like it in the archives, or anywhere else, and he doesn't think the FBI will find it in the secret labs either."

"Did you tell him that the liquid might have come from an Orgone accumulator?"

Mike laughed, "You can't be serious. Orgasmic energy was debunked years ago and Wilhelm Reich went to jail. What makes you think he was involved in this?"

"Mike, if you had lots of ingredients could you manufacture a liquid like this with today's technology? Is it something you could brew or distill or mix-up? Could you make it radioactive?"

"At the lab we've been talking about that and the answer is I don't think so. We can tell what's in the liquid and are doing some interesting spectrographic analyses, but reverse-engineering this liquid would be hard. The structure, the way the elements are joined together into molecules, is something we've never seen before. It would help if you could tell us more, but I understand that you don't want to talk about it."

"It's really not our secret to divulge. It's very special and you may have the only example of it on the planet so please be careful."

"Have you heard anything from the FBI? Are they giving you a bad time over this?"

"Not yet, but they're circulating the analysis to the government labs and a picture of the container: I don't think they've found anything. They did ask me to let them know if I lost any liquid or if you reclaimed the container. Eventually I'd like to write a scientific paper about this, with your permission. Although we don't know where this liquid originated or how it was manufactured, just the fact that it exists is very interesting in itself. My grad students are fascinated. They've never been in a situation where something totally new like this has landed in their laps."

"It's like a puzzle where you only have some of the pieces and a few of them fit together but the overall design is unknown, and you're sure that most of the pieces are missing," Jessica mused.

Mike smiled and agreed with Jessica, perhaps realizing for the first time that she didn't know much more than he did about the liquid.

"Well if we're done, Jessica and I are due at a friend's house for a working dinner, so we have to go."

Soon Keith and Jessica, Harry and Angela, David and Spunky were all in Harry's living room waiting for the big show. Keith gave a brief introduction, but first he swore David and Spunky to secrecy. He had suddenly realized that if the FBI saw their footage they might connect it to the fuel container and ask many questions. He would need to pitch his film project to the world as fiction, not fact, at least for the moment. Explaining the footage to outsiders was going to be tricky.

They all loved the film and Keith enjoyed the interplay between the soundtrack and the footage. The marching music, the nervous rattle of telegraph signals and shortwave sounds throughout the track, old speeches, explosions and screams, it all worked well together. He went home exhausted, but Angela was ready to show it to financial people, a discrete showing to a small audience, and the sooner the better.

When Keith had made his first film he had been represented by a sleazy agent who had arranged a dreadful contract for Keith and David, but they were relatively lucky, at least they were able to make their film. Now

Keith was moving in a different orbit because Angela's Agent, a Beverly Hills lawyer who dealt in millions, not thousands, had agreed to promote this project simply because Angela believed in it. Keith and Angela had briefed him on the actual story, and on the connection to the FBI, which in an odd way had vouched for the seriousness of the project. The Agent realized that when it was time to promote the film to the public, having the FBI interested, even if they were mad, would boost the film's ratings and authenticity. People would want to see why the FBI was making a fuss about it. To Keith's surprise, the Agent was more interested in distribution and marketing than in Keith's ability to write the screenplay. The Agent loved the trailer and saw possibilities immediately, suggesting plot twists that Keith had never considered as well as the names of actors for the key parts.

After their meeting, Angela took Keith aside, "How do like working in the major leagues? It's different isn't it?"

"Angela, I'm overwhelmed. Last time money was always on my mind, every penny counted, but now, at least my impression is, that we have a blank check and can do anything we can dream up. This is so different, I can't quite grasp it."

"You're exactly right. The big money is going to buy your film because it looks like it will be easy and profitable to market and distribute. Your responsibility is to write the best possible screenplay you can imagine. Forget about cost and practical details. Dream, live in the inventor's shoes, feel his struggles and emotions, write it down."

"I hardly know where to begin, but first, thank you, thank you for being my friend, for being Jessica's friend, and thank you for all you have done and are doing to help me make my way. I know Kristin is gone, but it is nice in a strange way I can't put into words, to know that I'm working beside parts of her body."

Angela hugged Keith and a tear rolled down her cheek.

A week later they ran the trailer in the Agent's screening room for a small group of friendly men and women, people the Agent had already signed up for the project. Angela and the Agent did most of the talking, stressing the uniqueness of the project and its appeal to a wide audience. Keith talked about the film, about its blend of real and fictional aspects, and how they would base much of the story on the actual diary which was being translated in Germany. Everyone smiled. Money was never mentioned. One of the visitors recognized Keith's connection to David's TV show and laughed, "We heard that you saved TV's first sex show and turned it from a flop into a money spinner. Bet you're having fun with those cute girls!" Everyone laughed, but Keith had a sudden realization: they all knew the truth, that it was hard work and clever ideas rather than sexy bodies that had saved David's show, and that it was Keith who was behind it. They were on his side, counting on him to bring them money too. All he had to do was move forward with the screenplay.

That night Keith and Jessica talked about Keith's project, about Remote Viewing, and about the diary and all that it implied. As they talked a vague idea formed in Keith's mind.

"Why don't you contact Fritz and the inventor in a séance and find out if they're alive and if so, where they are? We could visit them and learn about the fuel and everything else?"

"It's not like that, or I would have contacted the inventor a long time ago. I think about him all the time, but he doesn't come through and I don't know what else I can do."

"Have you tried to contact Fritz? Maybe you could hold Harry's camera or the film cans in your hand: they must have some of Fritz's essence on them?"

"There isn't any essence as you call it, but there is something to what you say. When I hold the diary, I know the inventor wrote it, he left something of himself on the pages, and these feelings are not on the Xerox copy, but I can't get further. Sometimes he sort of sends me a message like that night when I had the bad dream about being trapped in the tunnel and rescuing the diary: I had to escape. It was so real, I had to save the diary with my life if it came to that."

"How about Fritz? Maybe he's alive somewhere in Germany, maybe here in Nevada, he could be anywhere."

"Or he could be dead."

"Hey wait a minute, Fritz rescued the diary, or at least we think he did, so in your dream maybe you were re-living Fritz's struggle and Fritz was sending you an image from his memory, trying to make you understand how important the diary is. Fritz's fingerprints and hands must have been all over the diary, and we think he made the films in Harry's cans, so maybe you have been sensing him as well as the inventor and you have them mixed up."

135

"I never thought of it that way, I mean we know so little about Fritz except what Harry told us. He must be a little older than Ladislas, so he could still be around. And from what Harry said, he was an exceptional person, and so strong; maybe he survived."

Jessica thought over her dream and carefully described what she could remember about escaping from the lab. The memory of the dream was strong, but it was surprising how few details she could relate: she could see the lab, the people, and she knew she was holding the diary, but she couldn't find words to explain most of the visions inside her head. When Keith asked practical questions about the surroundings, the colors, how many people, how much water, could she see the flying machine, she was at a loss.

"In your dream you were climbing upwards to escape, right? So maybe you were escaping through an air shaft as the tunnel flooded and you had to fight with other people to get on a ladder or climb up steps? What I'm thinking is that maybe there's another way into the laboratory, a way from above that we could go down."

"I wish I could have that dream again, and look around more carefully and see if perhaps I was Fritz."

"And what were those abstract drawings I found scattered on the floor around you when you came out of the trance?"

"About the drawings, I haven't a clue, I made a few sketches before I fell asleep, but the others were like a little kid's random drawings: I couldn't understand them, and I don't think I can have the same dream again."

"It is amazing to think that your dream might have represented a traumatic event that happened to another person forty years ago and that you received it and can tell me about it. If this is true, there must be countless dreams and messages flowing around waiting to be received. Then again, you could have imagined everything based on Harry's footage and all our conversations."

"That's logical, but I can tell the difference between normal dreams, visions that relate to recent activities and thoughts, and psychic visits: this was the real thing, though I can't begin to tell you how I can sense the difference. Psychic dreams don't happen often, and usually it's not much fun."

"Fritz must have had other scary adventures, I mean, just think of that day when he and Harry worked for Lenni while people around them were shooting. We know Harry well so let's try to imagine the events of that day and approach Fritz from another angle: maybe you can find a way to contact him though your deeper knowledge of Harry? Think of them shooting plates, then the phone call, the rush to the scene, the work with Lenni. Harry and Fritz must have been so excited; they had no idea what they were getting into."

"I can imagine people fighting and shooting while a small film crew is covering the action, and I've seen pictures of Harry when he was younger, actually of him shooting plates all over the world during the thirties. He has lovely old scrapbooks from his travels, so I know exactly what he looked like then."

"I know what to do Jessica, it just came to me. I'll bet there's something unusual about the Magic Castle, about the room where you did your séance when you met Houdini. If we went back there you could contact Fritz or the Inventor; the environment is special and it would help you reach them."

"Why do you think that?"

"I'm not sure, but I see you in your white dress in that room talking to Fritz and the Inventor. I know I'm not psychic, but I have a strong feeling that you could do it, but only in that room."

"Are you perhaps viewing something in the future, an event that hasn't happened yet?"

"I don't know, but we could try. You have friends at the Castle and you still have the ethereal white dress. We could easily find enough close friends to fill out the table. We could even do it on a Monday night when they're closed. What do you think?"

"It would be fun with our friends and we could invite Max and Francine too. Apart from you and Clifford they are the only ones who were there with Houdini and me."

"We could set the mood by running the inventor's footage, not my trailer, but just the film and the stills from the box, so that everybody started thinking about the man in front of the camera as well as the man behind it."

"If we have everyone helping our message will be strong: it's a great idea. I wonder if your psychic side is developing, if this is perhaps the first time that you are seeing something happening in the future."

"I hope so, I'd like to hear more about Fritz and the Inventor, but I'd also like to bring you a success, a pleasant encounter with the spirits to make up for some of the troubles you've had with the other side."

The Magic Castle is a private club run by professional magicians, located in an old Victorian mansion in Hollywood. The Club contains small stages where the magicians entertain each other and their guests. There are bars, restaurants, lounges, a library, and one special room with a round table which has thirteen seats. Being a house of magic, not a psychic center, this room is equipped for fake séances. A hidden operator can make ghosts fly across the room, tilt the table, generate fog and many other effects. Normally a dozen people have dinner in the room. The dinner is timed so that the guests are having an after dinner drink as the clock strikes midnight. The lights go out, strange noises begin and a magician dressed as a psychic appears in the thirteenth chair and begins a phony séance. However Jessica had done several real séances in this room, to the delight and amazement of the professional magicians. She was the only non-magician allowed to perform there.

The Castle was delighted to hear that Jessica wanted to do another séance. Clifford would operate any needed special effects as before, Max and Francine (the couple who gave Jessica the apartment building) flew in for the event, David, Spunky, Harry, Angela, Sarah, and others filled out the round table of twelve. After dinner, at the stroke of midnight, the lights faded and the room became pitch black. Jessica floated down from the ceiling in a cloud of luminous fog and sat in the thirteenth chair. She wore her sparkling white dress as before, and looked just like an angel coming down from heaven. She explained that they were trying to contact the inventor they had seen in the film Keith had shown, and that they also were trying to contact the man, Fritz, who had operated the camera that had made the film.

All joined hands in a ring of thirteen as darkness enveloped the room. Soft French café music was faintly heard, a singer, an old piano, sad emotions in another language. Up in the control booth Clifford was amazed: he wasn't playing any music and the rest of the Castle was closed tonight. He hit the record button on his tape machine. Jessica talked quietly as though she was dreaming. Francine recognized that she was speaking in French, in the voices of two men, and followed a conversation between a Frenchman and a waiter. They were talking about the music, about another round of Ricard, and old times when they were both much younger. Eventually it all faded away and the lights came slowly back on. An hour had passed.

Everyone started talking, comparing experiences, and asking Clifford what had really happened. Francine described the French conversation and what the men had said. Suddenly Jessica stood up and exclaimed, "Fritz is alive, he's in France, we can track him through the music. We can visit him, we can go there right now, he's waiting for us. He's in Alsace, the German part of France, in a small café, and he's so sad, he's in pain and he's dying. I heard an old Alsatian folk song that only people, and they have to be very old people with long memories, would sing. Almost nobody there today knows the Alsatian language because the French schools force people to learn French and nothing else, and especially not German or German dialects like Alsatian. Let's go!"

After this outburst Jessica collapsed into Keith's arms as she shivered uncontrollably from the emotional strain.

Vergangenheit

CHAPTER 13

FRITZ

The news that Fritz was alive was exciting, but in the morning Keith and Jessica began to face reality. How many people live in Alsace? A million? Two million? And how many cafes have pianos and singers? And what does Fritz look like, how would they recognize him?

"Jessica, the séance was terrific and it's wonderful that Fritz is alive, but how are we actually going to find him?"

"It's obvious, what we must do now is so clear, I am surprised you didn't think of it yourself."

"What Jessica, what do you mean?"

"We'll make a picture of Lenni's camera, then we'll put an ad in the newspapers in Alsace with the picture and offer a reward for anyone who knows exactly what initials are engraved inside the camera and the name of the current owner. We'll write the advertisement in German, not French. I know it's a gamble, but what fun if he answers!"

Keith and Jessica poured over maps of Alsace, called tourist bureaus in little towns and bigger cities, learned how to contact the local newspapers, then wrote versions of the advertisement they hoped to place. Soon they had placed their German ad in their first ten papers and eagerly awaited a call or letter from Fritz.

While they waited Keith went to work on his new film, reading the diary, reading more of Schauberger's books, and kicking ideas around with David. Soon he discovered that his expensive new agent expected weekly updates on progress with the script and occasional meetings to discuss ideas. Keith had a proper writing contract, but he had gained unexpected responsibilities.

Unfortunately after days of anxiously waiting the only replies to the ad had come from people interested in the reward but who had no clue as to the answers to either question. Although Keith read the diary carefully, he began to realize that it was not going to be much help

141

in writing his screenplay. The diary seemed to be almost entirely technical laboratory detail of a most peculiar kind, much like Schauberger's books. If he hadn't seen the machine flying, he would have dismissed the diary as a work of fiction. Everything in his scientific training said that anti-gravity machines were impossible to make, yet here was a research diary describing the process of building one. After many frustrating hours, he had an idea.

"Jessica, this may be crazy, but I just had a strange thought, maybe you'll think it silly, but then I don't know much about the psychic world. My idea is that we should borrow the actual camera from Harry and go to Alsace and sit in different cafes with the camera clearly visible and it will act like a magnet to pull Fritz to us."

"That is weird, but I like old songs and a week or two in French cafes with the old camera would be delightful. Maybe touching the camera will give me some feelings or thoughts, and what's the harm. We can have a bit of a honeymoon together, read a few books, eat bread and cheese, drink coffee and wine, and let our minds wander. Let's call Harry and get the camera."

"I hope it still works so that we can shoot a bunch of grainy black and white film with it. It's just a 35 millimeter Arri, and Harry has lenses and magazines that fit. I'll tell the agent that the trip is part of my research, and send him a bill for the plane tickets!"

"I bet Harry would love it if you bring the old camera back to life. We can wander around and focus on cafes with Alsatian singers: that will limit our search to what, a thousand locations?"

"I can feel it in my bones, we're going to find him and you, you of all people, will be so surprised! It's like that song, '*I have a dream*' where the singer tells how dreams grow cold if you wait, so we'd better get moving: '*cold are our dreams if we wait too long*'."

"That's an old French song, '*Toi Que Moi Ressembles*', but you've got the meaning exactly, and you should hear Nana Mouskouri do it while crying on stage. I cried too. The words are so sad, so visual, I can see her dreams turning cold and fading away as she sings. It's like colors, mists, fogs, but I know they are living dreams that will die if she doesn't reach her lover. She's carrying her dreams, the secrets of her life, petals in her hands, in the golden sun, if only she can find her way to her lover before it all goes cold and fades away."

"Can paint your visions from the song? It would be such a

beautiful picture: I'd love to see it."

"I tried, a long time ago, but what I saw inside didn't reach my hands, and the more I tried, the more I cried with sadness and with frustration. The canvas grew cold."

"Hey, on a completely different subject, I read some place that psychics can dowse the location of things and find people by holding a crystal over a map. We could find Fritz if you can do that."

"Psychic energy is nothing like that, it doesn't relate to maps and compasses and crystals. It's much more serious. It comes from inside, like at the Castle when I could feel that I was inside Fritz and could hear the music in the café where he sat brooding over the past. That's what it's really like, it's hard, and it usually doesn't work, but sometimes it's so wonderful."

"Let's go to the library and find a book that tells which cities have the strongest Alsatian heritage, the places where people would know the old songs. That would be a good start."

"When we get to France, we'll go to Strasbourg first, the old capital of the Alsatian region, and visit the tourist office, then hang out for a while. We'll also go to Saverne and climb all over the ruins for exercise. And by the way, we already advertised in Strasbourg, but we can do it again if you like."

"Would a German guy like Fritz fit in with the Alsatians. I mean, would it have been a logical place for a German to go after the war?"

"Maybe his family came from Alsace. Lots of Germans still live there and it was part of Germany not so long ago. Bet he could blend right in, especially if he knew a bit of French. Could have been a good escape from the Nazis if he left before the war was over."

A week later found them in a Strasbourg café listening to music and wondering if anyone had noticed the ancient movie camera sitting on their table along with wine glasses and old books. Keith spent most of the time writing notes about his new movie, which featured romanticized versions of Fritz and Harry and their adventures with a professor and his flying machine. He had just mailed a treatment, a prose outline, of his film to David and began to look forward to the reply. Jessica sketched as she studied the darkening café, then on impulse hugged Keith and gave him a big kiss as the chanteuse, an emotional young woman, started singing *'Plaisir d'amour'*.

143

"Keith, do you know this song?   I wonder if it is our life, if the words are true for us. If our pains, our troubles, our disappointments will outlive the pleasures we sometimes enjoy?"

"I don't follow you, I've heard the song but I really don't know what it means in detail. Would you translate it for me? What's the connection with us?"

"The gist is that much of what people call love is pain that can last for a lifetime, while the pleasures are few and fleeting. There are dozens of verses in old books, but most people only sing a few of them. Love can be so sad and the French words are beautiful. After we're through here, let's go to Paris for a while and start your French lessons."

"French, I thought we were dealing with Polish and German?"

"Our need for those will fade, but we will be together and in love for a long time. I'd like to share my favorite French songs and love stories with you, to let you feel the pleasure that they bring to me. You need to understand the language, the emotions, the poetry, and not in translation!"

"Hey, speaking of emotions, I read recently that heartache is a real phenomenon. The example given was that when a husband or wife dies, the spouse often dies shortly thereafter from a broken heart. The doctors don't know why, but insurance companies change the rates for surviving spouses based on actuarial statistics."

"So let's not have any heartaches, OK?"

Later she wrote out the French and English words of the most popular verses for Keith:

> *Plaisir d'amour ne dure qu'un moment*
> *Chagrin d'amour dure toute la vie*
> *J'ai tout quittee pour l'ingrate Silvie*
> *Elle me quitte et prend un autre amans*
> *Plaisir d'amour dure qu un moment*
> *Chagrin d amour dure toute la vie*
> *"Tant que cette eau coulera doucement*
> *Vers ce ruisseau qui borde la prairie*
> *Je t'aimerai", me repetait Silvie*
> *L'eau coule encor, elle a change pourtant*
> *Plaisir d'amour ne dure qu un moment*
> *Chagrin d'amour dure toute la vie*

The pleasure of love lasts only a moment,
The pain of love lasts a lifetime.
I gave up everything for ungrateful Silvie,
She is leaving me for another lover.
The pleasure of love lasts only a moment,
The pain of love lasts a lifetime.
"As long as this water will run gently
Towards this brook which borders the meadow,
I will love you", Silvie told me repeatedly.
The water still runs, but she has changed.
The pleasure of love lasts only a moment,
The pain of love lasts a lifetime.

The next day was bright and clear as Keith loaded his backpack with ten pounds of camera and lens, a six pound battery, eight pounds of sensitive black and white film, one 200' magazine, a black changing bag, a Spectra light meter and a few odds and ends. A heavy load, but nothing compared to other 35mm motion picture camera outfits popular in 1938. Keith didn't have a tripod or a pan head, so he would operate the camera hand-held, just like Lenni on those streets long ago. As they set off Jessica commented, "Let me pick some interesting shots for you, places where we can capture the essence of old Alsace."

"Let's find a place without many people so that I can become familiar with the camera and the controls without anyone asking questions: this thing weighs a ton, but when it feels heavy I think of newsreel cameramen who carried Arris all over the world."

"Imagine doing this with people shooting at you: Lenni must have had nerves of steel."

They found an almost deserted park with ancient trees, a few benches with people reading newspapers, a peaceful area to start their film project. They began by shooting fixed angles rather than pans and movements. Jessica explained that these shots could be slowly dissolved in a sequence to elucidate the old way of life. There were no automobiles or things that could date the footage in their compositions. Jessica's artistic goal was to obtain scenes which could have been shot just before the war in 1938. She wanted the end result to be a dreamy sequence about the past. Finding appropriate settings, then figuring out the right lens and camera position, then actually making the shot when the background was clear kept them busy for days. Every time they had a chance they took the old camera into a different cafe for coffee or a snack.

After a few days of filming they spent an afternoon in the Strasberg Art Museum looking at an exhibit of old photographs and paintings. "Jessica, to me the best parts of this exhibit are the shots of Paris as it changed from a mess to a modern city as Housman's plans were implemented. You can almost smell the sewage in some of these old street photos."

"We're lucky that photography was invented in time to capture the old way of life before the city was rebuilt or these old scenes would be gone forever. No one bothered to paint things like this, the slums, the filthy street scenes, the buildings almost falling into the mud beside the Seine."

"But they did paint the Commune and all the killing that went on when Paris revolted against the government. I liked the side-by-side comparisons of the photos and the paintings: it really put me in the mood. Did anyone paint scenes like that in the thirties, as the war was approaching?"

"People painted, but I don't recall anything anticipating the coming devastation. The photos of Lartigue we saw are just domestic scenes, but when I look at them I feel sad because I know what happened after the photos were made. Think of the shots we're making now and your script about the inventor describing that era: we know what happened to these streets, to these old buildings, to these people, but they didn't foresee it at the time. The emotional impact of pictures, paintings and even music depends so much of what the viewer already knows."

"Maybe someday people will look back at our contemporary paintings and photos and feel the same way. I wonder sometimes if a big disaster is ahead and that we will wish we had seen it coming and had run for the exit, like your grandfather."

The days passed quickly as they moved from town to town visiting cafes and shooting footage which might have been made fifty years earlier. In spite of a variety of advertisements in a wide range of small and large papers Fritz did not contact them. Secretly Keith began to doubt the whole process: he worried that perhaps Jessica's vision of Fritz had been an aberration or a hypnotic trance and that he was nowhere near and that perhaps he was dead or far away if alive. As if to compound his negative mood, the weather turned foul with wind, rain, and unseasonable cold. Maybe it was time to quit and go home.

"Jessica, this weather, these cold gray scenes with the wind and rain, remind me of Winston Churchill's book **THE GATHERING STORM**, about the nineteen thirties when Europe was preparing for war but when most people didn't realize it."

"Just before the rain blew-in this afternoon did you have the feeling that the weather was about to change? Animals can sense slight changes in barometric pressure so they look for hiding places as a storm approaches, long before people notice. I felt it too, like something was coming our way."

"It's only wind and rain but it looks sad and foreboding. We can shoot in this weather and maybe capture the mood, especially at night with the puddles and light reflections. It's good practice for my film: these old buildings, people rushing to get inside and away from the weather, it's like the people feel apprehensive and are running to hide."

"It will be tricky to actually put that mood onto film, but we can try. They're lots of old buildings, dark streets with isolated street lamps, solitary people hurrying along. You should shoot some stills too, then I'll make sketches from them when I'm in a nice warm cafe."

"I wonder if psychics, people like you who can sense a bit of the future, saw the whole mess coming in the thirties and left the area, if they moved to safety while they could?"

"Like my grandfather: I don't think he was sensitive, but he was lucky, and maybe he had an intuition or presentiment about the future so he left. But Virginie's grandmother was sensitive and she stayed in her home through the war and the aftermath."

Keith shot reflections of lights in puddles, wind-driven rain, scenes with umbrellas and raincoats, night exteriors with an emphasis on bad weather rather than happy thoughts. They stood on street corners waiting for silhouetted subjects to walk past brightly-lit storefronts with Jessica holding an umbrella over Keith as he shot the scenes she selected. The old equipment was much more rugged than they were: it never complained about the weather.

Late one night they sat in a small cheap café, soaked from the rain, drinking coffee laced with cognac both for warmth and for the alcohol, as a sad chanteuse worked through an old Alsatian song. Jessica's upbeat mood had faded and they were both ready to call off the adventure and go home. From far across the room, an ugly bald old man, face and scalp disfigured by large cancerous reddish purple blotches, limped toward their table. During their visits to the cheap cafes of Alsace the couple had had many encounters with beggars and curious derelicts. Jessica felt something unusual deep inside as she watched the man, but she couldn't put her feeling into words. When the man reached their table, instead of asking for money, he pointed to the camera, "Mind if I take a look at your camera: I just want to touch it and remember the past. It reminds me of something from a long time ago. I saw you shooting in the rain and thought of the old days when I worked in bad weather too."

A violent shiver surged through Jessica's body as tears came to her eyes: she was unable to say anything but just pointed at the man. Keith realized what had happened and asked the stranger, "Did you help a cameraman named Harry shoot background plates in 1938 when this camera was new?"

As Jessica cried, overwhelmed with emotion, the man stared at her in shock: all three were unable to speak for what seemed like an eternity.

"Mine Gott, is this that camera, the one with Lenni's initials inside?"

"You're Fritz, the wonderful man who saved Harry's life while he shot street scenes for Lenni a long time ago," Jessica cried.

"Fritz, Fritz, that's not my name, but this is the camera she gave Harry isn't it?"

"Harry knows that isn't your real name, but he doesn't know any other."

"My name is Friedrich Hoffmier, but yes, I was there with Harry and you two must be his friends since you have the camera. Let me stop for a minute and catch my breath. This is so exciting, so unreal."

"Here, take my chair" Keith said as he quickly rose. A waiter appeared with a double shot of Ricard for Fritz and another chair. By the way the waiter treated Fritz, Keith could tell that they were old friends and suspected that this waiter was the one whose voice they had heard during the séance.

"Did you see the ad we put in the paper along with pictures of this camera?"

"No, I don't read the papers any more, the doctors say I'll be dead soon. I saw you shooting in the rain near the street lamps, like a blurry vision from the past and knew I had to see your camera. You must tell me about Harry and all that's happened. Mein Gott, what a shock."

"Fritz, or Friedrich, how can we help you? What's wrong? You're in so much pain, can we take you to a doctor or a hospital," Jessica asked.

"Too late. I'm dying from radiation poisoning, but the doctors don't understand it so they give me pain killers instead of a cure. I worked in a lab during the war with a wonderful old professor, a genius, but we were working with dangerous things and one of them has finally gotten me."

"We've been to the tunnel, at least we think it's the right tunnel, over in Poland, the one that leads to the lab where the inventor built the flying machine in the old movies. I took photos and can show them to you, and we've got copies of the pictures that maybe you made and the diary." Keith blurted out as fast as he could talk.

"What! Then Harry must have shown you the box and the professor's diary, and now you've actually been to the tunnel? Oh I wish the professor were here to talk with you. He became sick early on; he must have died soon after he flew away on the first machine. Many of the workers died before we knew how to handle the fuel and protect ourselves. I thought that I was immune, I was strong and young; nothing stopped me in those days, but look at me now."

"What do you mean when you said he flew away, did it really fly?"

"Oh yes, it was a big success but we had to be careful to make it look like it wasn't finished. The pressure to finish, to build hundreds of machines loaded with weapons, was intense. Human lives meant nothing. Making enough fuel would have killed thousands if it had gone that far." Fritz started coughing and bent over the table and whispered. "Sorry, let me rest for a minute, I cannot believe this is happening."

Fritz waved to the waiter and motioned for a round of drinks for all of them, then finished his glass. "I'm better now, just seeing this camera and the thoughts it brings back is the best tonic: I feel like I'm a young man again, marching along, filled with pride and excitement, and working with Lenni around the clock."

"How did you meet her? Did you use this camera too?"

Fritz picked up the camera carefully. The camera's weight didn't bother him as he easily lifted it to his eye and slowly panned around the room. "This is so wonderful, my mind is flooded with memories and feelings. I can almost see the old scenes as I look through the viewfinder. First let's have a toast, then I'll tell you about this camera and the old days."

The waiter left a fresh bottle of Pernod's Ricard Pastis, a strong anise flavored liqueur, on the table with extra glasses and a small pitcher of water then they toasted their new friendship. Keith was startled both at how strong the liqueur tasted and at how easily Fritz and Jessica consumed it straight. Fritz laughed and smiled for the first time, "Young man, you should mix it half and half with water, then you will like it better, but I can see that the beautiful creature here with you knows how to drink it properly." Then he refilled Jessica's and his glasses as Keith poured water from a carafe into his.

Jessica had stopped crying and now that she looked carefully at Fritz she realized that his eyes were strong, they radiated power in a strange way, just as Harry had described in his encounter with Fritz long ago. Even though the rest of his body was weak, the strength of his eyes was undiminished. When Fritz looked at Jessica she could feel his eyes surveying her body like a warm glow flowing over her skin, and her inner sensitivity recognized a kindred spirit, perhaps someone with sensitivity similar to her own.

Keith asked, "The box with the film and the diary, did you send it to Harry and what happened in Nevada, those guys shot at us when we tried to find them?"

"Shot at you? I don't understand. For many years I have waited for a chance to go back to the lab and bring out the other machine and all my films and drawings and material. But this year my illness became worse and I began to realize that I will never see the lab again and that all our work will have been in vain if I don't share my knowledge with someone. Harry is the only person I know in America, and I felt that America would be the best place to bring my secrets out into the open. Last month an old friend, a pilot, said he was going to visit friends in Arkansas, so I asked him to take the box discretely in his plane, then send it to Harry once he was inside your country. I plan to call Harry soon, but I have been waiting for my friend to return before calling."

"Was your friend going to Warm Springs, Arkansas?"

"Yes, I think that's the name of the town. There're a bunch of Germans from the war around there, at a rocket base in Alabama. Tell me

150

about the shooting and Nevada."

"We made a stupid mistake, or rather several mistakes. We went to an abandoned town in the desert, in Nevada, a town also called Warm Springs, and some people shot at us when we trespassed on their land."

"Lots of people have shot at me over the years, but I'm glad that we have all survived. Holding this camera brings it all back to me. In 1934 I was an apprentice cameraman, working hard to advance in the world. People in my position were slaves, but we loved the work and would do anything to learn more about cameras, film, light, composition and the thousands of things a professional cameraman knows by instinct. By a stroke of luck I was assigned to a team making a documentary film about the giant Nazi Nuremberg rally in September of that year. Lenni was in charge, but there were more than a dozen separate camera teams shooting aspects of the event. We even had a remotely controlled camera moving up and down on one of the poles supporting the huge banners behind Hitler. This gave us high-angle shots of the people marching toward the platform. Then afterwards she shot scenes from an airplane, the famous opening sequence where clouds drift by as the audience hears marching music in the distance. Near the end of the day I found myself working near Lenni as she directed one of the teams. I saw that she was very tired but still working full speed. I knew we had some beer hidden in a magazine case, so I opened the case and offered her a bottle. That moment was my first real break in the business, a simple act of kindness on my part. She smiled then said she hadn't had anything to eat all day and asked my name."

"We've both seen that movie, it was so effectively written, shot and edited: people still study it in film schools."

"Making that film was a first in many ways as women didn't get big assignments in those days. The story I heard was that Hitler personally selected her for the job because she was beautiful, so all the other Directors and cinematographers were furious. As a result her crew was short-handed so I moved up to Second Assistant cameraman, loading magazines and caring for the exposed film, and never looked back. I worked with Lenni on other projects and was on one of her teams filming the Olympics in the summer of 1936. Often I worked as her First Assistant when she was doing her own camera work. I was also influenced by Dr Paul Wolff and worked with him and his team shooting everywhere with Leicas. You may have seen his famous Leica photo of Lenni and a cameraman high on a platform shooting the Olympics with a long lens. Dr Wolff was everywhere in the twenties and thirties making wonderful photos from small negatives: he was one of the first great street photographers."

"It's no wonder that Lenni called you and Harry when she needed help on that day in 1938."

"We were friends, very competent co-workers in the thirties when everyone was excited. Our country was on the way up; the future was bright indeed for us before the war began."

"We have a car. Please let us take you to Paderborn, to my aunt's house. She's a doctor and has copies of our photographs. Aunt Gerta and her hospital can help you. Please come with us. I feel so close to you, I don't want you to die."

Jessica hugged Fritz, silently conveying her belief that she had recognized a kindred spirit. Keith was stunned and so excited both for the meeting with Fritz and for what it meant for his nascent screenplay; there was so much to learn now. "The car's a block away, at our hotel. I'll bring it over. We can be in Paderborn in five or six hours, and I'll call Gerta from the hotel to tell her we're coming."

CHAPTER 14
SÉANCE WITH GERTA

They arrived in Paderborn and went straight to Gerta's home, dead tired from the long all-night drive in their small car and five hours of continuous conversation and revelations. Gerta wasted no time on small talk. Hardly a word passed her serious tense lips. Her determination to help Fritz overruled any attempt at politeness. She didn't ask Fritz if he wanted to come with her, she just loaded him into her car and headed for the hospital. Maybe the French doctors couldn't help him, but Gerta believed in herself and somehow knew that she could not only halt his deterioration, but also bring him back to a semblance of a normal life. While she drove carefully but fast, she asked Fritz for details about his radiation exposure forty years before and any specifics that he could remember. How could he have been well and strong for years, then begun to collapse: it didn't make sense medically. As far as she knew, the symptoms of radiation poisoning appeared quickly once a person was sufficiently exposed: there was no delay, especially not a delay of forty years. Gerta frowned as she realized that he didn't know precise details. She had already guessed that the French doctors who had attempted treatment did not know about the flying machine and the unusual fuel that it burned. Tonight she would study the diary in Polish, especially the descriptions of the fuel and its formulation, but for now practical medicine and a thorough examination of his body filled her mind. Then it struck her: maybe he didn't have radiation poisoning, but only said that he did because the French doctors had misdiagnosed his condition. Gerta pressed the accelerator down; this was the diagnostic line that she would pursue.

Keith and Jessica wanted to ask Fritz many more questions, but Gerta emphatically told them to stay away, to go to bed and rest while she and her staff analyzed his condition. Resigned to their situation, they peeled off their tired clothes, climbed under the soft white eiderdown on one of the guest beds, and tried to sleep. But after so much excitement neither Keith nor Jessica could rest easily. Both minds raced ahead, speculating on questions and answers, trying to piece together Friedrich's story and to imagine the events of his life. Slowly the featherweight eiderdown worked its magic as their bodies began to warm. Hugging, then kissing, and finally a long slow sexual release enveloped their bodies and sent them into a deep peaceful sleep wrapped in each other's arms.

That night Gerta returned with Friedrich. He walked with

153

difficulty, but without pain as he breathed oxygen through a tube from a green tank. Gerta hovered over him like a mother hen watching a newborn chick, carefully easing him into the most comfortable chair so that he could examine Keith's photographs which were spread on a low coffee table. Friedrich recognized everything and involuntarily shivered when he saw the tunnel interior that Keith had photographed with his large flash bulbs. The pictures brought back memories of things, both good and bad, that he hadn't thought of in years. Keith and Jessica quietly explained the shots as they waited patiently for him to finish looking through the prints. Although both, especially Keith, wanted to ask questions, it was obvious that Friedrich was in a fragile condition, a condition that would not withstand extensive questioning or excitement. Gerta hadn't said a word about his medical situation or what she had done to treat it, but deep concern showed in every movement she made.

When he had finished looking through the photos, Gerta sat down beside him and took one of his hands in both of hers. "Friedrich, why don't you close your eyes and tell us a story about what happened. Tell us about the old lab and the professor and your adventures. Just talk slowly and you'll be alright. I'll give you more medicine if the pain returns or if you feel faint," Gerta said as she comforted Fritz.

"There is so much to tell, so much pain, so many mistakes, but what a fantastic invention. I don't know words that explain how excited we were, how we kept going no matter what the consequences. Your pictures, the things that happened there, the misery, the deaths, the thrills when we made discoveries, the elation and then the disasters, it's all coming back. When I start to remember, when I try to tell you about it, images and emotions and so many ideas come into my head that I can't put into words, it's so jumbled together. It's like a film montage, with the scenes blurred together, one after another, all going by too quickly."

Friedrich stopped and breathed heavily as Gerta watched carefully. Keith released that she was holding Friedrich's hand so that she could discretely monitor his pulse. "After Harry and I helped Lenni, she returned the favor a few weeks later by putting me in touch with a special military film unit, an incredible assignment. I hardly knew what was happening. One day I was an assistant cameraman, and the next I was given a powerful uniform and took the oath of allegiance to become an officer in the Waffen-SS. Skilled and politically reliable cinematographers were in short supply. Our unit's task was to make documentary films of secret operations, things the public never saw. Events were occurring that would never happen again and we were making a photographic record of these events for the Reich archives, for scholars to study in the future. In those days we were certain

154

of victory, of really making '**_Deutchland Uber Alles_**' come true and I was committed one hundred percent. I was strong and brave and worked day and night to make it happen."

"I was assigned to a unit that focused on industrial activities, especially the development of super weapons which would lead to victory. As the war dragged on the scope of our work expanded, but our numbers shrank. Some of us were killed in attacks, some were re-assigned, and I often found myself as the lone photographer and/or cinematographer as unforgettable events unfolded. I focused on doing the best work possible, treating the job as art rather than as straight documentary. Lenni's skill and her films had made a deep impression on me and I wanted to emulate her to the limits of my ability and subject matter."

"My superiors liked the results and I often found bits of my footage in popular propaganda films. I was promoted often and sent to ever more difficult places: by the end I held the rank of SS-Oberführer, a rank just below the generals, though I didn't command any troops. With such an exceptionally high rank I could go anywhere and film anything of interest without waiting for paperwork. When one assignment ended I was immediately sent on to another: no written orders, just a command to go at once. Headquarters wanted to be sure that I saw it all and sent back accurate pictures. I commanded a lot of respect wherever I went, a high-ranking SS officer with a bunch of cameras: nobody dared to ask questions and I could order almost anybody to do what I needed. When people saw me they were frightened, so I used their fear to advantage in my work. But in return, I led a very lonely life with few friends. Much of what I saw I couldn't discuss with anyone and most of the time I was on the move. My feelings, my emotions, those weren't supposed to exist for officers of my rank. I became an unfeeling machine, an extension of my camera. Although I was privileged in many ways, in return I had to witness horrible scenes and get them on film. People around me were starving and dying and my task was to remain cool, compose the shots, make useable exposures under impossible conditions, and send the footage back to Berlin with no excuses. My field-gray uniform and deaths-head insignia opened all doors. I hope you realize that I am skipping over a lot of awful things, things that I still cannot bring myself to describe. Not all the experiments I witnessed involved machines."

Keith almost stopped breathing: he never would have guessed that the weak, sick person in front of them, an old acquaintance of Harry's, was once such a powerful, and at least by reputation, horrible person. In all the old war movies the SS was portrayed as the vilest of Hitler's creations: cruel men who killed innocent people by the millions. Gerta hid her shock at this revelation: Friedrich didn't strike her as a cruel person. Once again she wondered how ordinary people could become so mean in wartime.

"One reason I survived was mechanical ability. My father had been a clock maker so from an early age I had taken things apart and put them back together. Tools and mechanical things came naturally to hand, so I was able to keep my cameras running no matter what happened. Near the end I was assigned to a top secret project, a project which hardly had a name, just a location. A brilliant professor was in a lab deep underground working on an anti-gravity machine, something that western science said was impossible, it could never exist. You've been to the tunnel, through the three rings of barbed wire, the mine fields and machine gun nests. Total security, there were no unexpected visitors, just carloads of fresh workers coming in from the camps: they never left. The professor was already weak when I arrived. I wish I had been able to escape with more footage of him and his work, especially the aerial shots as we flew around just before the end."

"Skilled and strong workers were rare in the tunnels so I applied my mechanical ability to the project and quickly became the professor's chief assistant. I could make things happen and we moved ahead fast. By this time neither of us believed in a military victory, but we were determined to bring this invention to fruition. What a discovery! We knew we could change the world if we succeeded. Every night bombs rained down, supplies went missing, but we improvised, we kept going: we knew we were close to the final breakthrough. Our superiors knew it too and pushed relentlessly. We hoped the war would end before our work was turned into weapons, but that almost didn't happen."

"The bombings had become more intense, so we decided to take advantage of the next big raid and escape in the confusion. The professor was probably dying from radiation poisoning and I didn't know if it would get me too. We decided to go separate ways in hopes that at least one of us would survive with enough information to bring his invention to the outside world. In the midst of a big night raid he flew machine number one straight up an airshaft and disappeared. What a sight, it's hard to describe the thrill I felt as I watched him escape with our invention into the night. Then I grabbed his lab notebook, where he kept all the formulas and details of our work, and ran down into the latrines, which were flooding from bomb damage. People running and screaming everywhere, with the guards shouting and trying to restore order: a horrible sight. I climbed up a small vent shaft into the midst of the bombing and started my motorcycle as explosions blasted the ground around me. Earlier I had loaded as much film as I could carry onto the motorcycle and filled it with fuel. I counted on my uniform and rank to get me through sentry posts, and headed for home in Alsace, my long black leather coat flying in the wind and rain. As I cleared the last sentry the general alarm sounded: someone had seen the professor fly away, so I had just made it out. Our plan was to meet in a small café after the war, the café where you found me. The professor never arrived."

Keith, Jessica, and Gerta were stunned into silence by the story. Finally Keith ventured, "You made it across Germany with the Allies advancing and the country in ruins: what an amazing escape."

"I changed into an American uniform after I crossed the front and spoke French or English when anyone addressed me. It wasn't that hard in all the confusion. One advantage of my career in the SS was that I had become an expert at clandestine activity: lying and deceit ensured my survival. I was immune to feelings about death and cruelty."

Jessica caught her breath at the coldness in Friedrich's simple statement: he could as easily have killed someone as not, and where did he obtain an American uniform? From a recently killed soldier? Better not to ask.

Keith continued, "I don't know where to begin, what to ask, but first, you mentioned the professor leaving on machine number one. How many did you build?"

"There were two identical units so we could test the effects of changes and improvements. One day we took both of them out together for a trial run which turned out to be a big mistake. The military was furious because they were afraid we would crash both and set the project back months. And when they saw us flying around they figured it was time to build hundreds of copies which would carry bombs and guns. Draftsmen were immediately set to making drawings of everything."

"Do you think the other machine is still in the lab?"

"Probably, unless they carried it away. It weighed tons, the structure was a special compound, mostly lead and steel, and I doubt that anyone else knew how to get it started or how to fly it. The war in Poland ended a few weeks after we left, so maybe they didn't have time to do anything except seal the lab and run from the advancing Russian army. I wouldn't be surprised to learn that they dynamited the entrance while the workers and anyone who knew about the project were locked inside."

"Could we get into the lab now? The landslide at the entrance is huge. Is there another entrance, like the one you used to escape?"

"You were in the railroad tunnel. There's a small parallel tunnel, a passageway a meter wide, part of the old coal mine. It runs behind the dormitory rooms and the labs. It may still be passable. There are small steel blast doors from the passageway into the various rooms. The workers used the passage to move from the dorms to the labs, the latrines, and the pit. The pit was a deep shaft in the coal mine: dead and useless workers were dumped there. I don't know how many. You don't want to go near."

Keith saw Jessica give an involuntary shiver as the blood drained from her face. She swayed and began to faint as thoughts of the pain and suffering around the old lab flooded her imagination. Although her face twisted in fear, she made a big effort and slowly regained her composure. "Maybe it would be better if you didn't talk about the dead people, the human misery. Jessica's very sensitive; she can feel their pain from far away. She fainted just inside the tunnel entrance when we were nowhere near the lab."

"I'm sorry. Jessica, this sensitivity, is it how you knew who I was when I approached your table in the café? I felt that you knew who I was even before we started talking."

"I had never seen a picture of you, but yes, I knew immediately who you were. I don't know how, but I could feel you approaching our table. We were in that cafe because during a séance I felt that I was inside you, in a small café, and I could hear an old Alsatian song in the background. We went to as many Alsatian cafes as possible to see if my visions might be true."

"Jessica can feel amazing things. One night she even conjured up Houdini: he was right in the room beside us. It was magical."

"I'd give anything to see the Professor again before I die, to talk with him even for a minute, to tell him that I escaped. I miss him. I yearn to know what happened after we parted. Sometimes I feel he's watching over me, apologizing for the radiation and my condition, but I know it's just my imagination."

"No Friedrich, it's more than imagination, he could be in the room with us right now although we can't see him. You just have to believe, really believe, and then anything's possible. He's close to you, I can feel it. If we work together, we can make contact. I've tried many times by myself but I've never met his spirit: we can try, he's here; I can feel it."

158

"Do you need a special room or a round table or anything to hold a séance to contact the spirits?"

"No, nothing except luck and a quiet place to sit and concentrate on what I seek. Positive thoughts from nearby people help while skeptics ruin my concentration: I just can't focus when people are negative. The night I contacted Houdini we were in a phony séance setting designed for entertaining tourists and having fun. Everyone was positive: no one in the room was more excited than I when it actually worked."

"Can I get you anything? Do you need darkness and a candle?"

"Keith I'm sorry, but what I'd really like is a glass of scotch, I need to relax and calm down. So much has happened today, so many thoughts are racing though my brain. And yes, turn the lights down. Let's sit quietly by the fire close together and see what happens in the twinkling firelight. Make yourselves comfortable, this can take a long time. Breathe peacefully and let your minds wander over thoughts of the professor and what he would be thinking if he were here with us. What would he be trying to tell us? That's all I need. Friedrich, sit beside me and hold my hand in yours, let me join our spirits into one."

Jessica had only finished half of her drink when her eyes closed and she fell into a quiet trance, resting against Friedrich. The others sat comfortably on soft pillows and blankets beside her, each with his or her own thoughts. Keith had been through this before and relaxed, letting his mind wander over what he knew of the Professor. He knew this would take hours, not minutes. Fritz had no idea as to what would happen, but he relaxed and sat peacefully, painkillers and oxygen flowing through his body. He might fall asleep at any moment. Only Gerta remained alert, extremely curious about the experience and what might happen.

Eventually Jessica appeared to awaken. Her eyes fluttered, then opened, but she wasn't conscious. She stared into space and started speaking in a language like Polish but with a strange and difficult, troubled, male accent. The words seemed to be directed toward Gerta, telling her how sorry he was about something but it was impossible to understand most of what he said. She recognized the word "Gerta", and sometimes the word "Friedrich" and once something that could have been the name of Jessica's father "Ladislas". The contact didn't last long. Just at the end the voice switched with much difficulty into simple French and implored Jessica to go to the lab and bring the other machine into the light. Then Jessica slumped over, closed her eyes and went back to sleep. Although the others were excited, they remained quiet, waiting to see if anything else developed.

After an hour Jessica slowly awoke. "I just had the strangest dream. Did anything else happen?"

Gerta couldn't wait to speak and replied quickly, "You spoke in a man's voice, in an old form of Polish, with much difficulty. I couldn't really understand it, but the voice was very sad about something and he knew my name, Friedrich's name, and once he mentioned Ladislas. It was so amazing. What does it mean: how could a spirit have known our names? Of course as a doctor, I have to point out that it is likely that you imagined the whole thing, drawing on your memories and fears, though how you spoke old Polish is beyond me."

"Perhaps you are right, but first let me tell you about my dream before it fades away. I was in the lab, the one in the old films, talking to a very kind old man, the professor, and he was giving me detailed instructions about the machine and how to start it and operate it. He was warm and friendly, like he was someone I already knew, but he was very insistent that I pay attention, as though I wouldn't have another chance to learn about the machine. It was as though he was passing the baton, his secrets, to me and I was to use them for the good of mankind."

"Friedrich, what was the professor's name, surely you must have known his name?"

"It was Polish, Gregorz, and he had fun making me pronounce it and spell it the way that he liked, without the extra 'z'. Why do you ask, doctor?"

Gerta's face lit up with surprise and shock, "Gregorz is the name of my uncle, my mother's brother, the one who left to study physics in Germany in the twenties. He is Jessica's great uncle. Even as a child he was brilliant, so he didn't want to stay on a rural farm with us. How can this have happened, it's impossible."

Keith exclaimed, "It all fits together and explains why he contacted you Jessica. At the end, just before he faded out, he spoke directly to you, and implored you to bring his machine out into the light. He said it over and over as his voice slowly faded away. We could go back and see if the machine's still there and take pictures and maybe get it running. What an adventure! Jessica, I know you don't want to go, but I could go with a few friends and check it out."

"No Keith, if you go, I'm going too. I owe it to Gregorz in a way I can't explain. Something about the way he talked to me, the way he implored me to pay attention. Maybe his spirit's fading and this was his last chance to meet us, I just don't know, I can't find words to describe what I feel, but I know I must go. It's tearing my heart out."

Things were happening too fast for Gerta. "Wait a minute you two. Just stop and consider what happened to uncle Gregorz and to Friedrich, and they knew what they were doing. You could both get radiation poisoning, and even if you didn't, your sperm and eggs could be damaged by the radiation. Are you willing to risk that, to risk maiming your children before they are even born?"

"And don't forget the soldiers over there, the ones you told me about who fire their guns into the woods for fun. You were lucky last time, but maybe this time you'll be caught or shot. Then what? Give the machine to the Russians and get yourselves carted off to Siberia? This is a job for professionals, not a couple of kids," Friedrich exclaimed.

"We're not kids, we're much smarter than that, and besides we've already been there twice, or at least I have."

Jessica grew impatient with practical objections. "If we just published the diary and all our photos now, nobody would take us or the invention seriously. Most people would say it was another example of secret wartime stuff that never worked; a bunch of old Nazi propaganda like those silly flying saucer books. And even worse they would say that Uncle Gregorz was a horrible Nazi scientist whose work killed thousands of people. Our family name would be ruined: no one would understand how wonderful he was. We need to have more information, pictures and details of the real machine, before we go public."

"Friedrich, are more of your films in the laboratory? Is there footage of the machine actually flying? What else might be there?"

"I was just thinking about that. If they sealed the lab just as it was, my film cabinet would still be there, and with it my archive of movies and stills. Also, it just occurred to me that you would be especially interested in Gregorz's personal diaries, the non-technical things that he wrote and kept locked up. He was a wonderful man, warm and compassionate, not at all like me. We disagreed all the time but we were a good team, compensating for each other's strengths and weaknesses. But if someone goes back to the lab, the most important thing would be to find samples of the fuel, if it hasn't eaten through the bottles or evaporated. The fuel was the key to the

161

whole thing. The guts of the flying machine are similar to a modern ramjet engine, but built in a spiral instead of a straight pipe. A machine shop could make one from the drawings in the lab, but without the fuel the machine would be just a curiosity."

"So much has happened that we forgot to tell you about our adventure with the fuel can that you sent in the box."

"What happened? I thought that it would all have evaporated by now, leaving just an empty fuel cylinder."

"There was some fuel left; a strange lavender liquid that's radioactive. We asked a chemist to analyze it and the radiation attracted the FBI so we're in a bit of trouble, but we haven't told them anything."

They were interrupted by a phone call from America. Gerta handed the phone to Keith. "David! We've just had a huge breakthrough." The call didn't last long and ended with Keith promising to call back within twenty-four hours. He turned to the others. "I've got a problem, or rather a great opportunity. I need to go home and meet with a bunch of people to work on my screenplay: things are moving quicker than I thought. They want to start production and I haven't even finished writing a decent first draft. Jessica, this could change everything. After production we'll have enough money to mount a real expedition into the lab and bring the machine out."

Friedrich's voice reflected his doubts, "You don't need money or lots of people, not at this stage. You just need a few skilled operatives who can slip into the lab and report on the situation, and with great luck, bring out my film, the diaries and drawings, and perhaps fuel. Anything more complex is crazy."

Gerta added a practical note, concern wrinkling her face, "Keith, you can put anything you want into your film, you don't need to go into the tunnel, you can do much better on a movie set by using your imagination instead of whatever is actually in the tunnel. Perhaps someday we'll find a few people who want to risk their lives to go into the tunnel and see if they can open the door to the lab. Think of Jessica and your future; don't risk your lives on a foolish adventure."

"It's not foolish. He's my uncle and yours Gerta, and we owe it to him to at least try to go back to the lab ourselves. Maybe the passageway is blocked, maybe the lab is empty, maybe everything is flooded, but we won't know unless we try. We can't ask someone else to do this, it's too risky."

There was silence as everyone thought over their predicament. Finally Keith perked up and asked, "Friedrich, how would you mount a small photographic expedition to the lab? You're an expert at secret activity and you know the area well. I'll bet not much has changed since you left."

"I could go to the lab myself; I'm feeling much better and hearing Gregorz's voice has given me new strength. Perhaps it's time for me to do something good for the world, to do a bit more to bring our invention into the light. The guards will be amateurs, peace-time recruits who have never killed with their bare hands, simple for us to outsmart."

"But you're too weak, you couldn't walk that far," Gerta exclaimed.

"When Keith showed us his short film and I heard the old marching songs, something inside me awakened; I'm feeling emotions that have been dormant for decades. Did you notice that all those old Nazi songs are fast, that you have to march quickly to keep up with the drumbeat? That was on purpose; we were young and strong. We could march all day and night at those fast tempos, unlike our soft flabby enemies. When I heard '*Die Fahne Hoch*' coming from Keith's film, I became young again. Doctor, you're about to witness a miraculous recovery. The best thing that I remember about the old days was the feeling of strength and invincibility that my comrades and I felt. We could do anything!"

"I could bring a cassette player loaded with the old songs and play them while we went to the tunnel if it would help you."

"The guards would run for the hills if they heard that music coming from the tunnel, but we won't do that, when we get there we'll be as silent and as deadly as cats on the prowl."

Jessica ignored their conversation and paced around the room, as conflicting ideas fought inside her head. Gerta's warning about radiation danger and deformed children growing in her womb had hit her much harder than she had realized. She had been sick that morning and had a strong suspicion that she was pregnant, but didn't dare discuss her symptoms with Gerta. She was afraid to tell Keith as he would immediately block any idea of a dangerous tunnel visit if he knew. Against this fear the spirit of Uncle Gregorz had gained irrational control of her mind. Its pressure was so strong that she toyed with going to the tunnel alone, driven by her mission instead of by practicality. And what of the spirits of thousands of murdered workers in the tunnel? Would she faint before she even reached the lab, would she become a limp body lying on the tracks in a deserted old railroad tunnel, rotting away before anyone found her?

Keith brought her back to reality. "Gerta, couldn't we take a Geiger-counter and use it to warn us about radiation. If the radiation were bad, we could leave. And we could wear lead clothes, like those lead sheets that people are covered with when they have a dental x-ray, to protect our reproductive areas? We could wear lead-lined hiking shorts."

Keith and Fritz started to focus on planning a quick and safe reconnaissance trip to see if they could find the passageway, get into it, enter the laboratory, then go home. They would carry minimal equipment, just enough to get there and take pictures. If they found anything interesting, they would bring out as much as they could carry. Keith knew he must return home soon to work on his film project before interest in it waned. Jessica knew that they were planning to do exactly what Gerta said they shouldn't do, and arguments continued unabated inside her head.

Late that night Keith and Jessica walked the dark tree-lined streets of Gerta's neighborhood, worrying over their hopes, dreams, and plans. They stopped in front of a peaceful house where dim candle-light came from one small window.

"Jessica, what's the song coming from this house, I can just hear it but can't make out the words?"

"The music's French, the song "*J'Attendrai*". It's so sad, the title means "I will wait" and the lyrics are about the seasons passing while I wait forever for my love to return. It was popular at the start of the war, especially among women who watched their men march away to death: it's so foreboding." The music resonated and amplified her inner worries and fears. As a trance began she reached for Keith and fainted to the ground, whispering "Keith, help me."

Keith dropped to his knees and lifted Jessica's head: her breathing was quick, coming in shallow bursts: her face tense with pain. Jessica's unconscious body lay on the damp grass beside the sidewalk as his strong arms lifted her to a sitting position. He hugged her, giving his warmth, trying to help the only way he knew, while his emotions tore through scenarios: would she recover, why had she fainted, was she sick or in pain, maybe they should go home right now? Then, when her eyes opened, she smiled and kissed him.

"I'm OK Keith, the song, it did something to me. I felt the same after I took the knife away from you; I fainted to the kitchen floor, crying as I saw a montage of sad old French scenes while *J'Attendrai* played in my head."

"I never realized that had happened to you while I moped around the house."

"I often see sequences of pictures and strange visions when I hear certain music, it just happens. Music can be so emotional."

"I feel it too, some songs make me cry a little, but I don't faint."

"The sad music, maybe that's why I just had a scary vision about the tunnel, but I know it's not true, we're not going to die down there."

"What, us, die in the tunnel? Wait do you mean? How can you be sure we'll survive if we go there?"

"Remember when we first met and I saw our whole lives flash by in an instant. We'll get through this."

"As I recall, you said that in that vision we died in each other's arms: maybe we die together in the tunnel?"

"But in that vision we died when we were old with six grown children, so there's lots of time left. We can do the tunnel, so don't worry about it."

Keith knew better than to argue such points: logic didn't apply. How could she take a chance like this, relying on one particular vision to be true and ignoring another which seemed much more realistic? He looked at the person in front of him sitting on the grass. She had just fainted after hearing an old song. The tunnel, especially the part they hoped to visit, would be far scarier than a bit of old music. Worried, he helped Jessica to her feet and held her tightly as they walked back to Gerta's.

The fainting spell troubled Jessica but she didn't want to voice her fears. She knew that they were in more danger than she had realized but her desire to vindicate Gregorz was if anything stronger now: she smiled with new-found determination.

Just in front of Gerta's house Keith stopped and wrapped his arms around Jessica. "When this is over, we'll go to Paris for a long romantic holiday: let's start thinking about the first of those six children." He had no idea that one was already on the way. Jessica smiled but said nothing.

Vergangenheit

CHAPTER 15

DEEP TROUBLE

The wheezing old steam-powered Polish train screeched to a stop at the Warsaw train station in a cloud of noise and coal smoke. Keith, Fritz and Jessica collected their backpacks and a suitcase containing cameras, a Geiger-counter, lead shorts, and a few clothes as well as empty bags to bring home any valuables they found in the tunnel. Instead of heading to a car rental agency, Fritz loaded them into a taxi and headed for a poor part of town. He had already acquired a large wad of Polish Zlotys and was determined to purchase a very cheap old Trabant, the least conspicuous car possible. There would be no paperwork connecting them to this car. Soon they were on the road headed slowly and inconspicuously out of town, just another dirty gray car smoking in the gathering dusk.

Fritz explained, "Warsaw is nowhere near the tunnel, and half the cars in the countryside have Warsaw license plates, so we blend in perfectly. We'll stay at an old hotel I know in Swidnica. The town's big enough to have a bunch of hotels, but small enough that there should be little military or police activity in the neighborhood."

In spite of Friedrich's confidence, training, and encouragement, both Keith and Jessica were worried as they discussed their plans during the drive toward the hotel. "I just realized why I'm more apprehensive than the last time I went into the tunnel," Keith commented.

"Why is that?"

"Last time I was filled with curiosity and I had no idea of what was there. I was focused on photography, giant flash bulbs, flares, movie cameras, and making pictures of an old tunnel. I didn't expect to actually find anything."

"So what's different? By the way, I bet I'm more afraid than you are," Jessica answered.

"I hope not. This time I know what's ahead even if we succeed. Friedrich, your descriptions and memories, I don't know, but they're so grim, I just can't put my feelings into words."

"Keith, we all just need to be very careful. You two must follow my instructions to the letter, and exit quickly if anything doesn't seem right. Remember rule number one: when in doubt, leave immediately, don't even stop to think about it. It saved my life more than once."

"And you didn't have Jessica's sensitivity. Her senses are turned up all the way so we'll know about problems long before we get into trouble."

"I hope you're right. I feel like Gregorz is with us, dragging us toward him and his machine, a relentless steady pull that flows like tango music in the song '*Si Tu Reviens*' (*'If You Return'*). The music moves strongly without end like a river, and his pull is like a tango, long slow purposeful steps. I hope this isn't a one way trip," Jessica replied.

"Don't talk like that. I'm counting on you to save us or I never would have agreed to this crazy idea. We could be sitting in the Hollywood Brown Derby eating Cobb Salad, drinking cold white wine, and talking up my next picture instead of travelling in this heap toward an old Polish coal mining town."

Jessica smiled, "And don't forget the thin pumpernickel toasts covered with melted Parmesan cheese that come with that salad. Now relax and enjoy the ride. I love you."

They checked into a modest hotel and paid cash in advance for two nights, the fewer records the better Friedrich pointed out. The next morning they drove over to the area near the tunnel and cruised slowly looking at the roads where they might park the car while they hiked into the tunnel at night. They looked first for the road they had used on their initial visit, the visit when they had both gone to the tunnel with the teens.

"Do you remember if we turned at this corner or kept going," Keith asked.

"I think it's up ahead a bit further. Remember the map, the road we want runs in a little overgrown valley," Jessica said.

"I really didn't pay attention to the roads last time because the kids told us where to turn and where to go, and it was late at night."

"But this time we have Friedrich's map, even if it is based on memories from forty years ago, the hills and valleys can't have changed all that much."

"We've been driving for over an hour since we left town and that time we were in the woods and parked in under an hour. Let's turn back and look for a turn that's closer to town."

"Do you think someone could have closed off the turn, maybe bulldozed some rocks across it or something to hide it?"

"Look over there. Please turn around Friedrich, I think we just passed the turn, look at that dirt path between those trees."

Soon they were on a narrow overgrown dirt road slowly going through the woods.

"I'm glad there were no other cars on the road when we turned; it must have looked like we just left the road and drove straight into the trees," Friedrich said.

"Drive slowly; we'll know it's the right road when we come to the barbed wire."

"It's so dark in here even in daylight."

"Relax, everything's going to work out, we'll be home in a few days looking at the great photos we're going to shoot tonight."

Ten minutes later they had the car turned around and parked near the barbed wire that blocked the road.

Friedrich climbed out and looked at the barbed wire, then climbed back into the car and started it quickly. "Let's go, quick, now."

"What did you see, what happened."

"When you were here before, you met a Russian who claimed to be a hiker, then you and the teens drove away. That fence has been redone very recently, but made to look like it's old. It now has a vibration monitor to alert the guards when someone climbs over it."

"Wow, I wonder what it's like at the second place we parked, the place where Jessica dropped us off but never returned."

"Keith and Jessica, we are not going to that place. If anything it will be more closely watched, but I would like to drive past it to be sure where it is if we can find it."

"It was easier to find that road, but a longer hike once we reached the wire."

"It's up ahead on the right, just go slowly and I'll tell you when we're near," Jessica answered.

"There it is, but look, there's a barricade across the road now, we can't even go down to the parking place."

"Your abrupt departure from the hotel in the middle of the night must have greatly annoyed the local police: I loved hearing about it, but now we need to be more careful. I doubt that they expect you to return, but they want to prevent others from following in your footsteps, so we will go a very different way, assuming that it is still open."

"Can we still get to the tunnel tonight?"

"Yes, let's do a little reconnaissance and see if we can find the old road on the other side of the valley, that's the road I escaped on with my motorcycle years ago. It leads to the mountain above the tunnel. From there we can walk down a path to the tunnel entrance."

"If it's on the other side of the valley perhaps the locals don't know about it, so it will be less visited and perhaps less well protected?"

"We can hope so."

"Friedrich, why do you think the police bother to guard this old tunnel? Anything valuable that could be moved was taken to Russia decades ago."

"I really don't know, and perhaps the soldiers don't know either. Maybe they are just following orders, orders that haven't changed in forty years. Often logic doesn't apply, and guarding this place gives them an excuse to hire more police, shoot their guns, repair fences, and practice for more serious duties."

"Maybe it's a training ground for new recruits?"

They found the old road a few hours later and it appeared that nobody had driven on it in many years. Weeds and young trees obscured it, but Friedrich was cautious. "If we drive down this road, our progress will be obvious; we will knock over trees and brush. Even a simple cop would be able to see that someone had entered recently. In many ways this road is worse than the others for that reason. We will park some distance away then carefully walk down this road leaving no trace of our activity."

"Where can we park, I mean, we can't walk all night, and on the return trip in the morning we hope to be carrying a pile of film and heavy stuff?"

"We will simulate a breakdown and leave the car, with no contents or identifying papers, at the side of the road. It will only be there four to six hours in the dead of night, so with any luck thieves will not bother it while we are away."

"Friedrich, do you think we have time to go back to Ludwigsdorf and look for the teens who helped us last time and see if they are alright," Jessica asked.

"That's a bad idea, please forget it right now. We are trying to be invisible, to leave no trace. Don't forget that if we are successful, we will want to come back and collect more material, so we don't want to run extra risks. Your friends may be in jail, or in Siberia if they haven't been careful, and if they are still here, they are certainly being watched."

That night they loaded only essentials into their backpacks: a little food and water, cameras and film, Geiger counter and lead shorts, flashlights and headlamps. Hopefully they would leave much of this behind and come out with their packs full of treasure. The goal was a fast efficient trip with no danger and no mistakes. After dark they left the car at the side of the road, inoperable, empty of identification, and innocuous, just an old car that had broken down on a lonely road through the woods.

The walk down the overgrown road was straightforward once they had left the area near the highway. They had been careful to walk so that they trampled no brush and left no footprints. It would be difficult to see, from the highway, that anyone had walked along the old road. Soon they were at an old sentry post.

"This hasn't changed since I drove through here forty years ago. Look at the rust on the gate's hinges and at the trees growing through the wire: nobody has been here in a long time. Be careful to stay near the center of the road from now on. The sides of the road were mined in some places, just to catch people who didn't know and shouldn't be here."

"What happened if soldiers or people walked here in the dark and happened to step off the road?"

"They died. Remember this was an extremely secret operation and the stakes were high."

"I wonder if we have similar sites in America, maybe out in the desert near Groom Air Force Base, where the government is supposed to be storing alien spacecraft?"

"I hope we never find out. Now be careful. After we cross the third ring of wire, we turn sharply down to the right and follow just inside the fence. It's an access path for maintaining the wire, and it leads down to the tunnel entrance. Stick close to the wire, don't stray from the path."

"When we crossed the last barbed wire, I thought of that old saying, the one that goes 'a little knowledge is a dangerous thing.' Last time it was just rusty old barbed wire, but after you explained things, the machine guns, the traps, the sentries, it all seems a lot scarier now," Keith commented.

"Think positive, stop worrying about what I said. You've walked around here before and we'll be in the tunnel in ten minutes."

"Can you feel Gregorz guiding you along the path Jessica? Is he with us now?"

"Hard to tell. We're all too tense to think straight, and you're right about all the stuff we've heard about the past. It does make a difference knowing about what it was like here in war-time, when visitors like us were shot on sight."

They walked quickly in silence with only one flashlight pointed at the trail, and Friedrich's hand blocked most of its light. After crossing the third barbed wire and walking down the path they came into the main valley.

"Look, there's the old dynamite factory, we're almost there."

"This backpack weighs a ton. I can't wait to leave the lead shorts behind," Keith whispered.

In little over an hour after leaving the car they were at the tunnel entrance. They hadn't heard a sound and Jessica hadn't detected anything unusual, but she could begin to feel the spirits of the people who had died building and operating this complex. As a cloud obscured the starlight, they crossed the open area by the tunnel entrance and slipped behind the edge of the warped railroad door. Silence and total darkness surrounded them until they switched on their lights.

"Are you O.K. Jessica? I was thinking of the last time you were here. We can turn around if you don't feel up to it," Keith whispered.

"This time is different. Gregorz is with me, leading me on, protecting me from the spirits: I'll be alright."

"I hope so."

As they started walking, Keith looked at the ruined railcars he had filmed with the flare. "Hey, someone's been here since I filmed this scene. Look at the beer cans and food wrappers. What a mess."

"Soldiers. You can tell by the kind of junk they left after eating. Your flare must have given them a surprise. I wonder what they thought of it. Let's get this over. We'll go down to the lab entrance then work backwards from there."

"Good, I need to keep moving, if we stop the spirits will dig into my mind, I've got to stay active and focus on the lab," Jessica said.

After an hour of fast walking they were in the middle of the tunnel looking at the pile of rock that blocked the entrance to the lab. Friedrich shook his head at the mess then turned and headed back the way they had come.

"The Russians didn't do this. You were right, this blockage was done to hide the lab as the Germans left," Friedrich said.

"Why are we going back instead of the other way," Jessica asked.

"Because there are no rooms and workshops further on, the tunnel just becomes an old railroad tunnel. We'll try the room next to the lab," Friedrich replied.

They entered an old workshop littered with bits of broken and rusty machinery and started looking for a door on the far wall.

"Why did they pile all the crap against the back wall just where the door should be?"

"Either the Russians didn't know about the door, or the Germans piled up the stuff on purpose to prevent the Russians from finding the door. Could be the same story in every room," Friedrich said.

"Hey Friedrich, over here, look, there's an indentation in the wall."

"And a pile of old junk in front of it. Let's shove it out of the way," Jessica said.

"Quiet, let's be very quiet, no reason to attract attention by making noise."

"Who would hear us," Jessica asked.

"Maybe I forgot to tell you, but the railroad further along is still active: a train might drive into the tunnel. Someone on it could hear us if we make too much noise. You never know."

"Damn this is so frustrating. This door is rusted in place, and there's no way to grab it. Funny that there's no handle or anything, at least on this side: must open from the other side," Keith said as he examined the door.

"I forgot about that feature. All the doors into the walkway are like this so that the guards could control access," Friedrich said.

"We just need to keep trying in each room, we'll find a way, I just know it," Jessica said with more hope than logic.

In the fourth room that they explored, a dorm room with old wooden 4-decker beds scattered at odd angles, their luck turned; the blast door was slightly ajar.

"Can you imagine sleeping in one of these beds: there's barely enough room to squeeze in," Keith said.

"They were thin and tired, there were no mattresses or blankets, they just collapsed until they were shaken awake to start work again," Friedrich replied.

"Check-out the back side of this door. It does lock from the passageway side, so the guards could control who had access to the passage.

Let's go. Ready Jessica?"

"Push me forward, don't stop whatever you do. As soon as we start to look around, to think about what happened here, about what it was like to live here, I lose my focus and the spirits start creeping into my head."

"What a stink, I could puke, the ventilation down here must be terrible, and it feels cold, much colder than the tunnel," Keith said as they entered the parallel shaft, a pitch-black man-sized tunnel with coal seams running through the walls and floor.

Friedrich pulled the door shut behind them and locked it. "Remember to always take precautions, even though we know nobody is in the tunnel, it never hurts to block access to pursuers."

Keith felt a tingle of fear run down his spine, "We're really in here now, locked in the secret old part of the tunnel, a place that's been sealed for decades."

"It's just a tunnel, stop worrying and get moving," Friedrich ordered.

As they started to walk they heard a distant rumbling and a few lumps of coal fell from the ceiling.

"Sounds like a train backing into the tunnel, just like I heard last time I was here," Keith whispered.

"I don't like that, there's no reason to park a train inside a tunnel in peacetime," Friedrich said quietly.

"Should we leave and come back another time, I mean you said to run at the first sign of danger," Keith asked quietly.

"No, we should be completely safe while we're in this passageway," Friedrich replied.

"Maybe I should get the Geiger Counter running and start taking flash pictures as we walk?"

"There's no radiation here and the pictures are a waste: save your film and bulbs for the lab," Friedrich commanded.

"Hey my feet are wet, what's happening, where did the water come from," Jessica said with surprise.

"This tunnel goes up and down, it's not even, and the water level's probably near the floor, you won't drown, your feet will be dry tomorrow. Don't stop," Friedrich directed.

They came around a narrow corner and froze, staring at a shoulder-high pile of large chunks of coal and rock that had fallen from the ceiling, blocking the passageway. Keith noticed that the water was almost up to his knees.

"Wow, I wonder when that fell down?"

"And if more will fall down while we climb over it," Jessica added.

"Move, crawl over it carefully, we don't have to come back this way, we can open one of the doors close to the lab on the way out," Friedrich commanded.

"Supposing we slide off and sail down into the pit?"

"We haven't come to that part of the tunnel yet, this is just a normal rock fall in a mining tunnel."

They climbed over, and only a few small rocks fell from above as they scampered down the far side of the pile.

"Hey look, here's the backside of another door. What a clever lock, just a heavy steel bar on a pivot: crude but effective. How much farther do we have to go," Jessica asked nervously.

"Three more doors, according to the map."

"Here's the airshaft that I escaped through, I wonder if it's still open at the other end."

"Too bad it's dark outside so we can't tell, but I feel a little breeze coming down it."

"Shhhhh, be still, turn out your lights," Friedrich commanded.

"I feel something, but it's not the spirits, it's different," whispered Jessica.

"Listen, do you hear that, it sounds like people talking," Friedrich asked quietly.

They stood silently in the coal black tunnel, their feet soaking in the icy cold water, nervously breathing the old smells from the latrines, the coal, and the long dead bodies. They could hear faint voices in the distance.

"The train probably brought a routine patrol into the tunnel. They walk to the far end, toss their empty cans, then walk back and take the train to their barracks. We'll hear the train depart in a few hours," Friedrich whispered.

"Can we wait somewhere dry, like near the door we used to get in here," Keith asked.

"No, you two go on to the lab, just be quiet, and unlock the door to the machinery room next to the lab, the door we first tried to open. Just leave it ajar an inch so that I can open it if I have to from the other side. I'm going back to make sure all the doors behind us are closed. Don't shine your lights at the backside of the doors in case the light leaks around the edges. You never know who might be looking and see it," Friedrich whispered.

As they turned their headlamps back on Keith noticed that Friedrich had produced a compact 9mm automatic pistol from his pocket. Without a word he silently headed back up the tunnel and over the pile of coal. Keith gently pushed Jessica forward, "Let's get to the lab, grab the stuff and wait for the train to leave. I'm ready to go home," he added.

"Me too, I don't feel good about this whole thing, and about being in here without him."

They walked slowly and carefully, feeling ahead as the floor went up and down, sometimes dry, and sometimes the water covering their knees. After ten minutes, they stopped in surprise, "Oh shit, I mean look, those boards with rough holes; that must be the latrine."

"Then the pit's just up ahead. The spirits, they're strong, run quickly, run, they're after us!"

"Stop Jessica; take your time, the floor's rough, focus, think of Cobb Salad, don't let the spirits grab your mind."

The beam from Jessica's flashlight bounced off the black walls as she ran in a crazy pattern, crying softly in pain. She grabbed her head then tripped and fell to the floor as her flashlight sailed down into the pit with a splash, lighting its gruesome black walls from under the water as it fell into the abyss. Keith rushed to her side and held her fast. They were inches from the edge of a midnight black vertical shaft that went straight down, with no guard rail or fence to prevent people from accidently falling in. Jessica was soaked from head to foot, trembling and shaking uncontrollably. Keith dragged her toward the far wall.

"Get up slowly, don't quit now, there's no way I could carry you out of here. Just look straight ahead, only two more doors and we're at the lab. Breathe slowly, stay calm. The spirits had fun scaring you, now they'll be quiet."

"You're crazy, it's not like that at all," she said though her mouth trembled with every word.

"Keep talking and start moving, tell me why I'm crazy"

"Spirits don't have fun, they don't tease people, that's not what it's like, and Keith, lots of these spirits were kids, little children, it's awful."

"I believe you, look, there's the next door. We're getting close. Keep going, you're doing great."

"One more door to go. Hey look at this sign, it's like the one in the tunnel near the lab, saying that unauthorized people will be shot."

"Not a very friendly greeting to our nice old lab. Get a good picture."

"The Geiger counter is showing a little activity, but we're still safe."

"This must be the door we tried to enter from the other side, can you unlock it?"

Keith turned a rusted steel bar and gradually opened the door a fraction so that Friedrich could enter from the other side. Then he removed the bar and placed it beside the door in case they needed to close it when they left. They walked a hundred yards further and came to another door.

"Look at this door, it's a lot more solid than the others, and what a sign, just a gun pointed at a guy's head, and the locking bar's a lot different from the others too."

178

"We're here, let's go, open it."

Keith fumbled with the heavy rust-covered steel bar that locked the door. The door was hinged so that it opened into the room, but the steel bar held it shut. After lifting the bar, Keith and Jessica both pushed but nothing happened. The door didn't budge.

"Damn, it's blocked from the other side. We're so close."

"Let's use our leg muscles with our backs against the door. Maybe we have enough strength to move it that way."

"I felt it budge a little, let's rock it back and forth and get it moving."

The door moved a few inches, then with a big shove from their legs it flew open and they fell backwards into the room, tumbling on the floor in the darkness. Keith turned on his flashlight, "Are you all right, holy shit, don't look over here."

"Why, what do you see?"

"The door was blocked by a bunch of corpses leaning against it."

"Look up there, toward the middle, there's the air shaft Gregorz flew up on his machine. My head's going crazy, there're so many spirits and he's so excited that we're in his lab at last. The film cabinet's over there, to your right, and the key to its door is on top of the cabinet on the left side, way at the back. He says you can reach it. This is fantastic, but I'm so scarred Keith, hurry up, we must get out of here."

"Easy Jessica, breathe deeply, calm down. Let's load the diaries first then all the film we can carry into both backpacks. No more spirit problems or outbursts, OK?"

"Easy for you to say. Look at all these diaries, put half in each backpack in case we lose one of them. There's so much stuff in this cabinet, we can't even begin to take it all with us."

"Someone will be back for the rest as long as we're very careful."

As Jessica loaded the backpacks, Keith walked around the room, stepping over desiccated and rotting bodies on the floor. The ceiling was twenty feet above with a large open shaft, perhaps ten feet in diameter rising up to the sky. Keith walked to the shaft, "Look, there must be forty years of leaves and dirt that have fallen down this shaft. I can see a few stars, so it's still open at the top."

"Over in the corner, there's the other machine, just like Friedrich said. Bonanza!"

"Let me take some pictures, while you grab the stuff, then we can get out of here fast."

Jessica explored the film cabinet while Keith took dozens of flash pictures of everything, especially the machine which had been under a large cloth. "It's in perfect shape, what a beauty. Have you found any drawings we can fit into the backpacks?"

Both were busily exploring as fast as possible, anxious to escape. Neither had given any thought to the ventilation aspects of the huge air shaft rising above. Suddenly they felt a gently breeze blow down the shaft, and since the room was sealed except for the door into the passageway, the breeze blew the blast door shut with a loud crash, followed by an eerie silence.

Keith ran to the door, but like the other blast doors, there were no handles or locks on the inside of the door. "Damn, it's stuck, look for some tools or something to pry it open."

"Stop for a minute and think carefully. The locking bar, how did it work, can it have dropped back into place when the door closed?"

"No, it was too rusty to move that easily, the door's just stuck."

"This is a workshop, there must be tools all over the place, we just need a big screwdriver or crowbar."

"Can you get in touch with Gregorz and ask him what to do?"

Panic set in as Keith and Jessica scurried around but tools were not to be found. Keith realized he was trembling with fear. His breathing was shallow and fast. He knew he needed to calm down and assess the situation carefully with a clear head, but fear had gripped him.

"It's as though the tools were removed on purpose, there're no screwdrivers or wrenches or anything that we could use to pry at the door.

In Friedrich's movies tools were everywhere and people were always furiously working in the background."

"Now we know why they were removed, don't we? What cruel bastards."

"Let's eat something and think this through. Hey wait a minute, what are we worrying about, Friedrich will be along soon, open the door and let us out. We need to finish packing, exploring and taking pictures so that we'll be ready to go when he arrives."

"Keith, I have a bad feeling about that, a strong feeling, but I wish it weren't true."

"What do you mean Jessica?"

Jessica started to cry as she sat down and held her face in her hands, "Friedrich isn't coming back. He's OK, but he's moving further and further away from us. We're on our own."

"How can you be sure about that. He's really clever, he knows we're in here and he'll come rescue us."

"No Keith, think about it. He would assume that we'll grab the stuff, wait for the train to go home, then walk out to the car just like we planned. How could he know we locked ourselves in?"

"Oh no Jessica, how could this have happened? Maybe we can find the fuel and it's so powerful that we could use it to burn a hole in the door. We can use the Geiger counter to search for the fuel. I'll do that while you contact Gregorz."

"Keith, it's not that easy, I'm trying, he's here, but he's silent."

Keith slowly walked around the room with the Geiger counter, it's clicking sound at first rapid, then slow. "Hey, there's another room over here, a little one with lots of warning signs, and the counter is going nuts. Time for the lead shorts."

With some difficulty they put the clumsy lead shorts over their hiking clothes. "I hope these work, the Geiger counter was going crazy over there."

"We don't have a choice, so let's open the door and take a quick look, then decide what to do."

Keith put the Geiger counter on the ground and used both hands to cautiously open the door. As his flashlight scanned the room he discovered rows of brass bottles, each perhaps one liter in size and sealed with a screw top, just like the one they had examined at home. He placed one bottle near the Geiger counter and its meter pinned, indicating super strong radiation. Keith quickly looked around the fuel room for anything useful. He saw several strange machines but had no idea what they were or how they worked.

"Well, we have the fuel, we could wrap a bottle inside a pair of lead shorts and carry it home, if we could get the door open."

He turned and saw that Jessica was sitting on Gregorz's machine crying softly to herself. "Keith, I never should have brought you here. Gerta and Friedrich were right, this was a task for professionals. We should be home. It's all my fault."

He put his arms around her hugging her sobbing body tightly. "It's as much my fault as yours: we're just two over-confident kids who screwed up. Hey, what do you remember of Gregorz's instructions for getting this thing running? From what you said he was explaining it in great detail, how to start it and how to fly it. He thought it would work. We could fly out of here. What can you recall?"

Inside, Keith didn't think that they could actually start the machine, let alone fly it, but he sensed that he needed to give Jessica something to do, something positive that she could work on while he opened the door. The longer she sat crying by herself, the more likely it was that she would go into a trance, lost among the spirits of all the people who had died and those of the corpses in this very room.

"It was so complex and I didn't pay attention. I'll try hard."

"Let me know when I can help. Meanwhile I'm going to pour some fuel on the door and see if it eats into the steel or the rock around the door. Maybe it's like acid."

"Be careful, if it's that strong it will burn your hands."

"Hey there're two dead guards over here with guns. Maybe I can shoot a hole in the wall next to the door to get a grip on it. I'll be careful, but it will make a hell of a loud noise."

"One thing I do remember about starting the machine is that we need electricity to get it going and there's some kind of electric generator that runs on the same fuel."

"Look in the fuel room and see if the weird machines in there remind you of the generator he showed you."

Keith didn't want to touch the forty year old corpses of the guards but his panic overcame all other emotions. He removed the pistols from both guards as well as the ammunition from their belts. Then he had a stroke of luck, one guard had a large strong knife strapped to the remains of his leg. "I found a big knife; I'll try it on the door."

He ran across the room with his flashlight and the knife and worked to open the door. As he frantically wiggled the knife in the crack around the door-jamb, the door started to move slightly. He pushed harder, afraid of breaking the knife, the door started to open, then he heard an ominous sound as the locking bar fell into place on the other side with a loud thunk.

"Oh shit Jessica, I almost had it open, I wiggled the door, then the bar fell into place. I'm so sorry. We're really locked in now."

"Maybe not, come help me with this thing, be careful, the insulation on the electric wires is fragile. We're got to move it over next to the flying machine and plug it in. It weighs a ton."

"I've never seen a generator like this, but look underneath, the electric part looks normal, it's just this spiral thing on top that's weird."

They moved the odd generator over to the larger machine and maneuvered it so that the electrical wire from the generator could be plugged into the machine.

"This runs on the same principal as the big machine: it's just a smaller version. I remember he showed me how they are similar. Get some fuel and pour it in here, this is the tank."

"I wonder if it's very noisy when it's running? Maybe the reason for the big air shaft is that these gizmos make a lot of smoke when they're running."

"I don't think so. When he showed me how to run it, I think

the generator was on, but I don't remember smoke. Of course I could be wrong."

"And this stuff's been sitting for forty years. Wonder if we need to oil it before starting? Did he mention that or any sort of prep we should be doing first? Let's think it through before we try to fire it up. See what you can remember and I'll bring a bunch of fuel bottles over here to get ready."

"Give the door another go while I try to contact him. I have a feeling we'll get just one chance with this thing: he was so serious when he explained it to me, like it was life or death, not a game or a joy-ride on a clever machine."

"Listen, do you hear that, it's the train moving again."

"Great the patrol is gone so if we can open the door we can leave the way we came."

I'll pour some fuel under the door and try to light it by shooting a few bullets into the fuel. Maybe it's like dynamite and it needs a shock to set it off."

"Let me get far away first, you too."

Opening a bottle proved more difficult than Keith had expected, but leverage with the knife helped. As he poured the fuel under the door he saw it's unusual purplish lavender color. It didn't eat into the stone or the steel, but smoked and vaporized slightly as it spread across the ground. Keith moved as far away as he dared, hoping that the old nine millimeter bullets would still fire after all these years. "Ready, I'll try a few shots."

The sound of the gun was deafening in the large rock-walled room. The first bullets missed the fuel, but eventually Keith calmed down and managed to hit the fuel with two shots. It ignited and burned the door furiously as they watched from the other side of the lab.

"Wow, that fuel's powerful, look the steel in the door is glowing red hot. We could bend it if we had a big lever. Somehow we've got to get the burning fuel to melt the locking bar on the other side."

"Try your knife on the door while it's hot, maybe it will give a little and we can burn it again."

Keith pried with the knife and the door did move a little, but not enough to be useful. "Good idea but it doesn't budge very much."

"Hey, the hinges are on this side, let's melt them with the fuel, maybe one at a time, then we can peel the door away from the hinge side and walk out."

"Great idea."

Keith wrapped rags and old clothes from the corpses against the hinges while Jessica focused all her psychic energies on contacting Gregorz and re-learning how to start the machine. Keith placed clothing against the hinges, then soaked it with fuel. A slim chance, but perhaps the only realistic escape. The air shaft was a concrete and rock cylinder, a tantalizing path to the outdoors, but smooth with no ladder or way to climb it to escape.

When he had the clothes soaked in fuel he yelled to Jessica, "Stand clear, we're going to melt the hinges off and walk out of here."

Jessica's muscles tensed, she could not remember ever feeling this excited, and this scared before. Her psychic senses were fluctuating wildly in the midst of her fear, of the dead bodies lying around her, and of the nearness of Gregorz. "Get your knife ready to pry it open while it's hot. Let's go for it."

Jessica covered her ears and crouched behind the flying machine in the far corner of the room. Keith fired at the fuel and finally it started to burn after five shots. Before it stopped burning he started to pry at the door, but it moved only slightly. Suddenly a voice yelled down the air shaft in Polish. Neither Jessica nor Keith understood Polish but the meaning was clear. Someone had heard the shots.

Jessica started pouring fuel into the generator. "Keith, I've made contact with Gregorz, fill this thing up, then start filling the machine through the cap over here. Hurry up, the generator won't run long, it has to be done just right. Use all the bottles, he says we've barely got enough fuel to escape. And grab your camera, Gregorz says we're in for a wild ride."

"Holy shit."

Keith worked fast, prying open the bottles and pouring them into the flying machine's tank. As the last bottle emptied into the smoking fuel tank, Jessica reached for a handle on the generator. She was in a trance, deep in communion with Gregorz. She started turning the handle, a crank on the side of the old repulsine generator, but she wasn't strong enough. Keith grabbed the handle and cranked and cranked as slowly the generator's speed increased, until suddenly it caught fire and started spinning by itself, emitting a strange warbling high pitched sound as it accelerated and rattled on its stand. Lights illuminated on the flying machine, it was coming to life. While Keith had been cranking, Jessica started turning around slowly and staring into space, then she ran to the door and started pounding on it as tears flowed down her face.

"Jessica what are you doing, get back here, it's time to go."

"No, I can't leave them here, they need me, I have to go back and get them and take them with us."

"Stop it, think, don't let them into your head."

"Help me open the door, where's the handle, hurry, they need us."

Keith looked at the air shaft. A light shown down as voices yelled. The noise from the generator was deafening. He had never heard anything like it. He slapped Jessica hard, and before she could react he dragged her to the machine and dumped her limp body into the passenger seat beside their backpacks and his camera while he climbed into the pilot's seat. Keith had no idea of what to do next but yelled out loud, "Gregorz, help me, help us get out of here before it's too late."

Keith moved control levers and knobs randomly, furiously trying anything. He didn't have time to consider the situation at the top of the shaft or the Polish guards who were yelling at them. Then underneath his seat he felt a vibration, something he had done was starting to have an effect, the flying machine was coming to life. It too had a strange warbling sound, not a pure whine like a jet, but a loud pulsating sound as the pitch increased, far louder than the generator. He had never heard anything like it, and for a moment wondered what the guards would think of this noise, and when they would start shooting down the shaft. Maybe they'd panic and run away! He put one of the Luger's in his lap and manipulated the controls and valves. Suddenly there was a jolt and a loud noise. They were almost thrown off the machine, but held on tight.

Keith exclaimed with joy as he felt hands on top of his, guiding his movements, showing him what to do. He checked Jessica's position; she was immobile, deep in her seat, slumped over the backpacks. Then a warm feeling washed over his body as a large smile came across his face. He moved the controls, left, right, front, back, up, down, then turned to

Jessica. "We're out of here."

He fired a few rounds up the air shaft to scare the guards away. The machine gained speed as he flew it around the room then started straight up the shaft, missing the sides by inches. As he gained confidence he accelerated and shot up at full speed.

Two guards stood in amazement at the edge of the shaft and Keith sorely wished that he was holding his camera instead of a gun as he sailed by their astonished faces, gaining altitude and heading toward freedom.

He turned to Jessica's inert body, "There's the big dipper and the north star. We'll go south to Vienna, following the road we drove last time. No one will see us if we stay low and avoid city lights."

Minutes later they were across the frontier and flying over Czechoslovakia, headed south over rural farm land and small roads. Keith began to take stock of their situation. He was cold in the open cockpit, with a wind of perhaps fifty miles an hour or more blowing against his face. As he experimented with the controls, he realized that the craft flew faster and quieter when it was close to the ground, perhaps an effect related to its anti-gravity propulsion system. He also realized immediately that when the fuel ran out he would sink like a rock, and so became constantly aware of soft landing spots in the fields below.

Jessica stirred beside him and looked over at Keith, "What happened?"

"The most wonderful thing Jessica, I'm part of your world. Gregorz came to me and helped fly us out of the tunnel. I can't describe how it felt to have his hands on top of mine, directing me, teaching me what to do, we owe him both of our lives. How could this happen, I don't understand it."

"You mean all three of our lives. I didn't dare tell you because I knew you would never have let me come along, but I'm pregnant."

"What, you mean you risked that just to gather some old books and papers?"

"They're not just papers, they're Gregorz's life story, and remember, I told you we would come out of this in one piece, so calm down and fly us home. I'm wet and cold, and I could sure use a drink if you see a bar that's open somewhere down there."

"Jessica!"

"Can you make it go any faster?"

"This is as fast as it goes, I hope we have enough fuel to make it to Austria and freedom, and no more drinking while you're carrying our child inside."

"Don't be so paternal, but OK, I understand what you're saying. Hey if we run out of fuel we'll have to land in Czechoslovakia, and they'd never let us keep this machine: the Russians will gobble it up, and probably keep us too unless we ran away: all our work in vain. Is Gregorz still helping you drive?"

"I feel his hands but he's growing fainter. I wonder what those guards at the top of the air shaft are going to tell their Commandant! I bet they'll be in deep trouble if they tell the truth. You should have seen the looks on their faces as we flew by: what expressions of surprise."

"If we make it across the border, what happens when we land? I'll bet the military will confiscate the machine anyway."

"I have an idea. If we can get on TV quickly and the world sees us flying around and we tell what a great invention it is for all mankind, and that it belongs to you since you're one of Gregorz's heirs; maybe it will be too hard for the military to grab it and hide it from the public."

"My machine, what a great idea, but first we need to get across the iron curtain and into Austria."

"And when the fuel runs out, we need to land in a soft field, not a lake or on top of a house or a highway."

"Where do you think Gregorz flew machine number one? He would have had a full tank of fuel, and he was an experienced pilot, so he could have gone a long distance."

"I wonder if he flew to Austria too. I think it had been liberated by then, so that would have been the safest place unless he wanted to go someplace special in Germany."

"Or Switzerland. We have no idea of how far he could have gone, and maybe he stuffed the passenger seat with extra fuel cans."

"Then he would want to hide the machine until it was safe to bring it into the world."

"Maybe he dumped it into a small lake high in the mountains. Fresh water could preserve it a long time, just like in *THE SALZBERG CONNECTION* by Helen McGinnis."

"What's that about?"

"A young couple poking about in little mountain lakes in Austria looking for secret Nazi treasure buried during the war."

"Gregorz's grave might be near the lake too."

As the sky lightened in the East they followed the main highway south from Brno and reached the town of Brecla, near the border. Keith realized that he would need to start travelling right over the road because the pass through the mountains was narrow and he didn't dare chance a crash in the rugged mountains on either side.

"Hey look down there, a car stopped and the driver is taking a picture of us."

"Is he a cop?"

"I don't think so, but the traffic's starting to get heavy. Where are we going to land if we don't get over the pass?"

"Look for soft snow. I'm going to slow down in case that makes the fuel last longer."

"Don't slow down yet or a Russian helicopter will start chasing us and we'll be in trouble."

"There's the pass up ahead, you can almost see the Austrian flag at the top."

"Quick, go faster Keith, as long as we can land on the other side we'll be OK."

Down below more people were taking photos as they approached the frontier and the sunlight made their dark craft visible against the clear blue mountain sky. Jessica couldn't resist waving to the Austrian border guards, "Keith, drop down and fly a circle around them and tilt a bit, like an airplane saying hello."

"They're waving back, but I'll bet at least one of them is on the phone to their air force."

"Just as long as it isn't the Russian military I'll be happy."

"What do you bet we pick up a TV helicopter soon?"

"As well as a military escort."

"Look, the highway signs have changed to German. Now all we need to do is make a soft landing, once we clear the mountains."

"See that spot in the distance, it's coming our way, and if I'm not mistaken it's a helicopter with a big number on the side."

"Let's drop down close to the farm fields in case we run out of fuel. It's time to slow down: we're on the home stretch."

"Smile, you're on TV Keith," said Jessica as she waved to the TV helicopter and snapped a picture of it with Keith's camera.

"I wonder if the TV guys have a live feed, if people all over are watching us?"

"Won't Gerta be surprised if she recognizes us?"

"Tell me what you sensed about Friedrich while we were in the lab. What happened, why did he go away? I hope he's far from the tunnel area because the cops around there must be going berserk right now."

"I hope they don't watch Austrian TV and put things together before we're safe on the ground."

"Seriously, what do you think happened to him?"

"It was strange, and not bad. I don't think he was hurt, more like he was protecting us in some way, but his spirit was moving away from us, growing fainter. I'll bet he did something to protect us from the patrol, but then couldn't come to the lab."

"In that case he would have gone to the car and waited for us."

"While he was waiting, he would have seen us fly out the air shaft and hopped in the car and driven away quickly."

"Look up ahead, the suburbs are starting, so we'd better set this thing down softly while we can."

"There's a little town, let's land just outside it, in the field next to the school where those kids are playing."

"There's a sign, welcome to Wolkersdorf."

They landed softly in a potato field with the TV helicopter close behind. Almost before they could climb out a reporter came running toward them, followed by a cameraman. The military helicopter wasn't far behind. Keith left the motor running slowly, still quietly emitting it's strange warbling sound.

Keith walked to the reporter and stopped him, "Stand back a little way please, this thing's radioactive and you don't want to get too close."

"Who are you? What is this machine? Where do you come from?"

"Slow down, I'm Keith, this is my wife Jessica, and this is part of a new Hollywood motion picture that we're making. The name of the film is *GREGORZ!* Incredible isn't it!"

Jessica was more surprised than the reporter when she heard this, but decided to listen to what Keith would say next.

"Hollywood, you've flown this from Hollywood, in America?"

"Not exactly. This is the world's first successful atomic-powered anti-gravity machine: it will revolutionize transportation once we get the bugs worked out. Jessica owns it, her uncle invented it."

Three uniformed men had emerged from the olive drab military helicopter and were listening intently to the conversation. Jessica walked over to them, shook their hands, and greeted them informally in the Austrian dialect of German.

A soldier approached the machine, which was still running, but Keith stopped him, "Careful, it's radioactive, we're wearing lead shorts to protect ourselves. Don't get too close. Please send for a Geiger counter and lots of lead sheets so we can protect people from it."

"Jessica, why don't you loan your shorts to one of the soldiers and I'll take him for a quick ride before the fuel runs out, if that's OK with them."

"Unload the backpacks first," Jessica suggested, then turned to the military men, "We don't know how much fuel we have left, and we probably can't re-start this machine once it stops running, so this will be just a short flight to show how it works. Eventually we hope to give this invention to the world, to help people everywhere travel more easily."

Jessica peeled off her lead shorts, glad to drop twenty pounds of excess clothing onto the ground, then the smallest of the soldiers put them on. Keith unloaded the backpacks and helped the soldier into the seat. The reporter, Jessica, and the other soldiers all talked at once as the TV camera covered the scene. Keith flew a few feet off the ground, then slowly went left, right, forward, back, up and down. Then as he flew up into the air and circled the field for a few minutes the engine began to sputter and Keith made a quick landing in another part of the field as the fuel ran dry.

The flying show was abruptly over, but Jessica's and Keith's adventure with the machine was just beginning. That night an astonished David saw the interview on television and heard his name mentioned as the director of the next great Hollywood film.

–finis–

AFTERWORD
THE TRUTH

Much of the story in this book is fiction, about things that perhaps didn't happen, but consider this. In 2011 an investigative reporter for *The Los Angeles Times,* Annie Jacobson, interviewed men who had worked at the top secret military labs at Area-51, the most classified part of the Nevada Test Range. This huge range is about the size of Connecticut and is completely sealed from public view. One of the many bits of information that she learned was the true story of the crash of a "flying saucer" near Roswell New Mexico in 1947. The wreckage was taken to Area-51 for analysis and it is probably still there. The device was built by the Soviets (it had Cyrillic writing inside). The Russians stole the design from captured Nazi scientists and equipment that had been developed in Eastern Europe during the war. The Roswell device was indeed a Nazi flying saucer and it used a strange method of propulsion, possibly an atomic anti-gravity motor. More detail is in her book, *AREA-51*, Little-Brown, New York, 2011. Remains of the German wartime underground factories are still scattered over Poland and East Germany. There are videos of people exploring them on YouTube, and various still pictures are scattered on the internet. The European locations in this book are places where these underground tunnels have been found. The book, *THE HUNT FOR ZERO POINT*, also describes these locations in detail. They really exist and you could go there and explore them yourself.

GLOSSARY

(Note: The film industry terms are circa 1980 Hollywood.)

ARRIFLEX: (AKA "Arri") German camera developed in the thirties. Electrically-powered hand-held 35mm professional movie camera with through-the-lens viewfinder. Unlike big Hollywood studio cameras where the camera operator looked through a separate viewfinder next to the camera, with the Arriflex, the cameraman saw the same scene that the film saw. 16mm versions were very popular also.

CAN: motion picture film is sold in steel cans, 100', 200', 400', 1000' in length. Professional film is 35mm at 24 frames per second, and 1000' of film runs about eleven minutes. This limits the longest scene to eleven minutes, so everything, including the length of carbon arcs, was sized to run for at least eleven minutes. During projection in a theater, two projectors are used, with a switchover after about eleven minutes, although some release prints are distributed on 2000' reels (very heavy) to make life easier for projectionists.

CFI: Consolidated Film Industries, one of the largest film processing laboratories in 1980 Hollywood.

CLAWS, PERFS: movie film is perforated on both edges and big heavy studio cameras will grab the film through four of these perforations, two on each edge, to move the film quickly between exposures (24 exposures per second). Cheap, and light-weight cameras may grab the film through only one or two perforations to move it with a more simple mechanism.

E-TICKET: When Disneyland first opened each ride required a ticket: the best rides needed an E ticket while the cheapest rides only needed an A ticket.

EXTRATERRESTRIAL HIGHWAY: N-375 really exists. Read the book "AREA 51" in bibliography for more information.

FEATURE MOTION PICTURE: a full length Hollywood 'movie', usually a bit less than two hours long, shown in regular movie theaters, A.K.A. "the big screen".

FOOTAGE: generic term for the film actually shot when making a movie of any type.

GRIPS: these are crew people who work for the Cameraman, AKA the Director of Photography. They arrange different camera platforms, move the camera during shots, and arrange flags to block light from the camera lens. Usually they are excellent carpenters and mechanics with a wide range of skills, able to build almost anything on short notice.

MAGAZINE: one of the Assistant Cameraman's jobs is to take the cans of film and camera magazines into a pitch-black room (or inside a black changing bag with arm holes and light-tight sleeves), and move the film from can to magazine or the reverse. The magazines are metal and mount on cameras.

PLATES, BACKGROUND: these are films that are projected behind actors so as to give the impression that the actors are far away in a different setting. Actually the actors are standing in front of a movie screen, and the plate is projected onto the rear of the transparent screen. A technique developed during the silent era and still in use, via electronic or optical effects.

SET: Usually built on a soundproof stage and constructed from ten foot high plywood flats, which came in one, two, and four foot widths. The flats could be quickly nailed together, then painted or wallpapered, and filmed the next day, then disconnected and prepared for the next film or scene. Flats might include doors and windows or other interior features.

SHOOTING HOURS: normal union crews worked ten hour days, but it was often expeditious to work crews overtime so that a particular location or stage set could be finished on a particular day. Crew people often drove an hour each way to locations which meant a typical "day" was at least twelve hours long, often with much strenuous work.

SOUND MIXER: the person in charge of recording the sound track as a movie is filmed. Sometimes he worked alone, and other times he had several boom men who moved microphones to follow actors and a recorder operator to make the actual recording. After the film was edited, a re-recording sound mixer would blend the various sound tracks, music, and effects together into the final movie.

TAKE, SCENE: Films are divided into scenes, each occurring at a specific place with scripted actions. When it is time to film a scene, various things may not happen correctly so the scene is filmed over and over until the Director is satisfied that he has captured the desired performance. Each attempt is called a 'take', and a Script Supervisor writes down what happened on each 'take' so that the Editor can assemble the best pieces into the final movie.

196

TAPE, CANS: new unexposed film is supplied in cans which are surrounded by white tape. Inside the can is a black bag holding the film. After film is exposed it is returned to the black bag, placed in the can, then the can is wrapped diagonally in tape to indicate that it is exposed film and not new film.

TAPE EDITING: In Keith's day, ca 1980, much of the world's sounds were recorded on magnetic tape a quarter of an inch wide. These recordings could be edited by running them back and forth on a flat tape deck to find the exact point where an edit was needed. Then the editor marked the spot with a white china marker and moved the tape to an aluminum block which held the tape securely. A single edge razor blade was used to perfectly cut the tape. Then pieces were joined while held in the block with pre-cut pieces of Mylar tape which adhered to the backside of the magnetic tape. In the movie world the same process was used, but the tape was 35mm (1-1/2") wide and the equipment was much bigger.

UNION: In Hollywood all feature films were made with IATSE (International Alliance of Theatrical and Stage Employees) crews, from cameramen down to janitors, each craft had an IATSE union. Their lock on film production meant high pay for the workers, but made Hollywood films very expensive to shoot.

VAULT: Scattered over Hollywood are odd small brick and cement structures which are fireproof buildings for storing films. A typical film, two hours long, ninety feet per minute, has a release print perhaps 10,000' in length. In addition there is a negative of the same length, original footage, both negative and positive, of about five times that length, as well as various title and special effects footage. Therefore a typical feature film might have a library of perhaps 100,000' stored in a hundred 1000' cans. Many films are made, but not released, so the vaults hold a treasure trove of old film footage.

WESTWOOD: beautiful area of Los Angeles, between Beverly Hills and UCLA campus, developed by the Janss Investment Company during the twenties: the Janss logo appears on sidewalks in the area.

Vergangenheit

END NOTES

Gerta's and Jessica's family tree:
Gerta born 1930, 5 years younger than Ladislas, and was age 15 at end of WW2, lived through WW2 in Poland. Went to university in Warsaw and to med school on scholarships. Finally escaped to Germany, studied more, worked her way up, now busy doctor: intense disposition, unmarried, no time for frivolity.
Ladislas born 1925, left for California in 1934, age 9
Ladislas' father, born 1895, university ca1915-1920, then married before 1925
Grzegorz, born 1900, university 1918-1928, then Nazi scientist
Gerta's mom, born 1902

Cameras:
1934, Zeiss Super Ikonta-c, 105/3.8 Tessar with rangefinder, 120 film.
1956, Super Ikonta IV, 6x6, model 534/16, 75/3.5 Tessar, selenium light meter, all metal, last camera in the series.

Geography & Internet:
A detailed map around Walim in Poland shows the areas in this book. This is just over the border from the German city of Gorlitz. This area is also just north of the Czechoslovak border. There are YouTube videos about this; search for the key words "Tajemnice Riese". Perhaps the best place to start is the Wikipedia article about "Project Riese". The test stand where the machine (AKA "the bell") was actually tested is known as "The Klodzkie Giant", and it is part of Complex Milkow.

The easiest place to find information is to go to both Google and YouTube and search for "The Bell", "Project Riese", "Nazi Antigravity", "Nazi Flying Saucers", and similar. Alternatively, go to the author's website, www.escottspencer.com, where there is lots of information. There are thousands of links to all of this. The following are a few related to the text of this book:

http://en.wikipedia.org/wiki/Project_Riese. This site contains a description of German WW2 underground workings similar to those visited by Keith and Jessica as well as maps, commentary, and references to other material.

http://mapy.eholiday.pl/mapa-walim-walbrzych.html. Detailed map of the area Keith and Jessica explored.

http://maps.thefullwiki.org/Ludwikowice_K%C5%82odzkie. Map of the Ludwikowice area.

http://ludwikowice.info/english/ufo.html. Information on flying saucers and other UFO phenomena associated with the Ludwikowice area.

http://www.polandforall.com/mysterious-subterranean-city-osowka-and-walim.html. Interesting news from underneath the Owl mountains.

http://www.thirdreichruins.com/mittelwerk.htm. Various interesting pictures and texts about the ruins of the V rocket factories.

BIBLIOGRAPHY:

Coats, Callum. *LIVING ENERGIES*. Gateway, Dublin, 1996. This book describes Viktor Schauberger's brilliant work with repulsine motors. Unusual science, complete with glossary of odd words. P287 shows a prototype of a Klimator.

Cook, Nick. *THE HUNT FOR ZERO POINT*. Broadway Books, NY, 2001. Modern factual investigation of anti-gravity research amidst clues to forgotten German inventions from WW2. Cook is a defense expert and wrote for ten years at "Jane's Defense Weekly." In Chapter twenty he visits the Polish site where Grzegorz might have flown his machine. Much present-day factual information and a good read as well.

Farrell, Joseph P. *SECRETS OF THE UNIFIED FIELD*. Adventures Unlimited Press, 2008. Much about anti-gravity developments in secret Nazi labs during the war. Page 248 shows the test stand where flying saucers were tested. Much information and detail.

Farrell, Joseph P. *THE SS BROTHERHOOD OF THE BELL*. Adventures Unlimited Press, 2006. Tells us that the Nazi anti-gravity machines are still being developed, long after the war ended.

Friedrich, Jorg. *THE FIRE, THE BURNING OF GERMANY 1940-1945*. Columbia University Press, NY, 2006. Describes what it was like on the ground during the fire-bombing raids on German cities during the war. Vivid photos and descriptions.

Hachette. *LES GUIDES BLEUS POLOGNE.* Librarie Hachette, Paris, 1939. Guide to travel in Poland before the war. In French.

Humphrey, Grace. *POLAND THE UNEXPLORED*. Bobbs-Merrill Company, Indianapolis, 1931. This book describes the travels of Miss

Humphrey in Poland where she spent a year exploring the country around 1929. At this time Poland was celebrating independence from foreign domination and national spirits were very high. Many rural parts of the country visited by the author seem like scenes from medieval times, unchanged for hundreds of years.

Jacobson, Annie. *AREA 51*. Little-Brown, New York. 2011. Much information on secret projects and a description of a German-Nazi designed flying saucer that crashed at Roswell in 1947, with Soviet pilots on board.

MacInnes, Helen. *THE SALZBURG CONNECTION*. Diamond Books, 1994.

Matheson. *THE LEICA WAY.* Focal Press, Chatham, England, 1963. This book contains a Leica photo of German businessmen in snow among other things.

Morgan & Lester. *LEICA MANUAL*. Morgan & Lester Publishing, New York, 1939, much information on Leica cameras just before WW2.

Overy, Richard. *THE PENGUIN HISTORICAL ATLAS OF THE THIRD REICH*. Penguin, Avon, 1996.

Reich, Wilhelm: *SELECTED WRITINGS: AN INTRODUCTION TO ORGONOMY,*
Farrar, Straus & Giroux, NY, 1973.

Reich, Wilhelm: *DISCOVERY OF THE ORGONE, I: FUNCTION OF THE ORGASM,* T. Wolfe, trsl., 2nd Edition, Farrar, Straus & Cudahy, NY, 1961

Reich, Wilhelm: *THE CANCER BIOPATHY, VOL. 2, DISCOVERY OF THE ORGONE,* A. White, trsl., Farrar, Straus & Giroux, NY, 1973.

Reich, Wilhelm: *ETHER, GOD & DEVIL / COSMIC SUPERIMPOSITION,*
Farrar, Straus & Giroux, NY, 1973.

Rezzori, Gregor Von. *MEMOIRS OF AN ANTI-SEMITE*. Vintage International, translated 1981, Viking Press. Much about life in German cities in the 1920's and 1930's. Atmospheric.

Schirer, William. *THE RISE AND FALL OF THE THIRD REICH*. Simon & Schuster, New York, 1960.

Spencer, E. Scott. **SENIORS HAVE IT TOUGH**. Horsington Press, 2008. This book is the predecessor to the book you are holding.

Stevens, Henry. **HITLER'S FLYING SAUCERS**. Adventures Unlimited Press, 2003, Illinois. A fascinating book for readers who want to know more about Nazi efforts in this area. P13-17 is about Der Riese (The Giant) as well as about underground processing of uranium in Poland. P17 is a map of the area in the Owl Mountains which is described in the fictional text herein. P25 is a schematic of an anti-gravity machine. P38 is a photo of the test stand where Grzegorz flew his prototype, called Mucholapka. P106 describes a nuclear-powered flying saucer. P121 talks about anti-gravity machines and Schauberger's vortex machine. P122 is a photo of this, while P123 shows how it works. On P126 there is discussion of Schauberger in the SS. P178 talks about "glowing magnetism" and P181 describes the 'Bloch Wall" and how it generates gravity waves. If you believe the material in this book, then you are ready for the rest of E. Scott Spencer's books!

Targ & Puthoff. **MIND REACH.** Delacorte. 1977. Mind-Reach is the book that led to the U. S. Army's psychic spy program and the subsequent prominence of remote viewing. The protocols that physicists Targ and Puthoff developed at the Stanford Research Institute are still in use today and have proven again and again in laboratory settings that psychic ability is universal.

Vogt, Hannah. **THE BURDEN OF GUILT, A SHORT HISTORY OF GERMANY 1914-1945**. Oxford University Press, New York, 1964.

End Notes

Vergangenheit